THE OMEGA HUNT

THE OMEGA HUNT

THE PACK MATES OF LUNAR CREST, BOOK THREE

by

GINNA MORAN

ISBN 978-1-951314-35-4 (soft cover)
ISBN 978-1-951314-36-1 (hard cover)

Cover design by Silver Starlight Designs
Cover images copyright Depositphotos

For Inquiries Contact:
Sunny Palms Press
9663 Santa Monica Blvd Suite 1158
Beverly Hills, CA 90210, USA
www.sunnypalmspress.com
www.GinnaMoran.com

Dedication

Dedicated to Noel Dreibelbies,

Without her support and friendship, life wouldn't be as fun and dirty. Thanks for licking all the men, but please share them with others.

"LYRIC, SHIT. LYRIC!" FLYNN'S VOICE rings in my ears, coming from nowhere and everywhere. Desperation lines his voice, the pitch full of fear. "Presithimy dobli et! Lyric, snap out of it. Fight the spell, damn it. Presithimy dobli et! Release her!"

Heat floods through my chest, burning pain through me. My skin buzzes with electricity, Flynn's familiarity helping to ease my panic. I know he's a distance away, but the magic flickering through the air feels as if his soul caresses mine.

"It's not working, warlock. Do something more," Caz says, his anger whipping through me. "She can't protect herself if she can't fight."

"Presithimy dobli et! Kcol nepo!" Flynn shouts, rousing more warmth through me. "Lyric, come on. Break free! Someone stop the bastard. I can't get a good enough aim. I keep missing."

Sagan growls, the low rumbly sound prodding at my attention. "Teleport. Do something else. If you head north, Flynn, you can cut him off. We will continue to chase him."

If only I could move. Fight. Do any damn thing. But I'm lost to a magical oblivion. My only sense left is my hearing, and that's starting to falter too.

Darkness shrouds my vision, making it impossible to see where I am. My back scrapes across the ground, my body frozen, unable to move or fight. I'm not even sure if I'm breathing. Numbness blooms from the skin over my heart. I had expected the lycan to gut me. I had expected to die a quick but painful death. What I hadn't expected was for the beast to jam some sort of magical amulet into my chest, leaving me immobile.

"Presithimy dobli et!" Flynn yells again, breaking through the strange fog weighing me down. "Release her, beast!"

Growls reverberate through my bones, the sensation drawing life through my body. Shapes form in my vision, still dark yet clearing the longer I stare. And then I blink. Flynn's spell is working.

"Again!" Caz says, his voice loud in my head. "I felt her in our mind-link. Try again!"

"Don't let him take her." Desperation lines Bastien's voice, his fear crashing through me at the fading numbness.

Sterling snarls. "Lyric, fight! You have to fight. He's going too fast. Wake up and bite his fucking head off!"

Except I can't.

Blinking my eyes again, I try to orient myself to what's happening. Dozens of emotions course through me, sending my mind whirling. Panic and anger and grief. Then sadness consumes me, and it takes me a moment to realize that the emotion belongs solely to me. My heart aches in disbelief and despair as everything that just happened crashes to me.

An image of Dax flits through my mind, dragging me back into darkness. I can still feel his blood splashing across my face. His body getting ravaged and discarded by the lycan plays over and over again in my mind. Fuck.

"Dax?" It takes all my willpower to project my thought out, my whole soul weeping in anguish. It's like my heart senses before my mind can process that there won't be a response. But I can't believe he's dead. I refuse to think a man so powerful could be taken down by a lycan. It's impossible...right?

Silence greets me, shredding my heart into tiny pieces. I concentrate on opening my mind, begging the universe to show mercy on me. All I ever wanted was to live a peaceful life.

To love endlessly, irrevocably, and without the fear my dad left behind in his absence. I guess that was too much to ask. If only my dad had prepared me for a short life. Perhaps knowing my end is coming wouldn't be so frightening if he had. All it took is getting caught off guard to ruin my confidence in my abilities, and now hatred twists and entangles with my despair.

"Lyric, I'm going to spank your ass until it turns into my brother's favorite shade of red!" Sterling shouts in my mind.

"Resist those thoughts," Sagan adds.

"You are not weak, blondie. You—"

"Presithimy dobli et!" Flynn's spell cuts Sterling off. I want to scream at him to try something else already, because whatever he attempts isn't working. It feels as if it's making things worse—

Bright light engulfs me with the thought, illuminating the darkness in my vision. My senses awaken and explode through every cell on my body. The lycan drops my legs, and I gasp and kick out as hard as I can. Flashing his fangs, the monstrous beast snaps his frothy jowls in my face. I try to kick him again, but he backs up with a roar. The forest dims around me as his guttural voice pierces my ears. His sparkling, iridescent green eyes are the only thing I can see through my blurring vision.

"Just submit, you bitch. If you submit, I will spare the last wolf." The lycan stretches his half-man, half-beast body, towering over me by at least four feet. I've never seen one so huge in my life. His claws look long enough to decapitate me with one swing. "I just need you."

My heart stalls at the guttural tone of his words. The last wolf? I don't understand. "What?" My voice comes out as a low whisper, and I gasp in a few more deep breaths, blinking the tears of pain from my eyes. I twist beneath his presence and try to get a view of the world around us, but I can't see anything. I no longer hear my guys or Flynn. Shit.

"Submit and I will spare your mate. Bow down to me or I will gut him like the others." The lycan stomps a few feet closer again, shaking the ground with his heavy body. He growls and punches the ground next to my head.

"Don't do it, gorgeous," Sagan whispers, his words making my head spin.

I brace my palms on the forest ground, expecting a huge crack to open up and swallow me whole. A whimper sounds from behind me, and I close my eyes, my heart aching more than I knew possible. Sorrow rushes through my veins in an icy wave. I want nothing more than to push myself up to run to Sagan. His grief is the worst feeling in the universe. It leaves my heart racing. If I didn't know better, I'd think it was about to pop from my chest to splatter on the ground with all the...blood.

Shit. There's so much of it.

My fingers sink into the cool mud a few inches, the ground softening as it drinks in the puddle of ruby liquid like the earth needs to quench its thirst. I jerk my hands out and stare at my fingers. Blood and dirt cover every inch of me. It's as if I've been buried in it and have managed to pull myself from my grave.

"Did you hear me?" The lycan asks, drawing my attention from my hands and to where he towers beside me. He snatches my hair and hoists me up. My scalp screams in pain, my body refusing to fight like it should. "Submit, or your mate will join the others."

Snapping my head back by my hair, the lycan forces me to peer around the forest in front of us. My heart slides into my stomach, and I release a small cry, shock and grief stealing my breath away. Three feet away, I spot Dax's body lying face down in the mud. I concentrate on his back, hoping to see even a blip of life, but he remains still.

And then I see Sterling.

My stomach twists, and I dry heave. He remains frozen between a man and a wolf, gray fur sprouting from his back, his hands stuck as paws. Slashes ravage his skin so much so that I'm certain if I tried to lift him, his body would fall apart.

"No-o-o-o-o!" My voice turns into a howl as my transformation grabs hold of me, freeing me from the lycan's grip.

I jump from him and dash toward Sterling. A whimper escapes me, my soul so heavy that I drop to the ground beside him.

That's when I see the others. Fuck.

Bastien and Caz lie dead on their sides in their wolf forms.

How could I not notice them before? Pain explodes through me, feeling as if my heart disintegrates inside my chest. But I don't die. I keep panting in agonizing breaths as my soul shatters into a million pieces. How did this happen? How could I have missed their last breaths? We're connected by our souls.

I squeeze my eyes shut, willing myself to wake up. This isn't real. It can't be. My guys are powerful and strong. We had magic on our side...but where is Flynn?

"Lyric, I'm here. Listen to my voice," Flynn calls.

I snap my eyes open, expecting to wake up from a horrible nightmare, but the lycan shoves me away, sending me sprawling on the ground. I skid across the bloody mud a few feet until I catch my bearings.

"Flynn, help! Please, help me!" I scream out with my mind, scrambling to get to my paws as the lycan stalks me.

"Last chance, Lyric Larson. Submit or your mate is doomed." The lycan clomps closer and strolls past without attempting to grab me. His body cracks and pops, his hair shedding into a pile at his feet, leaving him stark naked.

I stare in shock at Todd. I hadn't even recognized him in his beast form.

My eyes betray me and I dart my gaze downward and stare in shock at the smooth skin over his groin. No cock or balls or hair. Nothing. He looks like a mannequin come to life. It's so strange to see him in this state. I knew lycans lacked genitals in their lycan form, but I never thought of them as turning back into human. I don't know why.

"Fucking bitch." Todd clenches and unclenches his fingers. "You did this to me. You cursed me." Flaring his nostrils, he glowers, his body trembling. His mannequin-like features morph and change, revealing his flaccid cock, and now I wish it would go away again. "Now bend over and bow, bitch. Because you're fucking mine."

What. The. Fuck.

Anger rushes through me, and I prepare to bite his dick off. Todd shrieks at my attempt, the ear-piercing noise making my head spin. My paws fall out from under me, and I land on my belly as the world shakes. He stomps his feet in a tantrum and bends down, lifting a blond wolf into his arms. Something is incredibly wrong. Sagan wasn't next to us a moment ago. He was...whoa. The bodies of the others no longer lie around me.

"Submit. Bow down to me!" Todd yells, pinching Sagan by the scruff of his neck, exposing his underside to me. "Do it, or he is dead!"

Sagan remains lifeless, his head lolling. I shudder at the sight and jam my hands to the ground to push up. Confusion washes over me. I have hands again? When did I change back into a human?

"Lyric, damn it, fight! Come on, gorgeous. Pull yourself out of it. You can do it. It's not real." Sagan's voice stabs through my thoughts of desperation, tying around me and squeezing my very being, igniting pain in my soul.

What is he talking about? What's not real?

I jerk my attention to his lifeless body in Todd's arms. He remains still, but I'm certain I heard his voice in my ears and not my mind.

"Can't you do something, Flynn?" Caz asks, his voice drifting through the air behind me.

"She's trembling so much." This comes from Bastien.

I blink a few times and search around the forest. Todd remains frozen in his place like someone hit the pause button. Sagan fades from his arms, disappearing from sight.

"What the fuck?" I ask, trying to say the words out loud, but my mouth doesn't work. The words float through my mind, spinning and whirling.

"Did you hear that?" Sagan asks.

Warmth spills over me, swallowing the ice freezing my bones, turning my insides hot. My skin buzzes and static swirls through the air. Bursts of electricity light the forest around me. I tense, my muscles bracing for a witch to materialize in front of me to steal me away.

"Try again, warlock. She's opening up," Sterling says. "Hurry."

"Hold her still. She's going to fight and resist." A spark of heat sizzles across my chest with Flynn's words.

The world jostles—or maybe I do—and my legs wobble, sending me to the ground. A shadow blankets me, obscuring the light from above. That's strange. I stare at the sky, but it looks unlike anything I've ever seen. Electric light streaks across pitch-black nothingness. Someone stole the sun and clouds and replaced them with a starless, moonless void.

"Submit, Lyric." Todd's beastly hands smash into the ground on both sides of my head, startling me.

I screech and swing my arm, trying to punch him in his elongated muzzle, but a spark of power zaps me, shocking me to the core. Pain squeezes the air from my lungs as Todd bows low, getting into my face. He drips saliva on my forehead, but I can't move. Something invisible holds me down.

I twist my mouth and close my eyes, willing for him to disappear. "Why are you doing this? Is it for the cure? I know a warlock, and I bet he could help you."

Todd roars, sending my hair blowing from my face. "Submit to me!"

I glare up at him. "Can you say anything else, dickwad?"

"Submit to me!" Todd snaps his jaw. "Submit!"

"Fuck off," I mutter, narrowing my eyes. He's crazy if he thinks I'm going to submit. Especially to him.

"Submit!"

"No!" Swinging my arm up, I break free of the invisible weight holding me down.

I punch Todd in his snout, sending neon blood splashing across my face. My skin tingles, the strange sensation sizzling across my body, lighting me in an electric glow. Throwing my legs over my head, I somersault backward and catch my knees on Todd's hulking neck. He crashes face-first into the bloody dirt, howling in surprise. Locking my hands to his hairy head, I jerk his neck back and use all my force to bash his face into the ground.

"I'll never fucking submit. Never." My voice turns guttural with a growl escaping from deep in my chest, shuddering through my whole body as my she-wolf explodes free.

Sinking my fangs into the back of his neck, I bite off a chunk of his flesh, snarling and tearing away at the monster only to reveal Todd's human body. He slumps beneath me, going still. My mind whirls, my instincts taking over completely. I can't think about anything other than tearing this monster apart until I'm certain he won't ever hurt me again.

"Presithimy dobli et." Flynn's voice whispers in my mind, pulling me from my fit of savagery.

"Lyric, hey?" Bastien asks, his voice swirling around me in a tornado of his wild emotions. "Lyric?"

I pant and howl, my voice echoing through the air. "Bastien?" The thought rushes through my mind. "Bastien, where are you?"

"I got a connection," Bastien says, his voice bathing me in incredible warmth as if my soul sinks into his.

"Presithimy dobli et," Flynn says again. "Keep talking to her."

"Ma Belle, listen to my voice." Brilliant blips of light ignite in the air. It's like someone lit a bunch of sparklers and ties them to invisible strings to dangle through the forest.

"Where are you, Bastien?" I pad my way forward, stepping through the disgusting corpse of Todd's monster while his human body remains naked and unmoving beside the pile of guts. "Where is everyone? What's happening?"

A soft howl hums through the air, and then another and another. I close my eyes and listen to the four distinct howls, savoring them until I realize Dax's howl is missing. My heart stalls, my breath catching. I close my eyes and focus on the soft call of the wolves, of my mates, praying to the universe that Dax is okay. If he's not...I can't think like that. My soul would know, wouldn't it? I would have felt his pain beyond my own. I would know if his soul severed from mine. At least, I hope.

"Lyric..." The small breath of my name stirs something wild inside me. "I'm sorry. I'm so sorry."

Bright light blinds me, and intense pain ignites in my heart, burning through every molecule in my body. A wail escapes my mouth, and I dig my fingers into the muddy ground, trying to find something, anything, to hold on to as the world around me rocks and shakes, the earth breaking apart to devour me. Heat zings through my core, building fast and furiously, eating away at my very essence.

I scream, feeling my body stretch and break apart, getting pulled in six different directions. If the force doesn't stop soon, I'll be ripped to shreds. I just want the pain to stop. I want the light to fade. I want the agony to either release me or kill me. I can't take this anymore.

"Lyric! Presithimy dobli et!" Flynn's voice rams into me, forcing me into the mud until the ground swallows me whole, stealing the blinding light.

My mind whirls as a dozen emotions whip through me, twisting and entangling me in a web of fear and grief and pain. I rotate my body, trying to sever the hot emotions from my own, but they drag me deeper and deeper into the ground until everything disappears.

"No!" I scream. "No!"

The world stills, the darkness breaking with a beam of pale sunlight through the trees. I flail, swinging my arms and kicking my legs. My foot collides into something soft, and Sagan groans, snapping my attention from the sky.

"Fuck, right in the nuts," Sterling says with a groan. A silhouette pops into view, blocking out the sun overhead. "You're going to owe him a kiss to his tender loins, blondie." Bowing down, Sterling slides his hands under me and pulls me from the ground. "But first, let me check you out. Because fuck. I thought that thing was going to deflate your tit."

"Get the hell out of the way." Bastien kneels next to Sterling and pulls my hair off my shoulder to expose my chest to him. He motions for Sterling to adjust me in his arms to get a better look.

"Dax?" I ask, my voice coming out at a whisper, my throat tight and dry, hoarse as if I've been screaming my lungs out.

"Dax? Dax!" It's the only thing I can think to say, the memory of his absent howl hurting my chest.

"Hold her still," Bastien commands Sterling. "Don't let her see him."

Oh, fuck.

"Dax!" I scream again.

Sagan growls, his figure popping into view. "Damn it, Bas. Tell her he's alive. Can't you feel her panicking?"

Sagan's words register in my mind, and I gasp a breath and sink against Sterling.

"Let m-me s-see him," I say, trying to get my body to co-operate. Now that I'm snuggly in Sterling's arms, my body re-fuses to do anything besides relax.

Sterling nestles his chin into the crook of my neck and shoulder. "In a minute, okay? Flynn and Caz got him. They're taking care of his wounds. He's going to be okay."

I inhale a quivering breath. "Bastien, go to him. Help them."

Bastien leans closer and touches the back of his hand to my forehead. "Flynn is better suited to tend to him right now. Let me take care of you. Your emotions...the talisman did a number on your soul." Gently prodding his finger to my bare breast, Bastien inspects a medallion still piercing my skin. "We weren't sure if you'd come to with this in place."

I bring my hand up to touch it, but Bastien stops me, link-ing his fingers around my wrist. He tugs my hand to his mouth and kisses my knuckles, shaking his head.

"Don't touch it. Flynn managed to break the spell, but you could trigger it again. Wait for him, Ma Belle. He needs to remove it." Combing his hand through his brown hair, he pushes the dirty strands from his face.

I close my eyes and inhale a few deep breaths. "What the hell happened anyway? Where's the lycan? He was dragging me."

"He abandoned you here." Sterling props me up higher, allowing me to get a better view of the world in front of me.

I blink a few times and stare at an abandoned cabin twenty feet in front of me. Bones litter the ground of the front yard and some hang from a large tree, tied together by some sort of twine. I cover my mouth with my hand, the sight freaky as fuck. They're human, at least, I think, by the looks of the skulls lining the walkway.

"What the hell?" I ask, rubbing the heels of my hands into my eyes, trying to see if I can clear the grotesque sight from my vision. "What is this place?"

"Home, sweet home, to the fucking bastard," Sagan says, shifting closer to me. "I don't think he expected Flynn to be a warlock. He chose to flee instead of fight. Maybe had plans to come back later, because he buried you."

I shiver at the thought and glance down at my dirty legs. "Holy shit." I can't think of anything else to say apart from a hundred different swear words.

My mind reels at the idea that the lycan beast buried me like some sort of toy he planned to play with later. The thought leaves me with so many questions. Where did the fucker come from? How did he know we were opening the gateway to Lunar Crest to gather a few of my mom's belongings? What does he get out of this? And most importantly, where the hell did he get the weird-ass talisman from?

"You're going to have to wait a bit longer for answers, blondie," Sterling says, responding to my inner thoughts. "We gotta wait for Magic Man to do his thing."

"When? I don't want to stay here. This place is—"

"Freaky? Twisted? Sadistic? Completely bat-shit crazy?" Sterling taps his index finger to my bare knee as he lists everything. "I know. Looks like he's been eating people. Gross."

My stomach twists at the thought. "Oh, shit. We need to find him."

Sterling tightens his hold on me. "Not so fast, blondie. We have our own shit to deal with. Flynn will report this to whatever the fuck authority he belongs to and they can handle this. Not us."

"But—"

"Listen to Sterling, Lyric. That's an order." Dax's gruff voice steals my attention away from the creepy cabin.

"Dax!" I scramble forward, knocking Bastien onto his back.

Bastien tries to snatch me by my waist, but I accidentally

knee him in the gut in my attempt to rush to Dax. Wobbling on his feet, Dax stands between Flynn and Caz, using the both of them to remain upright. I know I should calm the hell down. I know that I could hurt him if I rush him. But Dax offers me a heart-melting smile and straightens his back, opening his arms for me.

"Brace yourself," Sagan calls.

"She looks like she's going to hump the hell out of you," Sterling adds.

Dax laughs, the sound of his voice so amazing that I launch at him and into his arms. He underestimates my force, and the two of us fall backward with me on top of him. He heaves a breath and groans, but all he does is roll me off him to get on top. I lace my hands around his neck and pull him to me, kissing him so passionately that he moans deep in his throat, his body hardening and throbbing between my legs, needing me as much as I need him.

If only pain didn't erupt in my chest.

I jerk away and arch my back. Heat bursts in my heart, and the edges of my vision shadow. The world spins. Dax props himself up on his hand to meet my gaze. Worry puckers his brows, his golden eyes sweeping over mine.

"Dax, give her to me. Now!" Flynn yells, his soft footsteps thumping in my ears. "You guys stay together. Head north and wait for me."

"What?" I ask, a whimper escaping my mouth.

"I'll get her somewhere safe and come back for you. I can't teleport you all at once without leaving behind a magical imprint others can track." Flynn ignores me as he speaks to my guys.

Dax doesn't hesitate to get off me, and Sterling scoops me up to hand me to Flynn before I have a chance to argue.

"You better take care of her," Sterling warns.

"With my life." Flynn takes me from him and holds me close. Glancing at me, he whispers, "Brace yourself, she-wolf."

I watch in fear as my guys disappear.

2

SPELLBOUND

"YOU NEED TO GET THEM immediately, Flynn. I mean it." I bounce on the balls of my feet, staring around the motel room.

He holds up a sheet. "I need to take care of that talisman first. Come lie down."

I cross my arms over my chest, wincing at the sudden pain exploding through my heart. Bending over, I clutch my knees, my breath escaping my lungs. I automatically reach for the medallion and lace my fingers around the cool metal to yank it the hell out of me so Flynn can get my pack.

"Lyric, stop," he says, grabbing my wrist. "Pulling it won't help any. I need to do it. Whoever the lycan got this bullshit from has some serious power. A lot of humans were sacrificed to make this blasphemous thing. Now come lay down or I'll pick you up and make you. It could be used to track you down by one of the Dark Ones. Probably why the lycan was fine with leaving you behind."

I crinkle my nose and sigh, slowly nodding my head. As much as I want Flynn to get the guys, I also don't want to risk someone coming after me again. Flynn motions for me to plop onto one of the queen beds, still unmade from this morning. Before I climb onto it, I stop and stare down at my filthy body.

"Maybe I should lie on the floor. No one's going to let housekeeping in here unless it's absolutely necessary, and I doubt you'll want to give up your bed or join our dogpile." I don't wait for his response and lower myself to the coarse carpet. "Someone always ends up on the floor, and it would probably be you."

Flynn doesn't respond to my comment and grabs a duffle bag from on top of the dresser. Shuffling his way across the room and into the bathroom, he wets a towel in the bathtub before returning to my side. I clutch the sheet around me, now ultra-aware that I remain naked. I usually don't care. It's not like he hasn't seen me naked a dozen times before, but something about being alone in this moment sends my skin prickling...and not in a bad way.

Flynn clears his throat like he senses it too. My guys have teased Flynn over and over again about being attracted to me, but he's never acted on it, so I've never been sure how to handle it. And I still don't. I'm used to the boldness of the wolves and not Flynn's type of subtlety.

What am I thinking? I have five pack mates.

Hovering his hand over my breast, he clears his throat again, tugging my attention from my wandering thoughts. "I need to clean the area to make sure the potion hasn't spread too much. It's still amazing that we managed to interrupt the spell and you're awake and conscious."

"Why?" I ask, touching my chin to my chest to peer at the medallion piercing into the soft skin of my breast to the right of my nipple.

Flynn tightens his jaw, thinning his lips. His lavender eyes dart from mine and to the talisman and back up again. "Something like this should've trapped your consciousness in what I can only describe as an alternate reality. But thankfully, whatever your father arranged with Fire Mountain includes some deflection of harmful magic. I still can't figure it out though. Witches usually leave a mark. You have no brands, tattoos, or anything."

"That you know of," I say, poking his shoulder. "How can you be certain? You have never done a close inspection." Why do I love the idea so much? I need to get it together. My guys are still out there. But I have so many questions, and I know they're strong and together.

Flynn's cheek twitches, his sparkling eyes darting down to my bare breasts once more, though the rest of me remains covered by the sheet. "Bastien assured me he looked everywhere."

"I guess you're right." I lick my lips and shove the idea away. "I don't really care about any of that anyway. Just hurry up and fix this. I don't like being separated for long."

"Neither do I. Now, try to hold still. I'll be as gentle as I possibly can." Flynn combs the stray strands of my hair away from my chest and stares at the medallion somehow lodged into my skin.

He gingerly grazes his fingers over the strange metal, trying his best not to touch my breast. I close my eyes and rest my head back. My skin tingles at his closeness, and I count my racing heartbeats. This is far more exciting to me than it should be.

"It's okay to touch my boob if you need to," I say softly, trying not to think about his fingers so close to a sensitive part of my body.

"I'll be fast." Flynn intakes a breath and cups my breast, sending a rush of energy straight through my middle.

I gasp and tense.

"Does it hurt?" Flynn asks.

Shit. I would say his touch is far from painful. I don't know how I feel about it either. My body should not be thrilled by his closeness. I mean, fuck. This is like me having the hots for my damn gynecologist during an exam. With Bastien, it's one thing. Flynn is an entirely different story.

Flynn clears his throat again, and I squeeze my eyes shut, fearing he might've heard my thoughts. If he does, he doesn't respond, which I'm thankful for. Because it's not like that between us. He's given me no indication that this is more than him wanting to help the High Council of Magaelorum get control over some dangerous witch covens. He's also been nothing but kind and friendly, never trying anything despite how much I suddenly want him to. I'm going to smack Sterling for putting the thought in my head about Flynn's intentions.

"I need you to take a deep breath," Flynn says, adjusting his fingers.

The inside of his thumb grazes my nipple, and I shiver under the sensation. Heat floods my face in embarrassment, and Flynn mistakes my gasp for a deep breath on his cue.

"Bokeena fli kig," he says, his voice lowering.

A sharp pain in my breast consumes me. I arch my back, my skin stinging. Flynn automatically covers my boob with his cool hand, the sensation snuffing out the burning caused from the medallion. Before my mind can tell my hand no, I reach up and cover his hand with my own, pressing it harder into my skin. But I can't help it. It feels as if his touch is the only thing to stop the agony from coursing through me.

"Give it a few seconds," Flynn murmurs, gently massaging

my sensitive skin.

My heart thrums against his palm, out of control and wild like my thoughts. It takes everything in me to let him go. My mind finally comes to its senses with the subsiding pain. It's already been minutes, which is too damn long to leave my guys by themselves and unprotected.

Flynn licks his lips, his chest rising and falling with his quickening breath. "You feel okay, Lyric?"

I suck in a few gasps of air and nod my head, afraid if I say anything that my voice will come out all breathy.

"Good," he murmurs, easing my hand away with his only to clasp it. "Why don't you take a shower, and I'll start retrieving your mates?"

Once again, I can only nod. Everything about the day catches up with me, leaving me a bit in shock and in need of something I can't explain. Assurance? Affection? I'm not even sure, but I can't get myself to do much of anything. I can barely think.

Flynn captures me in his lavender gaze, his eyes boring into mine. With his free hand, he strokes my jaw. I can't help squeezing his hand, not letting him go as quickly as I should. A dozen thoughts flicker in his expression, and he leans closer, shifting his gaze to my mouth. I lick my lips, wishing with everything in me that the world could stop just for a minute. I need sixty seconds to gather my strength. To pull myself back together when it feels like my soul splintered and cracked apart.

"I know what it's like to have your whole world taken from you. I know what it's like to not feel in control or safe. But I want you to know that it won't always feel this way. We're going to get things taken care of. I just—you're going to have to let go of me if you want me to get the others. They will eat me alive if they suspect I might disappear with you," he says softly, wiggling his fingers. I hadn't realized how tightly I clutch his. "But I promise you that it's safe here. No one can get in and out without me."

I finally manage to break free of the death grip my body has on Flynn. "Just be quick. I feel terrible...and I don't want to be alone." I pull the sheet higher up, gathering the fabric around me.

"It'll only take a couple of minutes, and you can dive into the dogpile you want." Flynn reaches up and touches my shoulder, his lips pursing as if he has something he wants to tell me but decides against it.

"Maybe you'll join in for once," I tease, forcing my mouth to smirk.

He chuckles. "We'll see."

Something about this moment feels incredibly heavy. It's like a blanket wrapping me in warmth to smother my trembling fear away. I don't know if it's because Flynn has saved my life once again or if it's because he willingly helps out the men most important to me, but all I know is something feels as if it shifts inside me. I don't tell him though. I can't. I'm afraid what it would mean for me if I said the truth in my soul out loud. I've claimed my pack mates after all. Admitting the shift in me could mess things up. It could make the situation more awkward than it sometimes is.

With a soft smile, Flynn touches my cheek once more and gets to his feet. He chants a spell, igniting the room with brilliant blue light. I blink, adjusting my vision to the fading brightness, and push to my feet. I clutch the wall for a moment until I regain my balance and force myself to head to the small bathroom. I hate the idea of leaving myself vulnerable, so I turn on the faucet, leaving the door to the bathroom open to keep my eyes trained on the door.

I never take my gaze away, blindly scrubbing my body until the filthy reminder of my shitty day washes down the drain. Nerves bunch in my muscles the longer time passes. Flynn said it would only take minutes, but it feels like hours have already ticked by. I dry off and dress, preparing to rush out of the damn motel room when a soft groan sounds from behind me.

Spinning on my feet, I watch Flynn help Dax into a chair. My heart jumpstarts, relief flooding through me. Flynn pats Dax on the back and blinks out of existence, leaving the two of us alone.

I rush to Dax's side and run my fingers over his shoulders and down his broad chest, my hands inspecting every inch of his skin. Hooking his arms around my waist, he pulls me onto his lap and crashes his mouth to mine just as passionately as he did in the forest.

"I was so scared," we both say at the same time.

I pout my lip and clutch his cheeks. "I thought I lost you," I add. "I thought I lost all of you."

"Never," he murmurs, lifting me in his arms, wobbling only a little as he carries me toward the small bathroom.

He's as dirty as I was when Flynn brought me here, but I don't even give a shit. I can't go another second without giving into my need to be as near to him as possible, my heart reacting to his closeness, the heat of his body, and how good it feels to have his arms around me.

"Lyric," Dax murmurs, breaking away from my mouth only to caress his lips to my throat. "You mean everything to me. Everything. What happened today—"

"It was none of our faults. I know you think you've failed me. But you haven't. We're all okay, and that's what matters." My eyes well with tears, my wild emotions setting me off. I've never felt anything truer in my life than the words he shares with me now. He means what he says, the rush of his feelings igniting a wave of warmth inside me.

He shudders a breath, squeezing me tighter in his arms. "You're right, my beautiful, fierce leader. Now let me savor you the way I want. I need your affection."

"And I need yours," I say, smiling through another kiss. "It's all I want. I need to feel you—mind, body, and soul—to assure myself that you're here and okay."

A deep rumble escapes his lips, vibrating across my mouth, sending tingles shooting between my legs. He tightens his arms around me, inhaling a deep breath of my scent, enjoying the fragrance of my skin. He strips me bare, and my back hits the shower wall as Dax reacts to me with fervent passion that steals my breath away. Hot water cascades over us, steaming the air. I gasp as he slides his cock into me, his need as intense as mine.

I clutch onto his shoulders, his body banging against mine, turning my pants into bursts of pleasure screams, the ecstasy of his lovemaking all-consuming. Our close quarters since leaving Lunar Crest haven't given me any alone time with my guys, and I feel it in this moment, knowing how hard it is on all of us in these uncertain times. I don't get enough of them. I don't think I can ever get enough—not with my body constantly yearning for more than the life we've found ourselves in, worrying about the wolves who hunt us, the lycans who want to ruin us, and the witches hell-bent on keeping us apart.

"No one ever can," Dax says, responding to my thoughts.

He moans and kisses me harder, thrusting fast and deep, pushing every thought from my mind until it's just him and me and our desire. Clutching onto my ass with one hand, he slips his other between us, rubbing his middle and index finger over my clit, ensuring I can't think about anything else except my body on the verge of exploding. I dig my nails into his shoulders and arch back, resting my head to the wall with my orgasm. Dax moans so loudly, his pleasure as intense as mine as we remain open to each other, enjoying everything we are together.

With a few more thrusts, he cums, sending an amazing shiver through my body as he shares his wave of pleasure with me, our hearts, minds, and souls bonded on the most intimate level. I can't help thinking about how he's mine, and how much I plan to enjoy him for the rest of my life. How much he means to me. How thankful I am that he's my mate.

How I'm falling in love with him.

An incredible, indescribable emotion crashes through me from Dax, and I intake a shuddering breath, the feeling overwhelming in the best way possible. It's now that I realize with our mind link, he heard exactly how I feel about him deep in my soul.

"I love you too," he says, easing away to glance into my eyes. "I love you more than life itself. I've been waiting all my life for this moment, and it's better than I ever imagined."

I laugh breathlessly and shake my head. "We almost died today."

He kisses me again. "The only thing I will remember about this day is this moment and how we live and breathe, and just exist together. My hero. My amazing woman. My true mate."

I grin. "Say it again."

"You're my true mate. Mine. Always."

"Always."

A crash in the motel room drags our attention away from each other, and Dax frowns and sets me on my feet. I follow right behind him, keeping so close that I bump into his back as his steps falter.

Dax releases a deep, guttural growl, and I take an automatic step backward. Sagan and Flynn stand together in the middle of the room with a naked man lying at their feet. Darting his blue eyes from the man and to me, Sagan quickly gives me a once-over like he needs to make sure I'm okay before anything else.

"What the hell?" I ask, gripping onto Dax to stand on my tip-toes for a better view.

"Grab my restraints," Flynn says, pointing at his bag. "Hurry. The spell won't last much longer, and I have to get the rest of your mates before the competitors figure out they're near the gateway."

I can't believe the competitors found a way through the sealed gateway, and now they're coming for me. And seriously—fuck. We escaped. We should've been in the clear. I swear to the universe I'm going to find the lycan that ruined our quick escape and chop his head off, especially if it turns out to be Todd. It was him in my magic-induced hallucination after all.

"Shit," I mutter, clenching my fingers into fists. "I'm going to neuter this bastard. Back up, Sagan. Flynn, your spell better hold a minute longer."

It's now that I realize the man is far from a stranger. It's Ryland. And damn it. I thought Eclipse Valley was out of the territory truce...unless this fucker has gone rogue and joined the hunt. It hasn't been that long since we left Lulupoterra. Could it be that Eclipse Valley decided to let their disagreements go because of the madness with Paige? Probably.

Flynn swears and raises his hand, getting me to stop.

Ryland jerks upright at the sound of my voice and surprise punches Sagan in the knee, sending him to the floor. Flynn summons power between his palms, but Ryland throws himself out of the way and next to the bed. Dax transforms into a wolf at the same time Ryland does. But Ryland doesn't fight. He howls, the loud sound ringing in my ears. Flynn summons more energy in his palms while Dax launches across the room. Ryland growls and snaps his jaws, bolting toward the window. He crashes through it and outside the motel.

"Wait," Flynn says, stopping Dax in his tracks. "Don't chase him. He's weakened the shield. If you go after him, it could destroy it completely. Only I can get us in and out."

Dax flares his nostrils. "But he's getting away. He'll bring the others."

"They won't get in," Flynn argues.

"I won't risk it. I can't trust your magic to protect us. They've already proved your shortcomings." Dax looks at Sagan. "Let's go. The hunt ends here."

"Dax—" I can barely get his name out before he and Sagan bolt through the door.

Flynn smacks his hand to the wall. "Fucking stubborn wolves. They'll jeopardize everything. I should just take you away. I'm not going to keep you safe otherwise."

I raise my palms at him. "Don't you dare, Flynn."

He rushes me, sending light bursting through the air. I can't dodge him, fight, or even move as he snatches me by the wrist. The world shifts, and I scream, only to have the breath escape my lungs as something crashes into me.

"Cherie, run." Antone shoves his furry head to my side.

I blink in confusion, my mind struggling to catch up. Growls reverberate through my bones.

"Run!" Antone shouts into my mind.

A witch materializes beside us, and Antone growls and knocks the woman off her feet. She chants a spell and wraps her hands around Antone's neck. His big wolf body drops to the ground, a strange red glowing light around his neck.

"Run," he says again.

But I can't get away fast enough.

The same witch flings her hands at me, and a searing pain wraps around my neck.

I touch my throat in shock.

I've just been collared.

3

Magical Collar

I HIT THE GROUND, EVERY muscle on my body seizing at once. My cheek rests against the dirt, and I stare in horror as the beautiful witch collars another competitor. Her short black hair swings with her movements, showing off glittering stones hanging from her ears. I try to scream, but my mouth refuses to open. The only thing I can do is dart my gaze at the battle unfolding in front of me.

"Such beautiful beasts," the woman whispers. "I had almost forgotten how much I adore you. Have the leaders not been treating you well that you'd come venturing into the Mortal World?" She speaks as if we can respond, yet she doesn't look at us, managing to waltz around to inspect those she captured while grinning at the beasts surrounding her with deadly growls. "Or is it because of this enchanting she-wolf? I suspected she would be like her mother."

Oh, fuck. She has to be from Fire Mountain. How else would she recognize me or know my mother?

Rage whips through me, making it hard to breathe. I clench my fingers into my fists. I can't believe I'm in this position. I'm better than this. We all are.

"Stay calm, Cherie," Antone says, his voice trickling into my mind. "You're going to hurt yourself."

Stay calm? How the fuck am I supposed to stay calm? This fucking witch just spelled me, stealing away my freewill. My throat aches. My vision blurs. I feel like an animal, even in my human form.

"If you fight the magic, it'll tighten. I just tried," Antone adds, his deep voice even and calm like he knows I need it to stay in control.

"I have to fight," I think back to him.

"Cherie, please." Antone lies just out of my view, though I can smell his familiar scent.

His sweet wildness prods at my nature, and my she-wolf awakens with a force strong enough to break me free. My muscles spasm with my transformation, and I feel my skin prickle as my blond coat breaks free. The witch doesn't even glance at me, continuing her mission in hunting the competitors, sending them fleeing in a frenzy. Men who thought they were tough now cower in fear, running away with their tails between their legs. I know I shouldn't feel so satisfied, but I do.

At least, that is until Bastien's beautiful white form launches at the witch from a hiding spot within the trees. Sterling and Caz follow his lead, charging at the witch in their wolf forms. The black-haired woman throws her arms out, building an electric wall out of magic, stopping all three of them in their tracks.

Panic ignites inside me. The witch saunters toward Sterling, her hands glowing with red light. He growls deep in his throat, snapping his teeth, trying to tear into the woman. My throat tightens at the sight of her gathering magic as she prepares to choke Sterling with the same burning magical collar that leaves me defenseless.

And I'm even more pissed. Not only at this fucked up situation but also at Flynn. Has he been setting us up all along? I thought he was going to kidnap me, not drop me in the middle of a battle between the wolves and witches.

With the thought of his name comes the rumble of his deep voice as he chants a spell. A flash of lavender light explodes through the air, surprising the witch. Guilt pours through me, spotting Flynn casting a counterattack spell against the woman. She yells, her face shifting into a hideous being, her teeth elongating as she grows taller, more threatening.

And then she attacks Flynn.

"No!" My howl whips through the air with my thought, my wolf call finally working against the faltering collar. I can feel it loosening.

And then it disappears completely.

The witch jerks her attention to me, her eyes widening in surprise as I break through her magic. Flynn takes advantage of her distraction and gathers energy between his palms. Thrusting it at the witch, he sends her stumbling a few feet. Bastien propels from the ground, joining in on the fight, but the witch disappears into thin air.

I gawk in horror, watching Antone and the other collared wolves vanish behind her. Pain tightens my throat, and I writhe on the ground, expecting the world to shift under the infuriating magic, but nothing happens.

"Ma Belle," Bastien says, rushing to my side in his human form. He drops to his knees and pulls me upright and against him. "Are you hurt? Let me pick you up."

I automatically bring my hand up to rub my neck. The strange sensation of the magic has already faded but the memory still lingers fresh in my mind. How can I even answer his question? I'm not sure. My mind reels, my heart aching. I continue to massage my neck, frozen in disbelief that our one trustworthy ally was just kidnapped by a witch—and Bastien's brother, no less.

"I don't know," I finally manage to say. "She collared me with magic. I couldn't do anything...and she took Antone. Damn it. I'm so sorry, Bastien. We'll get him back. I swear. She was a Fire Mountain witch. I know it. I could tell. Maybe Antone's with my dad and they can help each other."

Bastien frowns at my words and searches my eyes. "Are you certain? This looked a lot like what happened to my father—the collar, I mean—and I don't recall the Fire Mountain's High Priestess to be involved, but I can't be certain. It was—I like to block that bullshit out. The others might know."

"If it wasn't Fire Mountain, then who the hell was it?" I press my palms to the ground trying to push myself up, despite knowing that Bastien wants to gather me into his arms to hold me instead. "The Nightstars?"

A howl sounds through the air, stopping Bastien from responding to me. My heart flutters at the familiar call, and I sink against Bastien's chest in relief. I should be livid. I should get to my feet and threaten a world of punishment to Dax and Sagan for charging off. But all I can do is sigh a long breath and savor the sight of my beautiful pack mates returning to me in their most powerful forms, unharmed and safe. Dax and Sagan charge through the forest in our direction. Happiness floods through me at the sight of them. If Bastien wasn't hugging me, I'd catapult to my feet and tackle the two of them to give them the best rub down of their existence.

"You fucking hot-headed, stubborn assholes." Flynn surprises the hell out of me by blasting Dax off his paws with sizzling magic. His rage burns across the ground, smoldering the dry brush. It's intense enough that I dig my fingers into the ground, preparing to get between Flynn and my guys. "How could you do this?"

Oh, shit.

"What the hell were you thinking? You jeopardized all of us!" Flynn yells, his angry voice so sharp it feels as if it whips across my back. His features harden, and a glimpse of the terrifying monster that peeked through only once before when he was attacked in Lunar Crest morphs his handsome features. It steals my breath, seeing him like this. "You could've been hurt or worse. Do you know what they would have done to Lyric? We were lucky as hell the competitors weren't the only damn ones on a hunt." Lucky? How the hell were we lucky?

I open my mouth to ask, but Dax growls in his wolf form, stalking closer, his hackles prickling on his back. Rushing to my feet, I race to shove myself between them, holding my hands up to get them to stop before they try to attack each other.

Stretching his paws out in front of him, Dax transforms into a man and gets to his feet. His hulking form towers next to me as he tries to intimidate Flynn. I step closer and press my hand to Dax's chest, getting him to back up. He looks ready to punch Flynn in the face. I'm confused as hell over his sudden rage toward Flynn, and Dax seems to be in hit first, think about it later mode.

"Was this your doing?" Dax asks, testing my strength while taking a step forward. I have no choice but to step with him before he knocks me over. And damn it he's strong when he's determined. Waving my hand at Flynn, I get him to stay out of reach. Dax might charge him at any second.

"What's going on?" I give up on trying to keep Dax back with my hand and instead shove my shoulder to his pec, using my whole body to force him to stop trying to get to Flynn before we can talk. No one else moves, remaining quiet. I almost glare and command them to help me.

Dax growls at me, linking his fingers to my sides like he's going to flip me over his head and into Sagan's arms. "You set us up, didn't you? I knew I couldn't fucking trust you, warlock."

Aggravation whips through me at him blatantly ignoring me. I scrunch my face. "Dax, calm down. I don't want you doing something you'll regret."

"No, Lyric. I'm not going to calm down, because it's true. This bastard has been playing us this whole damn time." Dax grabs my hand and tugs me to him protectively. The rest of my guys shift closer, moving to form a semi-circle around us to jump in at one of our commands. "I have proof. He wears the mark of the wanted."

"I don't know what that even means," I say. "How do you

know? Who told you?" I huff a deep breath as Dax's words spin through my mind, making me dizzy.

"Ryland told me before he got away." Dax's deep voice rumbles near my ear as he bows into me.

My mouth drops open. "And you believe him?" Because I wouldn't trust any of the competitors in a million years, especially now. They'd do or say anything to try to tear my pack from me.

"More than I do this bastard," Dax snaps. "Now get out of the way. We need to figure out this bullshit."

I open my mouth to tell him to back down, but one look into his golden eyes shows me that he realizes that his anger at Flynn caused him to act in a way I don't appreciate. Frowning, Dax swallows, his jaw twitching, and he leans in to whisper something into my ear.

Dax's lips brush my earlobe. "Lyric, I—"

"I can explain. I want to explain," Flynn says, his soft voice sending my heart sinking into my stomach. The strange tone to his voice drags my attention from Dax. Flynn shuffles a teensy step closer, braving to face me with the looming pack of seriously growling, untrusting, ready to attack wolves around me.

I shift my gaze to meet his pleading lavender eyes. His pouty mouth looks unbelievably kissable in a moment most would go on the defense and automatically try to lie their way out of whatever kind of trouble they have brought upon themselves. But not Flynn. His sad eyes capture mine, his shoulders slumping in defeat. He fucked up. I know it. Dax isn't getting riled up for nothing. A part of me hates that Dax has a reason. Another part of me despises that Flynn gave my guys one. And lastly, the remaining part of me, the part tied to my heart feels like it's about to explode and kill me.

I lick my lips. "What is my mate talking about, Flynn?" My voice shakes with the words, and I break his gaze, my stupid eyes already threatening to leak with my aching soul. How could I have grown so attached to Flynn so quickly that my heart hurts at even the thought of his betrayal?

Dax drapes his arms around me, hugging me from behind as he senses my wild emotions, everything catching up to me. I just wanted a moment to breathe. Today was supposed to be easy. We were supposed to get in and out of Lunar Crest and then celebrate with ice cream. We were going to make an official plan to find my dad. Now, everything has gone to shit.

"Flynn," I repeat. "Tell me. You said you wanted to explain."

Flynn clears his throat. "Just us...just for a minute."

Sagan growls from behind Dax, setting the others off.

Spinning me around, Dax pins me to him, sliding his hand to my lower back. "We're not letting you have a second alone with our mate."

"He lied to us about who he was. He doesn't belong to the coven assigned as the gatekeepers. Tell her, Flynn. Tell her how you've been lying," Sagan says through our mind link, allowing

Flynn in for a moment so that he doesn't have to change from his powerful form.

Dax tries to keep me facing him, but I twist in his arms to face Flynn. The second my eyes meet his, I know that there is truth to Dax and Sagan's accusations. Flynn rubs the back of his neck and stares at the ground, silently trying to work out what to say. If I wasn't holding Dax back, he'd probably lift Flynn off his feet and shake the answers out of him.

"Are you not from the Tenebris Coven?" I ask, staring at Flynn, hoping the weight of my gaze will make him look at me. "Why would you lie about that? Who are you with?"

A minute of silence passes between us. Sterling, Sagan, Bastien, and Caz encroach on our space, caging us in even more within their circle to ensure Flynn doesn't try anything that will put me in jeopardy. Dax links his fingers around mine, tightening his hold like he expects Flynn to cast a spell and take me with him.

"Tell me. Please. Is that why you said you should steal me away from my pack? You have other plans?" I won't stop questioning everything until he gives me answers. His silence is killing me.

"He *what?*" Sterling snaps, his voice whipping through my mind. "You fucker!"

I don't have a chance to react as Sterling launches from the circle and jumps on Flynn, knocking him sideways. Slamming his heavy paws into Flynn's chest, Sterling pins him down and bares his fangs, releasing a threatening growl that vibrates in my bones, even at this distance away.

"Lyric, please," Flynn says, covering his face with his arms instead of trying to use magic to protect himself. He looks defeated. Hopeless. Just watching Sterling threaten to bite him leaves me conflicted. It pains me to be in this position in the first place.

I try to break away from Dax to intervene, but he doesn't release me. I jerk my elbow into his gut, and he swings his arm across my chest, pinning my arms to my sides. I could fight him harder to break free, but everyone's emotions crash through me. My mind, heart, and soul war with each other, battling it out about what to do.

"Dax, let me go," I say, my voice coming out a whisper, but at least it doesn't crack. "I mean it. I'm your pack leader."

"Gorgeous, I can feel you. Flynn hurt you, but you like him, and you're conflicted. You don't have to be in this position." Sagan's voice trickles to me, pushing through the others' heated emotions.

Sterling snaps his teeth inches from Flynn's face, yet still, he does nothing magical to protect himself. Caz and Bastien remain quiet yet observant, waiting for someone to command them. Whether it's me or Dax, I don't know.

"Lyric, control them. I just need a second," Flynn says, his voice rising to speak over the growls.

"A second to what? Come up with a believable lie?" Dax

says, his voice deepening, his wolf peeking through his golden gaze. "I knew I should've taken care of you when I had the chance." Pointing at Sterling, Dax adds, "Take him down. We're done with him."

My chest clenches, my emotions swirling wildly. I head-butt Dax in the chin, getting him to release me. Bolting forward, I lock my fingers around Sterling's tail and yank him back. "Sterling, no! Stand down. Dax is not your alpha, damn it. I will handle this."

"Handle this how? Like the last time? Just letting him do whatever the hell he wants while keeping us out of things?" Dax flares his nostrils with his words. He clenches his fingers as I stand between him and Flynn, keeping everyone back. "We're your pack. We have your best interest at heart, but I'm not sure if you have ours."

"Are you kidding me, Dax?" I yell, throwing out my hands.

Bastien nips the back of Dax's leg. "You don't need to be an asshole."

"I'm only speaking what's on all of our minds," Dax snaps. "She's let him close to her without discussing how we feel about it. We're a pack. She's our mate."

Dax's words explode pain in my chest as if he physically stabs me with them. The edges of my vision shadow. How can he think this of me? That I don't care or have them in mind?

"Don't act like you haven't kept shit from her," Flynn retorts, braving to speak from behind me.

"Stop. Stop!" I shriek, my voice echoing through the air.

I gasp and bend forward, trying to get my body to settle down. I just need the world to stop for a minute. I need to feel as if it won't implode and take us all with it. Everyone's anger and suspicion bat through me, making it hard to think about anything apart from Dax's accusations and Flynn's betrayal, whatever that may be.

And Dax's fury and hurt don't help any. I was obviously wrong to think we've moved past me not telling them about Flynn right away. I know he's going to regret saying the words he had, but it won't change the fact that he felt that way—that maybe they all do—and I'm afraid what that means for all of us. I don't have experience dealing with all of this.

A sudden quiet blankets the world around me, stifling the growls of my pack mates. Soft footsteps draw closer before Flynn touches my shoulder.

"As you wish, she-wolf," Flynn says, choosing to act on my thoughts that he eavesdropped on. "I've stopped the world for you."

I stiffen under the feather-light caress of his hand on my bare skin, my body reacting to my anger despite my mind trying to calm down. Swinging my fist up, I punch Flynn in the stomach, forcing the air from his lungs. I jerk my leg up and knee him in the chin with his bow, knocking him off his feet.

"Unfreeze the damn world, Flynn!" I shout, balling my

hands into fists. "How dare you use your magic against my mates. You weren't invited to listen in on my thoughts."

Flynn pushes his hands into the ground, propping himself up. "You were practically screaming them at me. I couldn't handle another second of Dax's hypocritical ass. And fuck, Lyric. I just want a damn minute to talk to you without a pack of wolves ready to shred me apart at any second. Your mates are overprotective. Dax struggles with following your authority. The others treat him like an alpha-mate, and I'm worried that they'll treat you like they do the leaders of Lulupoterra, and you're too blind to see anything otherwise."

"My relationship with my pack is none of your business," I say.

Flynn's eyes flicker with electric light. "Well, someone needs to keep them in line if you won't."

Fury swells through me, and I tackle him, grabbing his hands to yank them over his head. The heat between my legs presses against the skin of his bare stomach, his shirt rolled up from my gesture. Flynn has the nerve to flick his eyes right at my vagina, and his lavender gaze sparks with sizzling magic.

I slap him across the face. "Don't be a fucking perv! It's your fault I'm out here naked. You're the one who relocated me from the motel before I even had the chance to dress."

"You're blaming me? It was Dax who abandoned you and broke the barrier. Don't take out his shortcomings on me. I've been doing nothing but helping you. I've saved not only your life several times but also your mates." Flynn's face morphs with his words, his anger turning his handsome features monstrous.

"But why? Why do it? What do you truly get out of it? You still haven't answered my questions. What are you hiding, Flynn?"

"You are too fucking naïve, Lyric. I'm afraid no matter what I say, it won't make a difference. So what's the point?" Flynn's monstrous features soften and return to his pouty face.

"The point is to talk to me, damn it," I snap.

He grinds his teeth. "But you don't listen."

I raise my hand to slap him again in anger and frustration, wanting to beat the answers out of him like I would one of the competitors, but I stop short. Because he's not a competitor. He doesn't need to be manhandled. And...he's right. I have been naïve and overly trusting. I have put too much faith into others when my dad taught me better than this. He taught me that the only person I should trust in the universe is myself.

Tightening my jaw, I slide off Flynn and push to my feet. My fury runs too hotly, too out of control, that it stops me from thinking clearly. Who have I become? I don't like this version of myself. Everything is so messed up. All I wanted was to get the things I needed and find my dad. But it's like the universe wants to constantly get in my way. It wants me to live with a damn broken heart.

Flynn gets to his feet and shuffles forward, tugging his

shirt over his head. I stare at my frozen pack mates as my world moves on without them, Flynn continuing to still the world. He doesn't offer me the shirt to put on myself and instead slips it over my head for me. The soft fabric engulfs me with his fresh, minty scent, his magical fragrance somehow managing to calm my racing heart and thoughts despite how angry I am at him.

"I'm sorry, Lyric," he whispers, taking a step away. He rubs the back of his neck and searches the sky like he'll find out how to deal with this written in the vast expanse of blue. "I didn't want things to be this way."

"Then tell me the truth. We could've avoided all of this if you just told me the truth from the beginning. What was Dax talking about? If you're not with the gatekeepers, who are you with?" I swallow, my throat burning, the fire snuffing out inside me the longer I stand here, vulnerable and within Flynn's magical bubble.

"I didn't lie to you about my family. I am a member of the Tenebris Coven, but Dax was right. We're not gatekeepers. We're outcasts and criminals. I'm one of Magaelorum's most wanted warlocks." Flynn scrubs his scruffy jaw, darting his eyes from above to meet mine again. "We were framed for something we didn't do, and half of my coven is now imprisoned in Magaelorum. The High Council thinks we're responsible for the rise in lycans, and I want to clear our names. I want to go home." He sounds so earnest. Almost like a lost boy in need.

And what he says now, I already partially knew. He had told us that he was helping me not only from the goodness of his heart. I didn't realize to what extent. But why didn't he just tell me all this from the beginning? I trusted him. I liked him. I still like him, and more than on the level of desire I know we both crave.

"You should've told me, Flynn. I would've still helped you," I whisper, letting my hair veil my face. I feel so exposed and vulnerable when I know I should be strong. I just—fuck. Even after all of this, I want to help him. I want to forgive him. "I can still help you, but—"

He groans and shifts on his feet, flicking his gaze to my pack behind us. "Like your pack would let you. I would have to kidnap you. Dax reacted based on something he heard from your own damn enemies without even double checking to see if it was true. He's done with me. You heard him, and your pack clearly agrees with him."

His comment about kidnapping me unsettles me. It's like he still considers it.

"You don't know that. Dax is just upset and was taken by surprise. My pack does listen to me, despite what you think. We're just adjusting to everything. Can you blame them for wanting to keep me safe? Look at the shitshow that my life is. We have so many enemies that I feel like I can't trust any-one...and it sucks. I don't even know how to deal with this." I hug my arms around myself, stepping back as Flynn steps closer.

Magic flickers in his lavender gaze, and he gives me a once-over. "You won't be able to with them. You know that, right?"

I frown. "Just stop. They're my pack mates. Mine. So, no. You're wrong. I can't do it without them."

"But they keep you naïve." Flynn steps even closer. "Lyric, they—"

I hold my hand up, getting him to stop. "You do it too! You made a huge deal about no one being honest with me, yet you're not much different. Maybe we all have our shit we want to keep from each other. But even so, I was depending on you, Flynn. I needed you. I *wanted* you. How can I trust you? You keep insinuating that you want to take me away." I rub my lips together, trying to suppress my chaotic, messy feelings. I meet Flynn's lavender gaze, my heart hurting worse by the second. Now that I've said my feelings out loud, I don't know what to expect, and I hate it.

"Those were just thoughts. You don't understand because we're not like each other. Your pack might be okay with sharing you, but—" His comment fades and he shakes his head, trying to take my hand. "You can trust me."

I recoil, stumbling just out of his reach. "How? I liked you. I've been honest with you. Now I feel like I don't know you. And it hurts, Flynn. I don't even know what to do."

Flynn shuffles closer, holding his hands up as if I'm a wild animal on the verge of attacking. And who knows? Maybe I am. Maybe my she-wolf now dominates me, controlling my thoughts and actions with a disregard to what my humanity wants.

"Please, Lyric," he whispers, his face scrunching with the same hurt that mars mine. "Let me shield this place and take you somewhere that we can talk more."

Panic sneaks into my heart. "What? No. My pack mates nee—"

"I'm so sorry. I'll fix this." Flynn gathers magic in his palms. "I know I fucked things up."

I walk backward, keeping space between us. "So did I, Flynn. We all did." My back hits Dax's firm chest, my need to keep my distance. "I fucked up because I allowed myself to open up to you. I started to care about you, and you betrayed me. And you still won't just tell me everything without trying to separate me from my pack. You know, I was starting to fucking feel something for you—"

Dax growls, his body rippling behind mine. Hitting him must've somehow broken Flynn's spell and the world kicks on. Dax engulfs me in his muscular arms and lifts me off my feet. My words echo through the air, ringing loudly for my pack mates to hear.

I gasp at the rush of their emotions, spinning around me in a furious tornado hell-bent on ripping and scattering my soul across the universe. I know they suspected that Flynn was attracted to me. But having them hear me say shit out loud, without warning and in a time that feels as if our lives are about to explode...fuck my life.

"Lyric..." Sagan's soft voice fades with his words. "You have feelings for him?"

"I fucking knew it," Sterling snaps, his voice penetrating my thoughts as he remains open yet talks to the others. "I knew this would happen. I knew he'd hurt her."

I blink my eyes, tears threatening to spill on my cheeks. "St-Sterling, I—"

Flynn raises his hands, gathering magic in his palms. "I'm sorry," he says, shuffling away, putting more space between us. "To all of you."

"It's too late," Dax snaps. "We can't trust you. Get out of here before I—"

Flynn claps his hands, sending blinding light through the air. I wobble on my feet, disoriented as he vanishes before I can say anything. I bow forward and clutch my knees, my whole body trembling with anger, hurt, and now a sudden emptiness I never imagined. Flynn's absence leaves my world spinning.

If Dax didn't lift me off my feet, I'd smash into the ground and curl in on myself.

"Fuck. We have to move," Caz says, speaking up. "His shield would have gone with him."

I stare at the spot Flynn stood, wondering what the fuck we're going to do now. Without him, we have no protective magic. We are being hunted by basically everyone, and now I'm not sure I'll ever be able to find my dad. He abandoned me, ignoring the fact that I told him I'd handle my pack. Instead, he just listened to Dax.

"Damn it, you guys," I say, trying to sound strong, even though my voice falters.

"We don't have time for this. Caz is right. We have to move. Transform, Lyric," Dax says, his voice whispering into my mind. "Hurry up."

His command reminds me of what Flynn said about him acting like an alpha-mate.

Pushing the thought away, I tug off Flynn's shirt and stretch my arms over my head, breathing through my muscle spasms, my humanity struggling to let go of the form I find most powerful. Snatching Flynn's shirt from the ground with my teeth, I hold it while the others surround me.

With one last look around the forest, I follow behind Dax.

I let him lead our way.

4

ABANDONED

I HAVE SO MUCH TO say to my pack, but I don't know how to say it. I'm upset, angry, hurt, and in some serious need of cuddles. But now doesn't feel like the time. Everyone is on edge and spread out, watching the area. I feel practically useless, because I don't know what to do, so I just prove Flynn right and submit to the circumstances, allowing my guys to do what they feel is necessary.

I wish I could get my shit together. I'm better than just letting the circumstances control me. But I'm tired. My heart hurts. And in all honesty, I never expected to have such a blowout so soon in my pack. What a way to feel like I might doom them all. That's probably what Flynn can't comprehend and why he's so adamant. He'll never understand the bond that arose with my claim on my guys. He will never grasp that it's not about me or them, but all of us together. A part of me hoped that maybe I could include him too.

"I know this is screwed up, but please eat something, Lyric," Sagan says, dropping a dead raccoon in front of me. "For me. It's been all day, and I'm worried about you."

"I'm not hungry," I whisper through my mind. "I just—I don't know."

"You can talk to me about anything, you know. I overreacted earlier, and I'm sorry. I didn't think about your feelings and how you'd want to handle the situation. You never mentioned anything about Flynn, but I knew better. I just—I didn't want to believe it. And then when Ryland accused us of working with a criminal warlock and against the five High Priestesses...I was shocked. Angry. I didn't want to believe it, but he wears the same mark I've seen on the coven who killed my dad." Sagan's admission whirls through my mind. I understand why he reacted as he did. I can't truly blame him, especially now.

"Flynn isn't with any of those covens," I say, huffing air through my nostrils.

Sagan plops onto the ground and whimpers, nudging the

carcass closer. "I know, gorgeous. I just still don't know about any of this. All I want is to keep you safe...and fed. As content as I can make you. So please, try to eat a little. It's not so bad in your wolf form. I promise."

I flare my nostrils, my mind shouting at me not to even consider touching his offering, because...well, it's roadkill and half flattened. "If I hate it, we're breaking into someone's house and raiding their fridge...as wolves."

Sagan chuckles in my mind and uses his nose to push his scavenged supposed food closer. He knew I didn't want him to kill any animals, but this isn't exactly what I had in mind for dinner. But what are we supposed to do? We have no money, no shelter, and no protection at all in the Mortal World. Without an ID, I can't even go to a bank and get money from the account I left behind. I'm sure the she-wolves probably thought we might try that, and the last thing I need is for them to track us. Though, I'm not so sure they are. The witch who collared some of the competitors might've put a stop to it.

And now that I think about them...fuck.

I lie on the ground and rest my head on my paws, facing away from Sagan's gross but thoughtful attempt to feed me. I can't do it. My mind won't let my she-wolf take control. My human rationale refuses to accept these shitty circumstances. There has to be something we can do. I'm not so sure how long we can survive in the Mortal World without help. We might be better off somewhere else that's at least a bit safer. "Maybe we should just go back to Lulupoterra."

I hate even the thought, because the calamity that Paige left in her wake nearly guarantees a death sentence to my pack, but I don't know what else to do. How can we survive out here? There has to be a way to prove we weren't involved.

"You know the risk," Sagan says, nudging the carcass out of the way, knowing that I won't touch it, not with my stomach in knots. He nuzzles his snout against mine and licks me.

I tip my snout toward the ground and flatten my ears. "Then maybe I should go back. I can force the she-wolves to hear me out. I'll tell them everything. They need to know that the witches collared Antone and some of the others." I try not to think about what being collared means for him. It can't be anything good, but that's something else I don't know how to deal with. Antone and I haven't always seen eye-to-eye, but he's Bastien's brother and he's been an ally despite being an asshole half the time.

"They think we're working with a witch coven. Maybe if there was a way that would guarantee your protection, but I don't think it's a good idea to risk it. The alpha-mates will cage you." Sagan crawls closer to me until his big wolf body presses against mine, not allowing any space between us. He noses my neck and licks my ear, giving me the affection he thinks I need in this moment.

If only what I needed didn't include turning back into my human self, finding some clothes, and figuring how the hell to build my life again with only the help of my pack. I'm afraid I'll fail as their leader, and we'll lose more than what we already have. I can't bear to think that I'll be responsible for our doom if I can't get my shit together. I've lived in the Mortal World all my life. I should know how to handle this.

"We will get it figured out," Sagan murmurs. "You will not fail as our leader. None of us will let that happen, gorgeous."

I sigh a breath through my nostrils without comment.

He play-growls, licking the side of my face again. "Do you need me to convince you? That might require me to wrestle you until you admit I'm right. Who knows. Maybe I'll get to pin your cute ass down."

I don't get the chance to react. Two arms engulf me, and Sagan scratches his fingers into my coat, rubbing my wolfie body while he now sits next to me in his human form. His warm, inviting emotions encircle me. He fills me with his happiness over teasing me, snuffing out the bitter emotions from one shitty day.

"Get ready, gorgeous. I'm going to figure out the spot that makes your paw thump," Sagan says, chuckling. "Once I find it, you're going to be mine forever."

I try to nip his arm. "You better not. You know I'm already yours forever."

I squirm and growl as he moves his hands from my ears and down my neck to make his way to my belly. Flipping me onto my back, he smiles down at me and ruffles his fingers into my fur. It doesn't weird me out as much anymore that I enjoy this kind of affection from him in my wolf form. It's pure love and adoration with Sagan. I savor how much he loves playing with me, lightening both our moods. He scratches my ribs, shocking the hell out of me when my back leg actually kicks uncontrollably. I yip and wiggle, trying to push him off of me with my paws, but he has too great a hold, keeping me from moving.

It drives me crazy in the best way possible. The world outside the two of us no longer exists as long as Sagan keeps laughing. It's the best thing I've heard in a while, and I had no idea how much I needed it or how much I survive on my mates' good emotions, which have been scarce these last few weeks.

"That's going to have to change," Sagan murmurs, responding to my thoughts.

"Good luck with Dax," I quip, sending the thought to him.

Sagan scrunches his nose. "I'll ensure he comes whimpering to you with his tail between his legs later."

"No need. I'll get him to do it myself," I respond.

Sagan grins and scratches my belly again. "That's my fierce leader."

Closing my eyes, I will my transformation to take control of my she-wolf, forcing her to let my humanity break free. I can't stand not being in the same form as Sagan for a moment longer. I want to give him the affection I know he craves from me.

Sagan bows into me, caressing his lips to mine the second I finish. I tease him with my tongue, lightly brushing it to his until he hums with his hardening desire. His warm body pushes me into the ground as he deepens his kiss, and I comb my fingers into his blond hair, stopping him from trying to pull away.

I don't care if we're hidden just within the forest surrounding some small town I'm unfamiliar with. I don't care that someone could happen upon us during a nature hike. I don't even care that Caz and Bastien stand guard protectively just out of sight, allowing me to give all my attention to Sagan. All I care about is the softness of Sagan's lips on mine, how his hand sparks tingles across my body as he maps his way down my stomach in a torturously slow pace to tease and test me to see if I'll allow him to continue. All I care about is that we're together, wrapping ourselves in the love we've declared and trying to make good of this awful situation.

Sagan's fingers slip between my legs, and I gasp and shift my knee, giving him better access to my body. He moans with me, his mind open and connected, experiencing the pleasure he elicits with his index finger as he glides it harder over my clit, tracing his way over my sensitive skin. The tenseness melts from my body, the pleasure he creates a stress relief I had no idea I needed. I kiss him more fervently, clutching onto him while I roll my hips to show him exactly how hard and fast I want him to touch me.

Arching my back, I break from his mouth and close my eyes, enjoying the sizzling ecstasy he awakens inside me. Sagan kisses my jaw and makes his way down my neck. He traces his tongue over my breast and sucks my nipple, pulling it between his teeth, the sensation making me moan louder. I massage my fingers into his shoulders, listening to the sexy thoughts coursing through his mind. He hums, craving to taste more of me, fantasizing about making me tremble and scream his name.

My heart races with his desire, his mind focusing solely on my pleasure. His hard-on teases me, grazing my thigh, and I try to grab for him to guide him inside me. Sagan moans his disagreement and grabs my hand, pinning my arm to the ground.

"Not yet," he whispers, shifting his weight to kneel between my legs. "I've been dying to get my mouth on you. Your scent and taste intoxicate me. I can't get enough. I need to feel your pleasure. To experience what I do to you."

Damn. I want that too.

"So selfish," I tease, gasping a breath.

"Mmmhmm. I'm addicted to you. I can't help it." Sagan sucks the top of my breast into his mouth, leaving a hickey.

"What if I want to taste and suck you? Feel your pleasure?" I moan as he leaves another mark on my skin.

A rumble escapes his mouth, vibrating across my skin. He tips his head up to drink in my gaze and shakes his head. I grin and lean back on my elbows, loving how our bodies are as dirty as our thoughts.

Working his way down, Sagan kisses my stomach to my hips, positioning his broad shoulders between my legs. Pinching my ass cheeks, he pulls my body higher to his face, curling me as he holds me in place. I dig my fingers into the soft dirt, blindly grabbing for something to anchor me to the ground before I float away on our passion.

Sagan kisses the apex of my thighs, rolling his tongue over my excited body, until he sucks my clit into his mouth with enough pressure to steal my breath in the best way possible. I moan with the pressure, the sensation of his mouth so incredibly satisfying that I lose myself to our lust, craving more from him.

He eats me out, licking and sucking, tasting me as if he's starving and I'm the only thing that can settle his raging appetite. Whispering to me through our mind link, Sagan begs for me to look at him. I bite my bottom lip, trying my best to stifle any noise that escapes my mouth. Fluttering my lashes, I meet his intense gaze through my heavy lids. He hums and picks up speed by nodding his head up and down, the sensation bringing me to my peak.

My body explodes with tingles, my muscles spasming as I orgasm. I squeeze Sagan's head between my thighs, sinking back to the ground. He moans with me, the rumbling sound vibrating across my skin as he experiences my pleasure along with me.

I'll never get over the fact that with our mind link, we can feel each other on an intimate level unlike anything I've ever known or expected. A wave of warmth—of Sagan's love and pleasure, his pride in getting me off—crashes over me.

Reaching down, I grab for Sagan, wanting the weight of his body to smother me in its delectable goodness. He crawls forward, propping himself up on one arm and using his other to pull me up by my neck to kiss him. His muscles ripple, his erection throbbing and flexing between my legs. I mold my lips to his, exploring the sweet taste of his tongue, savoring his affection. The heat of his body warms me from outside in, and I rock my hips up, rubbing my dampness against his thick shaft.

"I love you," Sagan whispers against my mouth. "I love you more than anything. I want you to know that. My feelings will never change. I trust you. I know you will always guide us on the path you think is best."

I ease away from him, meeting his blue gaze. "You heard my thoughts about what Flynn told me." It's not a question. His reassurance sinks deeply into me, awakening the part of me my dad tried his best to get me to suppress. *Protect yourself. Keep your guard up. It's you against the world, Lyric.* But he was wrong. It's us—me and my pack—against the world, and Sagan's words solidify what I never knew I wanted so desperately until claiming the men to stand beside me.

Sagan's eyes flicker with something indecipherable, his features hard yet his gaze soft. "You never have to worry about me or us or what to expect from our future. You are my leader, Lyric. You are my forever, and I'm yours. Always."

His words fill up the emptiness I hadn't realized was consuming me. The uncertainty that was clinging to me vanishes with any ounce of doubt I carried. A smile spreads across my face as I feel the truth to his words deep in my soul as our essences mingle and join the way I yearn for our bodies to in this moment.

Flynn was wrong about my pack mates. I'm nothing like the leaders of Lulupoterra, and my mates are far from being anything like the asshole alpha-mates. I don't care if he thinks otherwise. Just because he thinks it, doesn't make it true. What it does is make me fight fiercely to prove him wrong. It...

I guess that doesn't matter now. Flynn's gone. He's broken his promise and abandoned me.

"And I'd never," Sagan whispers. "Now let me get your mind off everything, okay? I need to guarantee that not even an ounce of unhappiness touches your soul when you're with me."

I graze my fingers along his cheek, tracing his chiseled jawline. "I love you. You always know exactly what I need."

Sagan kisses me deeper, aligning his body to mine. I suppress all my thoughts of Flynn and the bullshit of today and focus on how perfect Sagan makes me feel. I don't want him to think otherwise. He deserves my full attention, needing my affection as much as I need his. The universe has been hard on all of us, and it's my duty as his mate to ensure I return the same to him. That we give and take equally. It's not about him or me. It's us. It's the only way I want things to work.

"I will give you everything you could ever want, my gorgeous woman," he murmurs, slowly pushing his hard-on between my legs, the pressure of him slipping inside me so good that I dig my fingers into his shoulders, forgetting everything else.

"You already do," I say.

I moan with his thrusts as he picks up his pace. He knows how I love it rough and wild when I'm in a mood, and he listens and follows my thoughts, giving me exactly what I want. What feels best in this moment. Sagan twists his hand into my hair, keeping me arched a bit to continue to kiss me. The position tests my core strength and awakens my body with lust and desire, ensuring such immense pleasure I know I'll think about for days.

Hooking my legs around him, I open my body wider to feel every amazing inch of him. I break from his mouth and hug my arms around his sides, clinging to him. He swings his body into mine, panting against the crook of my neck. I graze my teeth to his shoulder and suck on his skin to leave my own mark. The sky burns with reds and oranges overhead, the fiery sunset so beautiful that it makes this moment perfect despite everything.

Sagan moans, his heart beating in rhythm with mine. Our

bodies and souls merge as one entity as we share our pleasure and passion, our minds in sync with each other. Turning his head, he silently begs for another kiss. He steals the noise from my lips, keeping me quiet through our lovemaking, though I know how much he enjoys hearing me moan his name.

"You feel so good," I whisper to him through our mind link. "I just want to scream to the world."

He can't control his own mouth and groans against my lips. "You're indescribable. I will never get enough of you."

Something about the spontaneity and wildness of being together like this in the woods satisfies the she-wolf inside me. I want nothing more than for this moment to never end. I could share my passion with Sagan always and forever. With him, the world seems less complicated and more wondrous, magical...perfect. It's everything I could ever ask for and more.

Sagan smiles through another kiss, his happiness washing from him to me like snuggling together under a cozy blanket on a freezing winter night. He whispers his love for me again and again, the sound of my name a breath of perfection coming from his lips. His muscles flex and he tightens his arms around me with his orgasm. I tip my head back and moan as he cums, my body enjoying exactly what I do to him as I experience exactly what he does.

He cuddles me close, not pulling apart right away, continuing to give me his full attention and all the affection I could ever want. I could survive on his kisses alone and live the rest of my life in utter bliss. I know it's impossible, but it doesn't make me stop from wanting to try.

But then Sterling howls, his call pulling Sagan's attention from me.

And fuck. It's not his normal call. It's a warning.

I groan and cling onto Sagan, not untangling my legs from his waist. He slowly slides out of me but lifts me with him, not even caring that we're both naked, smelling of our feral passion in the forest. I consider asking Sagan to set me on my feet, but he seems determined to hold onto me forever like carrying me is his new sole purpose in life. So I let him.

Bastien responds to Sterling's howl with his own, and he and Caz dart past us in their wolf forms. I twist my torso and watch them run ahead of us to greet him. Dax howls next, the depth of his wolf's call digging into my bones. I try my best to silence my thoughts as I already start to guard myself, afraid Dax will say something about the fact that I seduced Sagan in the forest when anything could have come and threatened us. Dax was moody enough over Flynn that I'm afraid he'll take things out on Sagan, knowing well enough the others won't let him do so on me.

Sagan strokes his hand up and down the length of my back, striding toward our pack mates without hesitation. "You didn't seduce me, gorgeous. I seduced you."

I smirk and rest my chin on his shoulder. "We seduced each other."

"Then don't worry. If Dax says anything, I'll force his broody ass into submission. He needs to be put in check sometimes, and right now, he's obviously too frightened to see things clearly." Sagan kisses my temple with his words. "You can call him out on it. He'd deserve it."

"Uh-oh. Incoming, brother." Sterling's voice erupts in my mind in warning as his wolf howls again.

I tense in Sagan's arms, expecting a ferocious lycan to crash through the trees, snarling and preparing to devour us. Instead, Dax charges our way, his mahogany coat shining with coppery tones in the setting sun.

He growls, pushing off the ground to launch at Sagan, not even thinking about me being in his arms. Sagan spins out of the way and sets me on my feet. He transforms into his beautiful blue-eyed wolf a second before Dax collides into him. The two of them roll across the ground in a fight not unlike the ones they've gotten into during the She-Wolf Games. Fur flies as their teeth gnash into each other. Hot emotions smash into my chest. I heave a breath, winded, the intensity like being crashed into by a solid body.

"Stop," I command, bowing forward. Their mind links fuck with me in the worst way, and I can't concentrate on shutting them out.

Bastien, Caz, and Sterling bound their way in their direction, but Caz circles me, using his body to stand in front of me protectively. I clutch his tri-colored coat, bracing on his hulking wolf body. He rumbles with a warning growl any time Dax or Sagan gets too close in their fight for dominance. Annoyance rushes through me at the sight of Dax and Sagan snapping at Sterling as he tries to get between them. The two of them don't see eye-to-eye when it comes to me in this moment, each wanting to take care of me in their own way instead of working together as a pack. And it feels as if it's killing me, tearing me in half when all I want is to be together.

"That's enough!" I yell, projecting my voice both through the air and my mind. "If you don't quit it, I'll neuter the both of you."

Sterling latches onto Sagan's tail and drags him back. Sagan snaps his teeth at Dax in warning as he tries to go after him again. Bastien intercepts Dax, shoving him away with his head, getting more space between them. Tension runs hot, our emotions tangle and twist, trying to choke all of us.

What is happening to us? Where did the men who promised me loyalty, strength, and above all, themselves, go? Right now, I don't recognize my pack. I'm sure if I looked in a mirror, I wouldn't even recognize myself.

And I hate this.

I fucking hate everything about this.

Spinning away, I cover my face with my hands, sucking in a few deep breaths. I push everyone from my mind and shut them out completely. The sudden silence does nothing to help me. If anything, I feel worse. If this is how things will be from now on, I won't have a choice but to wall myself off from their madness, despite how alone I feel doing so. Because this sucks. Fucking Flynn. This is his fault. He abandoned us…

Or I guess, we sent him away. Dax might've commanded him to go, but I didn't even try to call him back. I haven't even stood up to Dax and put him in check like I should've. I'm just so tired. Weak. A disappointment to both my parents.

Tears splash my cheeks, my emotions sneaking up on me when I need to be strong. Why the hell is Flynn's absence getting to me so much right now? Maybe because we wouldn't be in this position if he stayed. But even so, I know we're capable of taking care of ourselves. I know we are. I have faith in my abilities and my pack mates. It just sucks. I never thought I'd want things to return to how they were. Playing the She-Wolf Games, getting time alone with each of my guys, not having to stress every damn second of every damn day was better than this, despite the situation and rules of the leaders—or the point of the games.

A cool nose pokes my ass cheek, making me jump. I twist around and attempt to whack Sterling in the snout, but he bows playfully, dodging out of my way. He races around me and nuzzles his big head right between my thighs, weaving through my legs.

"Damn it, blondie. I want to hump the hell out of you. You smell like my next fantasy. Bend over and brace yourself. I'm going to make you cream and scream while my scepter penetrates your treasure trove. Your boner-killing mood is about to get banged to the next century." Sterling stands on his hind legs and wraps his paws around my waist, humping me in his wolf form. The absurdity of his teasing cracks through the darkness consuming my soul.

Shoving him away, I make space to drop to my knees. I bow forward and stick my ass in the air, surprising the hell out of him. And everyone else. I can feel their gazes penetrate my surprise offering of my body to Sterling, my gesture kicking the fight and disagreement out of all of them. Gotta love my horn-dogs and the upcoming mating season that turns all of us to puddles of lusty mush.

I shake my hips. "Have at me. Whatever gets my mind off this bullshit. But you better transform into your sexy man-self or I'll send your red rocket blasting into outer space."

"What. The. Fuck." Sterling's voice sounds in my ears, and he drops down beside me. He folds his arms in front of him, resting his chin on them. Staring at the side of my face, he waits for me to look at him.

I shift on my elbow and meet his suspicious gaze, one of his eyebrows peaking up on his forehead. Leaning closer, I kiss him. "Hurry up. Ravish me," I murmur against his pouty bottom lip before sucking it into my mouth. "Unless you want me to ask one of the others instead."

Blinking a few times, Sterling gathers his thoughts, easing away to scrub his fingers into his cheeks. "My cock says hell yeah, give her what she asks for, but then my damn head doesn't think you actually want my cum cannon in your pleasure factory."

"Want to bet?" I surprise the hell out of Sterling by bumping into him hard enough to knock him onto his back.

He groans deep in his throat, his eyes shadowing with his heavy-lidded desire. I climb on top of him and kiss him, nipping his lip before sucking it into my mouth. His hands tighten around my waist, his fingers digging into my hips. He flexes his cock, thumping it against my back. I expect him to guide my body lower, but he waits for me to make my next move.

"Fuck, Sterling. Don't," Bastien says, stepping closer, cautiously like he's afraid one of us will attack him. "We don't have time for this, and it's your damn responsibility to control yourself. Lyric's nature as a she-wolf is far more powerful than her human sensibility."

Sterling growls against my mouth. "You try telling her no. She feels so good."

"You think I feel good? Want to know how amazing you feel to me?" I reach behind him and stroke my hand up the length of his shaft. "I want you."

Sterling groans again. "I want you more. You have no idea."

I dig my knees into the dirt, raising myself up to sit on top of him. I don't know what the hell I'm even doing, but it's like I can't control myself now that I got riled up. I deal with stress in two ways—fucking someone up or fucking them, and Sterling isn't in the former category, so…

Two big hands hook under my arms and drag me off Sterling before I start fucking his brains out in front of everyone. I yell out in annoyance, my body burning with an all-consuming need. I have a bad case of lady blue-balls. The ache between my legs grows more intense and out of control, nearly painful, like being on the verge of pure ecstasy but nothing helps to give relief.

"Let me go, damn it!" I yell, thrashing in Caz's embrace. His scent permeates around me stronger than ever, so tantalizing and intoxicating that it feels like a bolt of electricity strikes me in my damn clit, but the pain isn't agonizing. It's strangely enjoyable.

I tip my head back and try to strike him with a head-butt. "How dare you get between me and Sterling. I want him. I need him. He's the only thing—"

Caz flips me around to face him, crashing his lips to mine, stealing the complaint from my mouth. The cute bastard. He doesn't let me get carried away to attack him with my lust bomb next and eases away with a smirk. "Take a slow breath, Lyric."

"How can you so easily resist me?" I ask with a teasing tone to my voice. My heart and body settle down the longer I'm in his arms.

"Because you haven't boned him, blondie," Sterling says

from the ground, totally and unashamedly rubbing his cock. And damn it. I love watching him a bit too much.

Bastien presses his back to mine, drawing my focus. "I know this sucks. I know you're hurt and the upcoming season is messing with all of us, but we need to find shelter for the night. Somewhere we can easily protect ourselves."

"And when we do, I'll dip my stick into your wet well until you can't walk anymore. Because damn. I want to eat your sweet meat, tickle my pickle, and just fuck you until you're content, even if my cock falls off in the process." Sterling gets up from the ground and closes the space to the three of us. He slides his hand between mine and Bastien's bodies, giving my ass a squeeze. "And if that happens, I have back up."

I groan and hide my face against the crook of Caz's shoulder. "Your closeness is doing nothing for my desire."

Sterling dramatically sighs and bounces on his feet. "Damn it. I didn't want Caz to have to do this but you need some serious refocusing and someone who can kill your mood with one look."

Caz shifts me in his arms. "Dax, you bastard. Incoming."

"Protect your balls if you know what's good for you," Bastien adds.

Sagan crosses his arms. "And don't hurt her feelings anymore."

I don't get the chance to react as Caz spins and tosses me in Dax's direction. Dax catches me, his jaw tight, his brows furrowing. He's as upset with me as I am with him, clearly not wanting my closeness. I wiggle from his arms and smack my hand to his chest, annoyance rushing through me.

I'm not sure I can work through this with him until I figure out how to release my frustration over the whole situation. Since sex isn't an option, there is only one other way.

"I'm tired of feeling so bad. I get why you did what you did, but must I remind you that I'm your leader? Because I think I do. So, turn the hell around, Dax," I snap, placing my hands on my hips. I glower at him, even though he gives nothing away in his steely expression.

He lifts an eyebrow, tilting his head at my command. "What the fuck for?"

"Damn it. Just do as she says. Stop acting like a dickwad." Sagan growls with his words. He strides closer but stops short, waiting for my command. "You need to get over yourself and listen to and feel our mate. Don't you get it? She's starting to think you're going to treat her like your damn uncle treated Trista. You're testing her too much with your protectiveness, and I won't stand for it. Show her where you plan to stand in our pack and apologize for acting out of place."

Dax stiffens at Sagan's words, his hands curling and uncurling. Sweeping his gaze over my face, he searches my eyes for the answers I block from him.

If he wants access to my thoughts, he's going to damn-well earn it again. Because this whole situation is fucked up. We can't be fighting. We have enough enemies against us that we don't need this with each other.

"Lyric." His voice softens with my name. Reaching up, he touches my shoulder, playing with my hair. He steps closer and nudges me, putting his body between mine and the others, trying to get a bit of privacy. "Is that what you really think? Because it wasn't my intention. I just—you're my reason for being. You're my life. Without you, I'm nothing." A frown pouts his expression, but I still don't give my thoughts away. I must resist his puppy-dog eyes as he settles down and processes everything without the fire of his emotions. "Will you forgive me?"

I slowly nod my head. "Of course I will. But it doesn't change the fact that I can't get myself in control until I do what I feel needs to be done. Now, turn around." I twirl my finger, motioning to him to turn his back on me.

Swallowing, Dax releases a sigh through his nose and twists on his feet.

I trail my gaze down his muscular back and to his tight ass, his body flexing in anticipation as he tries to figure out what I plan to do. I give nothing away, standing quietly, dragging this out on purpose.

"She's so fucking hot showing her dominance like this," Bastien whispers to Caz.

These guys.

Doing my best to ignore them, I straighten my shoulders.

"Dax, I need you to know why I'm so angry with you," I say, lightly touching the small of his back, keeping behind him so he can't look at me. "I thought I lost you earlier. It felt as if a part of me died."

"I'm sorry," Dax murmurs, his voice gruff yet low. "I never want you to go through that again."

"Yet then you had to go and put yourself at risk by chasing the damn competitors. You accused Flynn of betrayal, which he might have not been forthcoming, but you're also not quick to give me answers. You constantly question my judgment and had the nerve to blame me for trusting a man you trusted too." I keep my voice low, trying as hard as I can not to yell. "I know you did. I felt it."

Dax cranes his neck to try to meet my gaze, but I move farther behind him. "Which is why I was so pissed off. Feeling your growing bond toward him made it all that much worse. It was—"

"I'm not finished," I say, flicking his ass cheek. "You will let me finish, Dax."

He growls, his muscles flexing, but he doesn't respond.

The others stand around and listen quietly, not moving or speaking or intervening. They give us as much space as they can, knowing that this argument is between me and Dax. It's our business to work out even if we're a pack.

"Your stubborn-ass attitude made me feel like shit. It made me question everything, and I hate so much that I do. Because

I love you. I love you and want to help you build an amazing life together as a pack with you standing beside me and backing me up like you promised." I tap my fingers against his bare skin, my mouth brushing against his bulging arm as I keep my voice low.

Admitting the words out loud opens my mind to Dax, allowing him back in. I need him to feel the truth of my words. I need all my guys to. I think we all need a little reminder that what we're going through isn't about running from the pack leaders or fighting witches and lycans. It's not even truly about finding my dad or surviving in the Mortal World.

Our current state is just a temporary grievance that we'll move past.

What we're going through now will help lead us to a life unlike anything we can truly imagine. It'll build a future born from both our shortcomings and our strengths. It'll be what we want. I know it. And I need everyone to remember why we chose each other in the first place.

"I want to give you the world, Lyric," Dax says, shifting on his feet, trying to turn to face me. I know it drives him crazy that I don't allow it, but I'm afraid I'll lose my nerve or get lost in his golden eyes. He blindly reaches for my free hand and misses. He might yank me over his head and into his arms if I allow it. "I want to give our pack everything we deserve, and I will do whatever I think is necessary to do so."

I slap his ass, surprising the hell out of him. Because,

damn it. "No you won't. Your thoughts about this are a huge fucking problem for me." I remain firm in my spot, pressing against him to keep him in place. "What you think might be necessary is different from what I think is necessary. I don't need you acting as if I can't handle myself or our pack. I need you to listen to me and trust that I can take care of you all in the world I grew up in. I do have twenty-three damn years of experience."

"I do. And I'm sorry for the bullshit today. If I could take it back, I would, but I'd still disagree with you about Flynn. He hurt you, damn it. I still feel it, and I hate that it happened," Dax says, hanging his head. "You're our girl. We should've seen it coming."

I sigh. "I'm fine. This isn't even about Flynn. This is about you cooling your hot-head off and listening to me. Trusting me. Accepting that I too can come up with a plan on how to survive in the Mortal World without protective magic."

Dax scrubs his face with his hands. "You're right. I'll do better from now on. I'm your mate, and you're my leader. Now let me hear your plan."

I tighten my mouth, feeling his slight defeat but also his determination to prove himself to me. "You will not only hear it, but you will think about it and work it through with me. Got it? I can't have you guys roaming around as wolves. Or eating roadkill."

"Stealing is probably a no, too," Sterling says, whispering

the words from behind me. He's been dying to speak up and can't help himself. "Huh, blondie?"

I frown and look at him. "What the hell did you steal?"

"Necessities," Dax mutters. "Clothes. Food you'll eat."

"You think clothes are a necessity *now*?" I rest my head on the back of his shoulder. "You know what, never mind. Hold still before you distract me anymore. There is something I need to do, because you're going to need this as a reminder."

Dax straightens his shoulders. "What are you planning to do? Spank me again?"

I purse my lips to keep a straight face. "How else will you remember? I'm going to smack it into your sexy ass so you never forget."

Sterling tips his head back and howls a laugh, making Sagan chuckle. I peek at Bastien and Caz over my shoulder, and they grin at each other, loving every second of the idea of me punishing Dax like this. And hell, so do I. He could use a damn good spanking and maybe it'll knock his bad mood out of him.

Dax groans under his breath, hearing my thoughts. "Is this how things are going to be?"

I trail my hand lower down his back. "Don't you prefer this over, you know, me biting your damn balls off? Consider this a better way to ease my stress."

"If you think this will humiliate me, it won't," Dax quips, his voice even and smug as hell. "Go ahead. Give me your best."

Grabbing his shoulder, I finally turn him slightly to meet his gaze. "I'm not trying to humiliate you. If you think I'd purposely do that, then you should spank your damn self."

"Then what's the point?" This cocky-bastard. "There are better ways to get your aggression out."

"Like I said, this is a reminder. Plus, I'm going to spank the damn bad mood out of you. Win-win for both of us. And if that doesn't work...then I have another suggestion." I can't stop thinking the thought of him jerking off, and Dax totally listens to my fantasy.

"Damn it," Sterling mutters with a groan. "You do realize you're just punishing me now."

I smirk at him. "You know I have other forms of punishment for you."

He play-growls. "You better fucking not."

Winking, I send him a thought about tickling him, knowing how crazy it drives him. Sterling fake-glares and backs away from us like I'll transform this second and pin him down in my wolf form to lick the hell out of his neck. Just the thought makes me smile.

"I'll hold him down if you want," Sagan says, sending the thought into my mind.

I can't stop the laugh from escaping my mouth. "Fuck, yes. When he least expects it."

Dax clears his throat, drawing my attention back to him. I

suck my bottom lip between my teeth and rub my hand over his tight, muscular ass, loving the feeling of teasing him, building the anticipation. He shifts on his feet, growing antsy because I don't do anything right away. And maybe that's the point.

"We don't have all night, Ma Belle," Bastien says, his soft voice whispering into my mind.

"And now you make me want to be naughty as hell, so I can line up next," Caz adds.

I twist on my feet and quietly step away, tiptoeing far enough to transform into a wolf. Dax links his fingers behind his head, stretching his elbows toward the sky. I wag my tail, bowing, trying to keep myself from releasing a bark. Because I think he may now need a huge dose of Sterling-style playfulness to get him to lighten up.

Dax swivels to peek at me. "Hurry up, Lyric before I—"

Sagan suddenly growls.

Caz barrels toward me.

A big hand grabs the back of my neck and drags me away.

"She-wolf, it's me," Flynn says, bear-hugging me from behind. "We have to go."

The world flashes with bright light, and I find myself alone in the middle of an unfurnished apartment. Flynn relocated me so fast and disappeared, it's like he was never here at all. A growl reverberates through the air, and I spin and spot Sterling materializing from thin air. One by one my mates join me until Dax appears before me last. Flynn disappears in a flash of light without a word.

What the fuck?

Caz crosses the small space to the door and twists the knob. Turning to me, he frowns. "The bastard locked us in."

5

TRAPPED

"IT'S POINTLESS, DAX. YOU'RE NOT breaking the door down," Caz says, offering me another bite of the sandwich we share. He continues to stroke his free hand along my leg in a calming rhythm.

Dax might be anxious as fuck, but I'm nearly certain that the fact that I'm more relieved than scared to be sheltered and locked away by Flynn than vulnerable and out in the open helps keep the rest of my guys relaxed. A part of me is still angry about feeling as if Flynn abandoned me after he said he wouldn't, yet another much, much more dominant part of me doesn't give a shit. I'm just happy he continued to be his stalker self. Dax won't admit it, but he's thankful too. I know he is. He's just pissed off that Flynn locked us in here, and he feels out of control.

"Come sit with me, Dax. I'll protect you from the big, bad warlock and his infuriating magic when he returns," I say, trying to project a wave of tranquility towards him.

The bastard waves his hand like he's trying to bat it away. "This isn't something to joke about, Lyric. He could be arranging a trade or something. Our species is coveted among witches."

"Which is why I don't think he would do something like that. If we're so coveted, why would he get rid of us so quickly? Look at the Nightstar Coven. They've been planning shit for ages." This comes from Sagan, resting on his back a few feet away. "So chill, Dax. You're making Lyric anxious."

Dax slaps his hand on the door. "I just want the fucker to face us!" He yells the words, not responding to us, but yelling them out in hopes that Flynn returns.

I rest my head on Caz's chest, my body fitting perfectly between his legs as he acts like a backrest. "Do I need to command you to join me? Why don't you let me feed you some of this sandwich before there's nothing left? I can't pick at it forever to save you some."

Dax punches the door again, the wood not cracking under

the strength of his fist. Groaning, he shakes out his bleeding hand and slumps his shoulders, looking as if he feels like a failure, losing a fight against the door.

"I'm going to kill him," Dax mutters. "First he breaks our girl's fucking heart and now this? He's a dead man."

I twist my lips to the side. "He didn't really break my heart. He pissed me off and betrayed my trust. I'd have to care about him to feel broken up." I'm lying and we all know it. I just can't let this continue to get to me. A part of me wants Flynn to grovel and sweep me off my feet, showering me with the affection I crave and never got. Another part of me thinks it's ridiculous to even think such things. He owes me nothing. He's never given me anything other than just friendship.

Sterling raises an eyebrow and slumps on the floor next to me and Caz. "Blondie, have you forgotten that we can feel what you feel? And it's okay if you liked him and wanted to bone his brains out on occasion. We thought he was cool. I was almost ready to hug him." Sterling steals the sandwich from Caz's hand and offers it to me again. "The fucker. He hurt me too. I envisioned a real bromance budding between us."

Sterling slings a leg over mine and nudges me with his shoulder to make room for him. I crack up as he hilariously shifts Caz's arm to drape it over his shoulder to be ultra-close while forcing Caz to hug him too. Caz doesn't complain and kisses the back of my neck.

I groan with a laugh, shaking my head. "You're misinterpreting things, Sterling."

"But am I, though?" Sterling leans forward and meets me with his beautiful gray eyes. Narrowing his gaze, he dares me to argue with him over it. "How can we help you work past this if you won't admit it?"

I lean in and bonk my head to his. "I honestly don't know what's going on with me. Flynn isn't even the same species as us."

"I've never seen a warlock cock before, but I'm sure it would work the same. He can probably spell it to be something familiar if it's...different. Fucking magical cock, I bet."

I gawk at him. "Really? We are not discussing this."

"You're my mate. We can discuss anything, even the fact that you think Flynn's hot," Sterling quips. "I've heard your thoughts on his tattoos. You want to see how far they go down into his pants."

"Sterling, watch it," Bastien says, speaking up. "Lyric will talk to us when and if she ever wants to about Flynn, or each other, for that matter."

"Yeah, brother," Sagan says from his spot still on the floor. "We agreed that those thoughts of hers weren't to be mentioned. Don't make me get up and remind you of the agreement."

I wave my hand at Sagan. "I got this. Just relax."

Sterling chuckles. "I'm ready to be handled like you handled Dax. I'll even bend over."

Dax growls from his spot still pacing in front of the door. "I'll help you, Lyric."

"Maybe in a sec," I say, smirking at Sterling.

Sterling glowers and warns Dax to stay back with a growl.

I twist in Caz's arms and mouth to Caz to grab Sterling. Grinning, Caz moves his leg, surprising Sterling with a bear hug to pin him to his chest. Sterling grabs my waist and stops me from scrambling away, so I rub my fingers into his sides at the same time I lick his neck.

He tries to throw me off him to swap places, but Caz snatches Sterling's wrists and yanks his arms over his head. Using his muscular legs, Caz traps Sterling in place for me, cracking up as he flails, trying to break free. I take the chance to will my transformation to take hold of me. Bastien and Sagan's laughter echoes through the room, sounding like the perfect melody to arouse happiness in my soul.

"Get him good, Lyric," Dax quips, finally breaking into a smile.

"Don't do it, blondie. I swear to the fucking fates if you do this I'm going to bend you over and spank you. You will feel it for days." Sterling tenses, trying to bash his head against Caz's, but nothing Sterling does can get him free.

I bark and prance in front of him. Sagan combs his fingers into the fur of my back, scratching the length of my body. I bow and wag my tail, loving how much my guys enjoy when I mess with one of them. Bastien ruffles Sterling's platinum hair, howling with laughter. He kneels beside him and Caz and makes kissing noises at me, smacking his hand to Sterling's chest.

"Come on, Ma Belle. This is the spot," Bastien says, grinning at me. He pats Sterling's thigh, getting awfully close to his junk, though he wears shorts.

"Fuck! Don't encourage her!" Sterling shouts, squirming and arching.

I don't even care that Sagan snaps his fingers in encouragement or that Bastien fucks with Sterling, pinching his nipples. All I care about is how hilarious and uplifting teasing my favorite horn-dog is, especially after all the crazy-ass shit he says to me.

"Hold him tight, Caz," I think, sending my voice to all of them. "I'm going to lick every inch of him."

Sagan cracks up. "Brace yourself, brother. Show our mate you can give her exactly what she wants."

"Give him a nip," Dax adds from behind me.

"Fuck off, you assholes. She's not open to suggestions," Sterling says.

"Maybe you'll learn that you can only say so many outrageous things before karma comes back for you." Bastian flicks Sterling's hard pec.

I pounce forward and hook my paws around Sterling's sides and drag my tongue up the side of his face. He laughs and continues to try to break free, threatening me with retaliation.

But I don't stop. I lick over his chest, tasting the sweetness of his skin. He shouts and laughs, unable to form words as I tickle him like crazy. Bastien, Sagan, Dax, and Caz encourage me to give him the punishment I promised him, and I bow and wag my tail in the air again, wondering how far I should take this.

"Fuck, blondie. At least show my cock a little attention," Sterling says through his laughter.

I release a growl, snapping my teeth between his legs, making him jerk even though I'd never actually nip him. Instead, I latch onto his shorts and tug them down his hips, making him inhale a breath. I lick his bare knee, up a few inches toward his thigh, fully aware of his hard cock on full display.

"Don't think I won't fucking lick you back, Lyric. You're tonguing a dangerous line I'm not sure you're ready for. I will lap my tongue against those soft lips between your legs until you can't think anymore. Woman or wolf, I don't give a fuck. You're my mate and I'm horny as hell for any form you take. My wolf doesn't care either." Sterling flexes his raging boner, wagging it like it's his damn tail. "Try me. Do it. I dare you."

I hesitate. His words turn me on, weirdly enough.

"Uh-oh. She's thinking about it." Sagan's laughter fades as the thought crosses his mind.

Ah, hell.

Silence falls over the room as my guys wait in anticipation to find out if I take Sterling's dare. I narrow my eyes, my wolf begging me to show him I don't give a fuck what form he takes either. He's my mate, my lover, and the damn ultimate pusher of all my buttons.

I slink forward, lowering my body to the floor, crawling closer. Sterling offers me his best cocky-bastard smile, flexing his cock again. I huff a breath, inhaling his intoxicating scent that prods at my nature. And damn it. My human rationale needs to shut the hell up. I'm a she-wolf. I have a wild side, and this isn't about sex or getting him off. This is about proving to him exactly what I'm willing to do to make a point that I will do damn near anything to lighten the mood of this uncertain situation. It's not like I've never licked his balls before...

"Oh, no you don't." Dax hooks his arms around me and flips me onto my back to cradle me in his arms. He ruffles his fingers between my ears and kisses my nose. "It's only punishment if he doesn't want it."

He tightens his arms around me like he thinks I might flail, knowing how much I hate feeling trapped in this form. Except I don't feel trapped in his arms. I feel relief that Dax isn't injuring himself in an attempt to break us free. I'm happy to lie complacent in his arms as long as he continues to look at me like I'm still the most important, beautiful being in the universe.

"Because you are to me," he murmurs, curling me up to his face to inhale a breath of my scent. He nuzzles his nose into my fur. "You're my forever and the future mom of my kids."

I huff a breath through my nostrils and lick his throat.

He's so damn lucky that I'm in a good mood now. If he had said such a thing earlier, he'd have gotten more than the threat of a damn spanking. Because our life isn't ready for such things. How could he even think about children when our world remains so uncertain?

"Because we know this won't last forever. We might not know how to deal with this now, but we'll get it figured out. Together. Lunar Crest is ours. It's our home and the home of our children. I'm not ready to give up on those plans yet." Bastien's words draw my attention to him, and my muscles shudder as I grab my humanity and tug it free.

Dax caresses his lips to mine the second I finish. Smiling against my mouth, he says, "He's right. None of us are."

I stretch out my arms, wiggling my fingers to get the others to come closer. My need to feel the warmth of their bodies surrounding me is all I can think about. I want to smother myself between them and absorb their strength and love and devotion. I want to feel the touch of their ten hands, savor each one of their kisses.

"What about feel the sting of my hand smacking that naughty ass of yours?" Sterling asks, rubbing his hands together. He bites his bottom lip with his cocky-bastard smile and strides toward me, ready to snatch me away from Dax.

I wag my finger at him with a laugh. "You can try."

Dax surprises the hell out of me by flipping me onto his shoulder, giving Sterling the perfect view of my ass. My long hair sweeps back and forth as I egg him on, wiggling my hips to show him I'm far from scared of a little spanking. I crane my neck to peek around Dax's bulging bicep and stick my tongue out at him, silently daring him to do it.

Standing in front of Dax, Sterling positions himself at my ass and rubs his warm hands down my butt cheeks and to my thighs. He slides his hands around to hold my legs in place and squats down.

Sterling kisses my ass cheek and sucks a spot hard enough that I know he'll leave a damn hickey in his wake. And then he does it again, working his way to the apex of my thighs. All I'm wearing is a long shirt, and if he wanted to get me going, he could easily do so. I'm not so sure I'd stop him either.

He hums his pleasure at my thought against my sensitive skin, sending a trail of vibrations through my body. The bastard inhales a breath and nips my smooth skin. "Keep it up, blondie. Your ass is incredibly lickable. You know I'm not afraid of tonguing that balloon knot and working you up just right. You did say you'd consider letting my pleasure pole sneak in your back door."

Oh. My. Fuck.

I squeeze my thighs together as heat flushes through me. And damn it. The others all notice my reaction, and my body's excitement at his teasing me with something I can't exactly know for sure if I'll enjoy or not. "Nothing about that pain in my ass will be sneaky."

Sterling chuckles and pats my butt while leaning to meet my gaze. "I can handle that dainty booty button with the most care. I'll not just lick it and stick it. I'll—"

Sterling's words cut off with the flash of brilliant blue light. I shield my eyes and clutch onto Dax's arm and side. And fucking Flynn. He just had to pop back in here while I'm trapped on Dax's shoulder with my damn ass in the air. Like come the hell on. This is not the position I want to be in confronting him, especially because familiar silence blankets the room, and Dax feels like stone holding onto me.

"Are you kidding me? You couldn't wait until I wasn't in the middle of cheering my pack up?" I swing my body, trying to break the spell he casts over my mates.

"It'd be eternity. Between the five of their grumpy asses, they seem to take shifts in carrying bad moods. And so you know, you all looked ready to get carried away. I know they want to. It's all they ever want to do in their spare time." Flynn's shadow casts over the wall as he hovers behind me. The bastard is probably staring right at my ass too.

"Which you've given us hours of, so don't pull that shit, you peeping warlock." I smack Dax's back this time, but still, Flynn's magic sticks. He's not taking any chances this time.

Flynn's shadow shrinks as he moves closer. "You should know by now that I'm always around. I was hoping your mates would settle down and sleep or something, but you all never let down your guards."

"Because you locked us all in a room after leaving us amid a lot of wild emotions and hurt feelings. You didn't even try to let me handle things." I twist to try to look at him, but he stands just out of view.

"I never left you. I just cloaked myself. You wouldn't understand. Those five beastly men want your babies, not to gut you." Flynn's voice softens with his groan. "None of them would have seen reason had I stuck it out."

"So you thought relocating us was the best idea? You better have a damn good explanation for locking us in this room, Flynn," I snap, squirming in an another attempt to break Flynn's magic freezing my pack in place. "My guys hate feeling caged. They think you're going to trade us or some shit."

"I would never, she-wolf," he says. "I'm sorry I put you in this position in the first place. I just don't know how to handle all of this, especially now. Your pack is...aggressive and protective, which I can't blame them for. Look at what I'm doing. You're just so—" Flynn stops talking with a sigh. "You're just so you. I can't explain it."

"Don't even think that trying to kiss my ass with some bullshit excuse and compliment just makes up for all this." I regret the words immediately, wishing I could take them back because of the dirty innuendo.

"I don't. Plus, it looks like Sterling has the ass kissing covered," Flynn responds, his voice low and taunting. His footsteps thud against the carpet as he strolls the rest of the way to me. I spot his boots first from my position, and he kneels to meet my gaze from beneath me.

I tighten my jaw, steeling my guard against his sorrowful eyes so full of pity that you'd think Dax gave him lessons on giving me a puppy-dog gaze. Licking his lips, he stares at me in silence, gathering his thoughts to speak his mind.

"I'm sorry. That was uncalled for, but none of this is easy for me. I'm still trying to grasp the dynamics of your pack. I'm not used to the bond I see between you all. It makes it harder for me to get through to them. I didn't tell you all the truth because I was afraid of how you would react." Flynn hangs his head, dropping his gaze to the floor. "And I was right. They will never be able to move past this with me. They—"

I reach out and brace on his shoulders, trying to push myself up to get off Dax's broad shoulder. "They have already moved past that. They are upset that I was upset and hurt, and now they're pissed that you locked us up. They can't help thinking the worst...at least, Dax. They've been through a lot with witches. You know this."

"I only brought you here to keep you safe," Flynn says, dropping the rest of the way to the floor to sit cross-legged. "I know you're fearless and tough as hell, but I couldn't just keep standing by, watching and praying to the fates that my magical shield would hold up, especially because you kept moving and separating."

"I never asked for that," I say, letting my hair hang down

to veil me from him. "I'm not your responsibility, and all that you're doing makes me question your intentions. You never told me everything. What exactly do you plan to do? What are we for you? Dax thinks you want to use us for our magic. Is that it? Was I reading too much into things between us?"

He rests his elbows on his knees. "I feel as if whatever I say to you will be wrong. In the beginning, I might have thought that way. I mean, about how you could help me. But I see it's different. It's not one sided. Because I can help you."

Ice travels through me with his words. "What would you have done had I not put up a fight?"

"Lyric, please. It doesn't matter. I'm not sure any of this does now, to be honest. Your pack basically banished me from your life, and you will probably accept it. Despite how hypocritical you are, I still can't just abandon you to the wilds of the Mortal World." His words burn fury through me. What a way to just brush off my questions and avoid answering me truthfully once again.

"Of course you can't. It seems that since you keep avoiding telling me the truth, I'm going to assume that I was wrong about you. Your motives are worse than I thought. You probably stick around and help us to protect us so no one else gets us, right? How else will you use me if someone else manages to get a collar around my neck," I snap. I can't help accusing him. What if I've been blinded by thinking we had a connection? What if it was wishful thinking to assume him saving my life was because he cared and not something else? I guess I'll find out. "You've gotta keep track of your damn magical investment."

Flicking his hand, Flynn sends magic sparking at me, lifting me off Dax's shoulder. He keeps my pack frozen in time, the sight of them smiling at the spot on Dax's shoulder now without me a bit unnerving. I wish he'd just release them. They deserve to hear him too.

"You did lose some of your life to save mine. I know how magic works. You told me that you wanted nothing in return, but I can already feel the cost adding up. So, don't you dare call me hypocritical, Flynn. You can't twist that onto me." I try to swing my fist at him, hoping to break the spell to free my pack, but Flynn drops me a few feet away onto the carpet, pinning me down with a flick of his hand.

"But you are. Look how you keep forgiving these guys over and over again even though they've kept things from you. It's no different than what I did. I knew if I told you right away, you'd try to gut me. You were practically brainwashed into thinking all witches are evil." He rubs his hands together, sending sparks of purple across his skin.

I glower at him, his words digging under my skin. "The relationship I have with my pack cannot be compared to me and you, Flynn. They're my mates. We've bonded and have accepted that our futures belong together. The claims we have on each other are soul-deep, and irrevocable. So shoot me for learning to forgive and work things through with the men I will spend my life with. Yeah, shit with us has been up and down and fucking sideways, but it helps us work through it. They're not using me. They care about me more than they do their own lives."

"You say that as if I don't care about you," he says, his voice rumbling with annoyance. "I care a helluva lot more than I knew possible and way more than I know I should, considering who and what you are. This whole situation kills me. I fucked up, okay? I fucked up and regret that I ruined everything."

His admission sinks deeply into my bones as he admits something I wasn't sure I could believe to be true no matter how often my guys mentioned it. It hasn't been long since I met Flynn, but our undeniable attraction constantly pulls me in a direction I thought I shouldn't want. Because he's right. We're too different. Hell, we're not even the same species. He's a warlock and I'm a wolf with five men as my mates.

"Flynn, don't," I say, my voice lowering with my words. I can't do this right now, exposed and vulnerable with my pack frozen under his spell.

"Don't what?" He meets my eyes, his brows furrowing and his body tensing. "Don't tell you how I feel? Don't try to reason with you? Don't do everything I can to try to salvage something that had turned my shitty life into something exciting?"

I hang my head, the action being one of the only things I

can do because of his magical hold on me. "Don't mess with my heart. You've hurt me enough already. I cared about you. My mates cared about you. They welcomed you into our pack, and I don't know if I can trust you completely."

My words hang in the air between us, the truth of them ringing loudly in my soul. Sterling was right. Flynn isn't just hot to me. He isn't only the warlock who has been helping me figure out the disaster of my life. He's been my friend. My confidant. He's been around, supporting me through every damn frightening moment over the last couple weeks. I mean, I've looked forward to waking up to seeing him curled up and sleeping on the other bed in the motel room.

Flynn scoots from his spot, closing the space between us. Touching my cheek, he combs the hair from my face and tucks it behind my ear. "The last thing I ever wanted was to hurt you. You're the most magical, fearsome woman I've ever met."

I cock an eyebrow. "You're a warlock. You are the most magical being in existence."

"But my magic comes from outside me, summoned through spellcasting." Pointing his index finger at my chest, he gently pokes the sensitive skin above my heart. "Your magic sizzles in your very soul. I want to protect it...and you. I don't know what your father had planned with the Fire Mountain Clan, but I can see how special you are."

"Flynn..." I don't know what to say.

His words touch me so deeply that I can feel them radiate

in my soul. The pressure of his finger lightens, and he shifts my hair, pushing it to my back. I remain frozen, unable to move, but I wouldn't, even if I wanted to. Something about this moment with Flynn, with the world stopped in time around us, awakens something unfamiliar and exciting inside me. I should be angry he refuses to unleash my wild pack, and with them, my heart, but I feel safe and protected and content just staring into his lavender eyes.

"I know I shouldn't say this, because I can't have you like I want," Flynn says, tipping his head back with a groan, "but I can't help myself. I need you to know that your feelings aren't unreciprocated. I've been trying to resist you. I know it's what's best. But my heart and mind refuse to agree. And today...fuck. I will do anything to make it right between me and you and your pack. I realize you come together or not at all, and I will do anything just to be around you and your wild heart."

Whoa. Did he really just say what I think he said? He's finally confirmed that I wasn't crazy for feeling something intense between us. The same spark I experience with my pack, I feel with Flynn. I've never thought much about the fates all of them have spoken of one time or another, but I'm starting to believe that it was the fates that brought us together, even if a little magic helped us along the way.

Flynn's heavy gaze bores into me, and he waves his hand, releasing me from his spell. I lie back on the floor and stare at the ceiling, my emotions running rampant with all of the what-ifs flitting through my mind.

What would my pack say if I told them I still trust Flynn? Would they argue with me? Would they think this was a huge mistake? How would they react, knowing that I can't stop thinking what life would be like if I opened myself for six men? How could I handle it? Would my pack feel as if they're being taken from instead of given more like they think about each other? They consider our pack a family. They consider me their leader. How would they handle Flynn?

I know a part of our agreement was that they would accept my choices if I chose another outside of them, but I don't think anyone considered the possibility that the person my heart wants might be someone from a completely other existence. I guess I'm about to find out. I can't just ignore my mess of emotions taking me on a roller coaster with far too many free falls to be enjoyable. I need to just get this all off my chest and get through it.

"You want me?" I finally ask out loud, wanting—no, needing—for him to confirm that I heard what I heard and my mind isn't playing tricks on me.

"How could I not? You're powerful, fierce, confident, and not to mention the most beautiful woman I've ever laid eyes on. You awakened something inside me I didn't even know was there." He eases himself onto the floor next to me, resting his arm against mine. We stare at the ceiling together like we can somehow see something about our situation written in the glitter of the old popcorn spackle. "I've spent the last few years of my life thinking I was doomed to be alone. I thought I'd never be able to allow anyone into the bullshit my life had turned into. But then I felt your presence interfere with my magic shield. It called me to you."

I crane my neck to look at him, though Flynn continues to train his eyes at the ceiling. "We're not that much different, you know. I had been alone, surviving on my own, thinking that's how my life would be. I was too afraid to let anyone in. And then the packs came for me."

"Funny how the fates work, huh?" He finally turns to meet my eyes. His fingers draw over my hand as he tests my reaction to his touch. I don't link my hand with his right away, just savoring the sensation of his cool skin against mine. "I've spent what feels like forever wondering what the hell they were doing...but now I see things more clearly. I just wish...I wish we could start over. I want to be honest with you and your pack, Lyric, though I'm afraid they'll never trust me and won't give me a second chance. I know I don't deserve it, but damn it. I can't abandon you."

I gently caress my pinky finger against his, waiting for him to link his fingers through mine. I swear sparks shock my fingertip when our palms press together. I suck in a shuddering breath as the sensation courses through me, sending tingles through my body. He feels it too, his lavender eyes crackling with his power.

I lick my lips and squeeze his fingers. "I want that. I know people make mistakes. Hell, I make a ton of them. But things will need to change. Things work between my pack and I because we have an agreement. We share a bond that goes beyond anything of this world. And honestly, we're still learning how to live together and what we need to do to make this work. Dax—"

"Dax will never go for any of this," Flynn says, tightening his jaw.

I sigh. "You can't just assume things. I'll tell my pack the same thing. They will have to accept this. We need you." I cringe inwardly at the way the words come out, like I'm only considering allowing Flynn to stay because he's useful. "But more importantly, I want to help you too. I want you to stay...if this is really what you want. We can work together."

Rolling onto his side, Flynn offers me an adorable smile, the side of his mouth stretching up in the corner. "I won't take this second chance for granted. I'll be nothing but open with you about everything. I'll do anything to prove to you and your mates that we can make this work and accomplish what we need to."

I sit up and stare at my pack, still frozen in their places. "You might want to start with agreeing to never use your magic like this against them."

"How else will I be able to sneak around with you?" His smile widens with his comment. Flush burns across my face at the thought, and he reaches and caresses the heat burning my skin. I know he's teasing, but damn it. I love the idea of not necessarily sneaking but of what he's implying.

"Flynn," I say, his name coming out breathlessly.

It makes him smile wider. "I'm not exactly used to the whole naked bonding thing."

Laughter escapes my mouth, and I shake my head, sending my hair sweeping over my neck to pool between us. "Trust me. Neither was I at first."

He chuckles, his musical laughter filling me up in the best way. "I guess that gives me hope since..." Waving his hand, he points out the fact that I'm only wearing one of the T-shirts he magically sent us after locking us in the room. "You know, you fit right in."

I whack him and scrunch my nose. Leaning closer, I leave only a couple inches of space between us. "Then maybe get naked right now before unfreezing them. It'll prove how serious you really are. Be one with my pack." I'm totally teasing—well, sort of—but I keep my jaw tight to stop from laughing like I want to. I'm far too curious to see his reaction.

An indecipherable expression flickers with the electric light in his eyes. Sucking his top lip in his mouth, he holds my gaze in consideration. "I'm not sure I have your confidence to do that."

"Why not? You should," I say in all honesty. "Have you seen yourself in a mirror before? You're hot. Modesty is not in my pack's vocabulary. They wouldn't even think anything of it."

He cocks an eyebrow. "It would be the first thing they notice."

"That's usually just me." I lock him in my stare, my whole body tingling, silently begging the universe to nudge him into agreeing. "I can't help myself. I think it's a she-wolf thing. It's even encouraged."

Now that I'm thinking about him naked, my curiosity consumes me. I'm used to all the competitors wanting to show off their bodies that Flynn's now obvious shyness only makes me want to rip his clothes off for him. I want to drink in the sight of every inch of him and familiarize myself with his tattoos, tracing each of them with my fingers until I reach his happy trail that I always peek at if he goes without a shirt. Thinking about that sexy strip of hair that leads into his jeans drives me a bit wild. I suddenly wonder if he wears boxers or briefs or if he goes commando like my guys do most of the time.

"Boxer-briefs." He groans softly in his throat with his words, and I realize I projected my thoughts to him. The spell he casted to link our minds when he was stalking me in Lulupoterra remains in place, active when I feel myself opening up.

Excitement zings through my middle as he answers me honestly, already proving he won't hide or avoid my questions.

And my damn eyes.

I drop my gaze down the front of his fit body and zone in on his jeans, devouring the sight of his growing bulge pressing against the sturdy fabric. I should be used to the sight of an erection, but Flynn's is suddenly the most fascinating thing in the universe to me. I can nearly imagine unbuttoning his pants to see his cock pop free, unrestricted and fully throbbing and wanting me.

I wonder how big he is and if he man-scapes like my pack. I wonder if because he's a warlock, if he's built differently or if he can cast spells to make things crazy-interesting in bed. I wonder if Sterling could be right about his cock being magical...

What am I even thinking?

Another groan escapes his lips, and I squeeze my thighs together at the sexy rumble of his voice. My vagina clenches in appreciation, loving that I got a vocal reaction to my wandering thoughts.

"Lyric," he murmurs, bringing my hand up to kiss the back. "I should tell you..."

I flutter my lashes and turn my attention from the hard bulge promising to escape his pants if I just tug down the zipper. "Tell me what?"

Flynn scrubs his palms over his face. "I need to unfreeze your guys. I'll give you a minute to prepare your pack."

I'm nearly certain that wasn't what he had intended to tell

me, but his chest heaves and his magic flickers intensely in his eyes like he's losing control over the spell.

"I might need more than a minute." I huff a breath and curl my torso to sit up. Because fuck. I'm losing myself to my fantasy. I don't know if it's because Flynn admitted his growing feelings for me or if it's because my body goes crazy with the need to mate, but I might need an extra ten minutes so I can hop in a damn cold shower and rinse away my dirty thoughts that leave my vagina tingling, wet, and so damn horny that for the first time in a while, I think about masturbating to chill myself out.

Flynn releases a breathy moan, his gaze flicking toward my thighs, barely covered with the shirt. "Lyric..."

Heat blossoms on my face, and I laugh, the sound escaping my lips soft and seductive. "You might consider breaking the mind-link spell because I can't filter my thoughts when I'm...in a mood."

"You never have to with me." He brushes his fingers through my hair, playing with the blond strands. "I just—it's time for me to face your pack. I need to make things right before anything else."

I smile at his words, loving how he cares enough about my pack not to give in to my raw desires to push the weak boundaries set between us. "Maybe give me five with them, okay?"

He bobs his head. "Tell them I'll do anything to prove to them I'm your pack's ally."

"I will. Trust me," I say.

Smirking, he says, "I do."

With a clap of his hands, Flynn sends sparks raining around me as he disappears with his light. The world kicks into action before I have a chance to get to my feet, and I suck in a few calming breaths through my nose, preparing myself to face my pack.

"Shit, where did she—" Bastien's words snap off as he spots me on the floor where Flynn left me.

All five of them rush to my side and drop to their knees like I'm injured or something. Sagan and Sterling both flare their nostrils, and Dax sniffs my hair, his instincts probably driving him wild.

It's disorienting getting spelled. I can't imagine what crossed all of their minds after I just vanished from Dax's shoulder to end up here across the room a second later. Time passes by but they don't feel it like I do, not unless they were with me in that moment.

"What the hell, blondie? You smell even fucking better than a second ago. How the hell did you get over here? Fuck, I want to mount you right here, right now, and wet my dipstick in your oil well." Sterling slips his hand over my thigh, and I automatically ease my legs open without thinking.

"Damn," Sagan murmurs with another breath. "I can already taste her."

Growling, Bastien whacks him on the back and then

snatches Sterling by the wrist, stopping his wandering hand from slipping his finger inside me. The thought of him getting me off right on the floor in front of him only makes things worse, my body still incredibly turned on from just the thought of Flynn that—

Everyone freezes as my thought projects from my mind to theirs. I will the universe to take it back, to give me another minute to prepare them for what I need to, but Dax grabs me and flips me around to face him. The second our eyes meet, he growls deep in his throat, his golden gaze searching my face for answers I'm not quick to give.

"He was here," he says, his voice turning nearly guttural with his anger. "He got to you, didn't he?"

I clutch Dax's face. "Hear me out."

It's Sagan who crosses the room and punches the door. "Warlock, show yourself!" he yells.

Footsteps sound from outside the room, and everyone turns their attention in Sagan's direction, staring past him at the door. Curling his fingers into fists, he prepares to lunge at anyone attempting to intrude on us.

"Please, calm down," I say, wiggling to pull myself from Dax's lap. "I need you to trust me on this. Flynn and I—"

"He spelled you," Sagan says, pointing at me.

"He didn't," I say. "So just hear me out."

Tipping my head back like Flynn will magically fall from the ceiling to land next to me, I steel myself for my pack's oncoming anger.

"Flynn," I call, raising my voice. "They're not going to calm down unless they hear what you have to say yourself."

With a flash of blue light, Flynn reappears.

Bastien and Caz launch at him from their spots.

I stare in shock as the two of them attack.

6

WARLOCK CONFRONTATION

"STOP, DAMN IT!" I YELL, pushing past Dax.

Rushing across the room, I jump on Caz's back, stopping him from reaching Flynn. We both fall to the floor, and my knees hit the carpet at his sides. I use my strength to get him to stop moving. Pinning him in place, I shove my hand to the back of his head. I slide forward a bit for a better hold. My half-naked body rests flush against his spine as I straddle his back. I'm still turned on despite the sudden shift in my mood. Caz freezes beneath me at the sensation of the heat of my body pressing against his skin. His muscles ripple and flex in his arms, and he sucks in a deep breath, arching his back.

A throaty, human growl rips my attention from Caz. Bastien wrestles Flynn, outmatching him. Flynn gasps as Bastien flips him off his feet and onto his back. Sterling, Sagan, and Dax do nothing but watch.

"Bastien, stop! I said, stop!" I screech, unable to get up fast enough to intervene as he swings his arm, punching Flynn in the nose.

My movement knocks Caz from his lusty haze, and he breaks his arms free of my hold and hooks his hands around my fingers, stopping me from getting off him.

"Let him get it out of his system, Lyric," Flynn says, rolling out of the way from another one of Bastien's jabs. Blood trickles from his nose, and he clenches his jaw and straightens his back, daring Bastien to do it again.

I expect Flynn to shock him with power, but he doesn't even try to protect himself. The force of Bastien's punch sends him stumbling into the wall. Bastien rushes him again, snagging the front of Flynn's shirt in his hand to drag him off the floor. He hoists him up, slamming Flynn's back into the wall. All Flynn does is turn his head, closing his eyes, and braces for another punch.

"Someone stop him," I say, struggling to yank free of Caz's hold. I manage to get up, but Caz flips me over his head. I land on my back and roll out of his way before he can grab me again. "He's gotten in enough punches."

None of the guys try to intervene.

Flynn takes another jab to the jaw, his lip splitting with the force. "I'm fine, Lyric. I won't let him kill me."

"Fuck, I don't care if you can handle it. Bastien, stop!" I shout again, getting to my knees. "I'll blow whoever the hell stops him. You'll get all my damn attention and be rewarded for listening."

Again, no one moves.

Frustration courses through me. I know they're upset, and I know the fact that Flynn had basically given them permission to beat the shit out of him gives them a reason not to rush to get in between, but fuck.

Getting to my feet, I straighten my shoulders. I might regret what I'm about to say, but I need to get them to focus on me. If they just look at me, I can talk to them rationally instead of letting them get their aggression out of their system until they're good to talk things through.

"Okay, that's it. Whoever stops Bastien can take my ass virginity." That gets everyone's full attention, even Bastien's, and he drops his bleeding hand to his side.

My heart stalls at the sudden intensity burning through the room. Talk about boner triggers. The idea of anal sets every single one of them off, and I clench my damn ass cheeks together. Because ah, hell. I can already hear Sterling teasing about double the peen again.

"Is she serious?" Dax asks Sagan.

"Fuck yeah," Sterling responds. "That ass of hers is mine."

"Not if I can help it." Sagan punches Sterling, knocking him back.

Sterling and Sagan make a mad dash toward Bastien, not even caring that he finally stopped attacking Flynn. I tighten my jaw and glare at the two of them. Bastien tries to dodge out of the way from Sterling and Sagan's determination, but he can't move fast enough as Sterling tackles him. Sagan dogpiles on top, pinning both of them beneath him.

I jog toward Flynn, tugging up my shirt in the process to press the soft material to his bloody lip to staunch the bleeding. Silence falls through the room as my guys watch me baby Flynn as if a split lip can be fatal. It's enough to make me drop my shirt back down to stand in front of him. All of our emotions tangle and twist together. It's hard to separate whose belongs to whom. So I push them all away, clearing my head. I just need a moment of quiet to process my own feelings.

Placing my hands on my hips, I sweep my gaze across the small room, giving Dax a look as he remains guarded with his arms across his chest. Caz stays on the floor, though he sits up and hugs onto his knees. Rolling off Sterling and Bastien, Sagan pushes to his feet and purses his lips. His blond hair falls across his forehead, but he does nothing to move the veil of golden tresses from his eyes.

Shoving his hand between Bastien's shoulders, Sterling uses Bastien's back to stand. He bends down and offers out his hand to pull Bastien from the floor. I watch quietly as Sterling punches Bastien's arm like we're not all waiting for them to look at me.

"Sorry, Bas. I want to slide my hotdog between her buns way more than I want to see the bastard beaten into submission. You know how she feels bad and will want to make him better. I'd prefer she make me feel like the luckiest cock on the block instead." Sterling whacks Bastien on the back. "But thanks for your service."

Oh. My. Fuck.

I squeeze my thighs together, my ass totally clenching at the sound of Sterling's excitement. "Don't get too excited. I never said when I'd let you."

Sterling smirks. "Tease."

"Enough, you two," Dax says, his rumbly voice cutting through the room. "I'm ready for a fucking explanation for all of this shit."

I bounce on the balls of my feet, my nerves getting the best of me. I have no idea why I'm suddenly reluctant to get into this. Maybe I'm afraid that they won't agree. Maybe I'm afraid they'll question my judgment. Fuck, I don't know what I'll do if they're completely against this. My biggest fear is that it'll rock our newly formed pack in a way that'll destroy us.

Be strong like I raised you. My dad's words flit through my mind. Sucking in a breath, I steel myself. "You will get it as long as you all control yourselves."

"I have been," Dax says, flicking a stern look to Bastien.

"Shockingly, he's right," Sagan mutters.

Flynn clears his throat, interrupting the two of them before they start growling. "And I'm thankful for that, Dax. I never wanted things to turn out this way. I want to make things right."

Striding across the room and to my side, Dax towers over me in an attempt to intimidate Flynn, but Flynn remains emotionless. "You obviously have a thing for our mate if you've risked getting your cock chewed off to cage us in this fate-forsaken apartment. So tell us why the hell we should hear you out."

"Dax, how are you all even so sure?" Caz asks, slowly making his way closer. "Flynn could be using her. We know she cares for him, but we can't be certain the feeling is mutual. We can't bond and feel him like we can with each other." Because getting claimed by me binds them all together.

I extend my hand out to Caz, getting him to clasp my fingers and get a good look in my eyes. "It's not using me if we all benefit from the situation. Please, just settle down. Everyone needs to hear him out. If you still feel strongly against allowing him to stay around, then I'll understand. We're a pack, and what you guys want is important to me."

Sagan groans and scrubs his hands across his face. "What you want is important to me too, but how do you expect us to believe him? He's been lying and withholding information. He didn't even try to fight to be heard earlier. He just backed down and disappeared."

"What did you expect?" I scrunch my nose at the memory. "How you handle situations is different than how he handles them. His power comes from his magic and not his ability to overpower or dominate someone into submission."

Sagan's face darkens, and I immediately regret my words. Because there is more to my guys' strength and power than just how hard they can hit. They're all brilliant in their own right.

Offering me a small smile, Sagan softens his features, hearing my thoughts. I send him a dozen thoughts about all the things I love about him, ensuring he knows that even if I stand up for Flynn, I'll always stand up and have Sagan's—and the rest of my pack's—backs too.

"What if I cast a truth spell?" Flynn asks, straightening his shoulders and catching Sagan's attention, tugging it away from me. "You can ask me anything you want. I won't be able to lie. It will prove to you that my intentions are good."

"Fuck yeah. I'm down. Cast the spell right now." Sterling slaps his hands together and rubs them like a cocky bastard already thinking of a dozen unimportant things to ask Flynn. He shifts his gaze to me and winks, knowing that I know exactly what he plans. "I have a lot of questions that I need honest answers to."

"Sterling," I warn, narrowing my eyes at him. He might

want answers that I'm not sure I'm ready for. What if Flynn says something that hurts me? Or what if Sterling's unashamed curiosity about another's desires embarrasses Flynn. He's modest in comparison to my pack. "How about we keep focused on what you all need to hear to trust that Flynn isn't out to get us? The other stuff is something we can find out later."

Sterling huffs and fake-glares at me. "You know you're curious about the same things I am, blondie. You can't deny it."

"Hell yeah, I can," I retort, challenging him with my gaze.

Flynn touches my shoulder, and a spark of electricity zings through me. "I'll answer anything, Lyric. It's obviously important to help him make a decision about me. I don't want to deny anyone anything. I'm okay with sharing every aspect of my life with you and your pack. This way you can really get to know me."

When Flynn puts it like that...

A blip of excitement rushes through me. "If you're okay with it, but I have to warn you."

"Sterling already comes with a warning label," Flynn responds, smirking at Sterling. "I think I can handle him."

Dax flicks Flynn's hand like he can't help himself, getting him to remove his hand from my shoulder. "As long as you know your place, warlock. This is for my mate only. Do you understand?"

Flynn crosses his arms. "I do."

"Then let's settle this," Dax says, motioning toward the

stretch of unfurnished carpet. "We have shit to do."

"This is a truth serum of sorts, but I need a little bit of your blood to tailor it to you specifically. I don't want to risk your safety by leaving myself open to be controlled by anyone." Flynn stands in front of a make-shift altar he arranges on a massive wooden table that takes up the dining area and part of the living space of the apartment.

Seeing him summon furniture with only a couple strange words made me extremely jealous for some reason. I just remember thinking how annoying moving into my apartment in Evergreen Beach was with having to drag a damn couch all by myself because I knew no one and didn't want to waste money on movers.

"You're never going to have to worry about that again," Caz says, caressing his fingers to mine until I take his hand.

I know my pack is on edge, but Caz is especially clingy in this moment. I don't mind, though. He's always so quiet and cautious and never pushy, even as the others dominate my attention, and I want him to know that I will give him what he needs when he needs it. And right now, while the others need answers from Flynn, Caz just needs anything I'm willing to offer.

"Me first," Sterling says, extending his hand to Flynn without hesitation.

"If you ask anything too crazy, you can kiss your chance to

stake a claim on my ass goodbye, Sterling." I smirk at Caz, tugging him along with me to the table. "I'll give it to Caz."

Sterling growls. "Damn it, blondie."

I grin and stare at the altar. A few objects surround a bowl of liquid Flynn keeps crushing some different herbs into with a stone. It thickens and pops, changing from brown to brilliant blue with a drop of Sterling's blood from his index finger.

"Anyone else?" Flynn asks, smacking the side of his bejeweled athame dagger against his palm.

He looks to each of my guys, though they all stare at each other. They're obviously nervous of the idea of Flynn needing their blood. They'd have to trust him enough to believe he won't use it against them. Sterling is definitely going to get a reward later for his bravery.

"If you don't want to, you can always filter questions through Sterling," Flynn adds, looking at me. He remains expressionless, but I can tell by the flicker of lavender magic in his irises that he worries that he won't succeed in winning anyone else over, and it's important to him.

Dax stands from his seat and stretches his arm out to Flynn as an offering. Everyone stares in surprise. He tightens his mouth, clearly not wanting to do this, but he also doesn't want Sterling to be the only one able to ask questions. Sterling wouldn't interrogate Flynn like Dax would.

Dax curls his fingers into a tight fist. "If this is a trick, I swear to the fates that I'll—"

I reach out my hand and cover his before Flynn pricks him with his athame. "Dax, you don't have to do it if it makes you nervous. I can handle it." If I didn't know any better, I'd think I offended Dax just by suggesting such a thing. Admitting any sort of weakness is excruciating for him, and I can't blame him. I hate admitting my own.

He growls and yanks my hand to his chest, pulling me against his body. Sliding his other arm around my waist, he hugs me close and leans down, brushing his lips to my ear. "Absolutely fucking not, Lyric," he whispers, his low voice surprisingly even and almost gentle. "You trust Flynn already. It must be me. I don't want even a drop of your blood to spill. You've been hurt enough. It will be torturous to know you experience an ounce of pain on my behalf. I can handle this, okay?"

I laugh in exasperation, lacing my fingers to the back of his neck. I keep him close and tilt my head to meet his intense, golden gaze. Our lips hover an inch apart from each other's but neither of us lean any closer. Everyone's gaze penetrates us as they wait to see how this plays out. "Seriously? You were nearly killed. Stabbed with damn claws too many times to count. It should be me worried about you experiencing even an ounce of pain."

"I'm not risking your safety. If something goes wrong, it will be me facing witch servitude or death or whatever bull shit, not you. You are too important to all of us. It is my duty—all of our duties to put you first. Without you, we don't have a future. It's one of the few things I can agree on that my mother taught me. If you have a problem with this rationale, you're going to have to spank me into submission. Otherwise, take a seat and let one of them cuddle you." Dax's eyes flick over my face, a teasing smile threatening to soften his stern expression. The bastard. He damn well knows that even if he thinks I'm the most important being in his world doesn't change the fact that he's one of mine.

Plus, spanking him into submission? Challenge accepted. His cocky smile is far too inviting as he silently dares me to try.

So I slap his ass hard enough to make my palm sting.

And shit. Dax doesn't budge or react, acting as if the strength of my hand was a mere tap. His muscles ripple with his movement, and he shifts slightly, giving me better access to his ass like he wants to see what I got. And I will show him. The sting of my palm will be well worth it to leave a reminder that I will always take his damn dares.

Positioning my body, I get ready to swing my hand at his ass in full force. Linking my other hand to the back of his shorts, I tug them down to reveal his tight ass cheeks to me. Bastien and Caz both laugh. Flynn watches in silent curiosity, not interrupting to tell us to hurry up so he can get this over with.

"Do it," Sterling says, encouraging me with a wickedly handsome smile. "Get that feisty ass of hers, brother."

Ah, hell. He wasn't goading me on after all.

Before I have a chance to try again, Sagan grabs the hem of my shirt and tugs it up, showing off my ass. I laugh and try to spin out of his reach. His determination is far too powerful to fight against, so I give in to his dominance and playfully shake my ass and submit to his desires. He teases me with a growl and smacks my ass with his open palm so hard that I catch myself on the edge of the table, using it for support. The sound of his skin slapping mine rings through the air, the sensation of his stinging spank weakening my knees in a way I never expected it would.

I bow forward, resting my elbows on the table, a dozen thoughts rushing through my mind. My body refuses to react or put up a fight. Is this what true submission is like when you willingly give away your dominance? It's the strangest thing. I didn't think I was capable. Now that I've opened myself to compliance, it's like something comes over me. My body does nothing but willingly and eagerly leaves me open for more of Sagan's hot punishment.

And then Sagan spanks my ass again, sending heat swelling across my bottom.

"You naughty she-wolf," Sagan says, positioning himself behind me. "You're in trouble, you know."

His body molds flush against mine as I rest my head on the cool table, working through my surprise and thrill of the unexpected spankings from Sagan in front of everyone. Who knew this was something I'd enjoy? I hope my skin aches for hours as a reminder that Sagan has a wild side I want to explore more. I'd expect something like that from Dax or Sterling, but Sagan seems to be getting bolder and more playful by the day.

"You're crazy if you think Dax is the only one willing to endanger his life for you. We all would," he adds. The cute bastard. He's so lucky he caught me off guard in my mission to show Dax that he doesn't need to protect me. If he hadn't, it would be him getting this punishment.

"Doesn't mean you should," I quip and brace for another spank.

"I'd love to see you try." Sagan bows into me instead, sending my mind whirling with lust and desire, just imagining him tugging his cock from his shorts to slip it inside me while I'm in this position. "You can't be the alpha all the time, gorgeous."

"Uh-oh, brother. You're in trouble now," Sterling says, bending his body over the table beside me to drink in my reaction. "Lyric will get you back for this."

Sagan kisses the side of my neck. "I'll be ready and waiting."

Flynn clears his throat, finally taking advantage of the small moment of silence as everyone focuses on me instead of his athame. "If you want to participate, I'm going to need your hand now, Sagan. There is a time expiration on the spell, so we need to get a move on with it."

Sagan reaches between our bodies and rubs my ass, spreading and closing my butt cheeks, letting me feel his hard shaft against my excited flesh. I try so hard not to react the way I want, because now that my mind clears from my lust-filled haze, I realize how this could be giving the others all sorts of ideas. "I'm good. These fuckers can handle it. I think I need to cuddle Lyric until she regains her senses."

A part of me wants to remain where I am, bent over and exposed, ready and waiting for Sagan to have his sexy way with me, but I really do need to focus on everything despite my sizzling desire.

Chuckling in my ear, Sagan slides his hands under my stomach and hauls me upright and off the table. He spins me around with a huge smile and brushes his lips to mine. "Maybe next time you won't offer something so thrilling to my brother."

Shit.

I shiver at his hum against my lips and drape my arms over his shoulders, letting him lift me off my feet. Sagan carries me a few feet to the end of the table and plops into a chair with me on his lap. I give him more of my affection, teasing him with my tongue. Talk about a distraction. I can't help wondering if life will always feel so...primal. Lusty. My mind wanders too much now. I can't imagine how mating season will be. It's a bit daunting and nerve-wracking.

"It'll be a lot of fun," Sagan says to me telepathically.

I wiggle on his lap, feeling his excitement. "I bet."

I only pull away from him at the sound of something crackling. Twisting on Sagan's lap, I watch Flynn sprinkle some sort of white powder into the bowl. His magic sparks with his potion, sending smoke into the air. He meets my gaze from across the table. The way he looks at me—his bottom lip sucked between his teeth and his brows low on his forehead—is like a soft plea for this to work to get back into my pack's good graces.

I offer him a small nod with a smirk, silently giving him my assurance. I have faith that my guys will see reason and accept my decision to work with Flynn. I'm nearly certain they already have. This is more about easing their worry. About getting to know Flynn in such a way that guarantees he will be honest and helps trust to work both ways between my guys and him.

Flynn puffs a breath and flattens his palms on the table on each side of the bowl. Sterling, Dax, and Caz sit on the chairs around him. Bastien plops in the chair at the corner of the table beside me and Sagan and grabs my legs to pull them onto his lap like he doesn't care which part of me he holds as long as he touches me.

"Tru tinia et si raquiestota," Flynn mutters, sending blue smoke wafting from the stone bowl. It fills the small apartment in a haze, the scent of burning herbs and his ever-present fresh mint fragrance consuming my senses. I've never watched him create a potion, and it's fascinating as hell. He mentioned that his magic comes from outside him, and it makes me curious of the extent of things.

Bringing the bowl to his mouth, Flynn chugs the liquid down, his face scrunching as if the serum tastes disgusting. He wipes his mouth with the back of his hand, ensuring none of the liquid remains on his face. Everyone watches him in silence, but he never takes his gaze away from mine. We lock each other in a stare that sends goosebumps over my skin. Sagan tightens his arms around me, adjusting me on his lap, and I rest my head to his shoulder, my anticipation to find out what happens next and what my pack will decide on driving me a bit crazy.

The haze in the air clears. Flynn suddenly breaks eye contact and slumps into his chair in front of his make-shift altar. Blinking his lavender eyes a few times, he shakes his head and shivers as a strange glow lights his skin for a moment before fading. I suck in a worried gasp. If Sagan wasn't holding me, I would rush to check on him. Flynn manages to compose himself and straightens his back. He licks his lips and rests his hands on the shiny ruby fabric, lacing his fingers around what looks like a jagged crystal to occupy his idle hands.

"You okay?" I ask, breaking the silence.

He nods. "It's a bit unpleasant at first. Have you ever felt the intense need to speak up but your fear keeps you back because you're afraid you'll say the wrong thing?"

"I can relate," Caz says, smirking at me.

I stick my tongue out at him.

"Getting started will help with the feeling," Flynn says, knowing that we all get distracted easily.

He jumps right in, far braver than I would be. I know what it's like for everyone to hear me without a filter like when I arrived in Lulupoterra. It was basically a truth spell with my mind open to everyone.

Flynn finally releases me from his gaze and flicks his attention to Dax and adds, "So the serum works simply. For the next hour, you can ask me any question, and I won't be able to lie to you. You can start whenever you're ready."

Sterling claps and rubs his hands together, bouncing in his seat in excitement. The cocky bastard acts as if this is the most excitement he's had in a while, which makes me want to knock him upside the head and remind him that this isn't supposed to be fun and games. "Let's get the important questions out of the way. I'll start with the ones I know are on blondie's mind. What size is your—"

Dax smacks his palm on the table, cutting off Sterling's question. I guess there is no need to remind him with Dax able to focus, but now that Sterling started to ask the question...damn.

"How long have you been on the run from the High Council?" Dax asks, shifting in his seat to focus all of his hot intensity on Flynn. Neither questions are really that important to me, but I'm already completely engrossed in discovering the answers.

Dax can't help flicking his gaze to mine. I can feel the penetration of his stare, but I don't want to look at him, knowing he heard my thoughts. His curious eyes shift away, releasing my attention.

"Twelve years." Thank the universe for Flynn's response.

My eyes widen. "Twelve years? That's so long."

"Feels like eternity." His deep voice softens, and his eyes crackle with his ever-present magic. But instead of looking powerful, he looks awfully sad.

Flynn's response now captures everyone's attention, so they lose focus on me and my wandering thoughts. Flynn's eyes flash once again with his familiar light purple electricity. Without having to ask him, I know thinking about his past strikes a nerve. All of us feel like that. It's probably one of the reasons I can tell Flynn will fit in.

"Damn, how old does that make you? I know warlocks can live over a millennia...is this how you really look or are you spelling yourself to look like our mate's next fantasy? Because if you are...shit. Is that monster look you get when you're pissed off your unsexy true self?" Sterling asks, unable to keep his questions to himself. I can't pretend I haven't thought about the strange morphing of his appearance either.

"It's a defensive spell intended to trigger fear. You all are predators. I can't exactly intimidate your species as I am. And as for my age, I'm thirty-three," Flynn responds, "and the youngest member of my coven."

Sterling rests his elbows on the table. "What a baby. So young."

Bastien raises an eyebrow at Sterling. "He's older than all of us."

"Not by much," Caz says, tapping his fingers to the tabletop.

"None of that matters." Dax groans at how easily Sterling, Bastien, and Caz get distracted and scoots his chair closer to the table. His hulking presence gets them to quiet down and save their conversation for later. "What's important is that we know exactly what and who we're dealing with, like what were the convictions against your coven? If all goes to shit, we need to be prepared."

"Unauthorized use of dark magic, endangering Magaelorum, the murder of Liohts' High Priestess and transferring her magic, coercion toward a gatekeeper, and spreading the lycanthrope virus," Flynn says, his voice remaining even.

Dax doesn't respond, and the rest of us remain silent, his answer sinking in. Those are some serious charges. And what the hell? Whoever this High Council is must be insane to include Flynn with his coven for those convictions.

"Where is the rest of your coven? What happened to them?" Caz asks, his curiosity flowing through me as he breaks the silence blanketing the room.

Flynn's eyes glass over with his thought, but he blinks the

sadness away. "My High Priestess, parents, and three of my coven sisters and two coven brothers were executed by dragon fire."

"Shit, man. That's fucking awful," Sagan responds, speaking up.

Whoa. Did he just say dragon fire? I knew Magaelorum was full of witches and warlocks, but I never really thought about much else.

Flynn's eyes darken at his comment and he continues, saying, "It is, but I'm not the sole survivor. I have two other coven sisters, one who I share a blood bond with, and another brother with life sentences at the Maximum Magical Penitentiary. They're who I'm trying to help."

"How did you escape Magaelorum? It took five High Priestesses to help our ancestors." Sterling leans on the table, now as engrossed with Flynn's responses as the rest of us.

"My aunt gave her life to the fates to ensure I made it to the Mortal World. I was training as a High Priest to take over the Tenebris Coven in the next century before we were framed. It is my duty to do what I can to get the High Council to overturn their decision and also for me to seek justice against the coven who wronged us." Flynn licks his lips, flicking his attention back to me. His face lines with a mixture of his emotions, his anger and grief of talking about his past and the injustice his coven faced nearly palpable. "I think it has something to do with one of the covens that have been trying to re-populate your species. It took some serious magic to do what they did, and there aren't many capable of such things. They'd have a reason to pin shit on us, especially if they had plans to use you."

"And if you're wrong?" Dax asks, his puckering expression mirroring Flynn's. He feels bad for him. All my mates do. I can feel it in my soul.

"I'll still have something they'd want by turning over those covens. If I can find the proof I need that someone else was responsible for some of the crimes, like the lycans, I can prove to the High Council that they were wrong." Flynn sighs and drops the crystal with a thunk. Bringing his hand to his neck, he rubs the back of it. "I just want the same thing you all do. A chance to create a future without having to constantly worry about my life. I want to reunite my family and get them out of that fateforsaken place, and I fully believe we can all get what we want if we work together. If the High Council can get the five covens that have been hiding you and manipulating your species, you can stop worrying about them and the cost it takes to stay protected. You can focus on getting the alpha-mates in control. It will also help with your lycan problem."

"If those assholes are taken care of, we could focus on more important things," I say, imagining a future I wasn't sure was within our reach.

"Like bearing my children." Dax smirks at his own comment, staring at me from across the table, waiting for my reaction.

"Or, you know, building our territory," I respond. "Teaching the future leaders how to fight and lead without fear."

"And our litter of children," Dax adds telepathically to just me.

"So what do you think? Will you work with me, so we can help each other?" Flynn asks before I can respond to Dax's comment.

Dax's eyes darken, and he leans back in his chair and stares at the overhead lights. Sagan and Bastien remain utterly silent with me. I don't have to ask them to know that they've already chosen my side and will agree with what I want. Caz and Sterling hold a silent conversation between each other as they decide if there is anything else pressing that they need to know before deciding if they can fully support Flynn's desire to work together and help each other.

And me?

My mind is set. I hope my confidence and stubbornness are enough to influence everyone to believe what I feel deep in my soul. Flynn is a good person. He won't let us down. He's lost so much and can understand us unlike the covens who want to use us. My emotions run rampant with my thoughts. Flynn shifts in his chair, keeping his attention split between all of us as the silence drags on. All I can think about is launching myself across the table and tackling Flynn, giving him the hug he looks like he desperately needs from me. I want to hug everyone and tell them that I truly believe in us. We're going to be better than okay.

"So, I can feel that Lyric is already fully on board with this situation, and I can't deny her that decision, so I need you to answer some more personal questions," Sterling says, speaking up again. He sits straighter with his arm muscles flexing. "I'm sure you already have an idea of what I need to know, but I need to hear you admit as much out loud. I can't just keep on wondering and pretending that you're not on a mission to steal our mate from us. She's the sexiest, fiercest, smartest, most incredible woman in the universe, and I can't blame you for your desires, but she is ours. Now tell me the truth. Are you planning to try to take Lyric from us?"

"I don't want to steal Lyric," Flynn says, his eyes flashing with magic. "That would break her heart."

"Yeah-fucking-right. I know you want her." Sterling swings his attention to Dax. "I think he's bullshitting us. I know he has a boner for blondie. We've all seen it."

"Sterling, come on," I snap, glaring in his direction. He's turned from excited to paranoid, and I don't understand what triggered it. "If he wanted to kidnap me, he'd have already done so. He'd have put me in some cage and turned all of you in."

Sterling flares his nostrils at even the thought. "I didn't mean kidnap you. I meant steal you from us, meaning that he will try to win your heart and make you become exclusive to him, which I'm not fucking cool with. I can see he's uncomfortable with our pack and relationships with you. He looks like there is some weird reason to pity you, like it's some horrible thing that we all want to ensure you experience maximum ecstasy daily."

Heat warms my cheeks. Sterling is crazy to think that I'd ever turn my back on them or that Flynn pities me. Maybe he did in the beginning, but he knows that we're a packaged deal. "Flynn, tell them that's not what you want."

"It isn't," Flynn confirms.

I stick my tongue out at Sterling. "See? You have nothing to worry about. You guys are mine, and I'm yours, and no one can change that."

He growls again and flexes his arms as he clenches his hands into fists. "Then what do you want to get out of this besides clearing your family's name? I know you have a hard-on for Lyric. It's undeniable."

"I..." Flynn tightens his jaw, his face reddening as he tries to resist answering but can't. "I want you to share her with me. She is amazing and everything I could ever want. I just want to be with her, even if it means only getting part of her and sharing her with you."

Wow. When he says it like that, my heart can't help beating out of control.

Sterling throws his hands up. "What have I been saying?"

His words are directed toward Dax, Caz, Sagan, and Bastien. "I knew he wanted to fuck her, but how can we be certain you won't change your mind about sharing?"

"Then that's his problem," Bastien says, speaking up.

"Lyric holds our souls. She will never hurt us," Dax says, meeting my gaze. "Trust her."

"I do," Sterling says. "I just—what if he breaks her heart? Today was rough. He could hit it and quit it since he doesn't bond like we do. That wishing well of hers is ours for life."

I pout my bottom lip at his words. I can't help melting a little bit over his worry, which isn't something I thought about.

"I would never. Sex isn't everything to me, and it's not the only thing I want." Flynn scoots his chair from the table and links his fingers to the back of his head.

I shift in anticipation on Sagan's lap, devouring Flynn's responses to Sterling's questions about me. I mean, I knew Flynn cared about me because he told me as much, but my damn horny ass wants to know more details.

"Do you want to join the Lunar Crest pack or something?" Caz asks, shifting his gaze to mine for a second. "Because we've all worked hard as fuck for our spots."

"And there are only five damn spots. The leaders will never in a million years allow a warlock to compete in the games," Sterling adds.

I puff a breath through my mouth. "The games are over, guys. This isn't a competition anymore."

"You want him on our pack?" Dax asks, swinging his attention to me. "But—"

"If he swears loyalty to me and promises to remain by our sides..." My heart races at the thought.

"Don't you dare say it, blondie. I can already feel you staking your claim on him, and it doesn't work that way. He's not even a wolf." Sterling taps his fingers on the tabletop, distracting himself the best he can. His need to come to me courses between us, but he won't try to steal me from Sagan's arms.

I cock an eyebrow at his exasperation. Everyone stares at me, their eyes drinking me in as they try to hear exactly what's on my mind.

I shift again on Sagan's lap, swiveling my body to get to my feet and walk to the other side of the table. Sterling's gaze burns over me, his emotions running wild.

"I can claim whoever I want," I say, sauntering closer, my skin prickling under the weight of everyone's attention. "That was part of our deal. And while I consider what we want as a pack, and I do want you to be okay with this, don't tell me what to do."

"Then I need a fucking date first. I need to know he can romance you. I want to know he's capable of a bromance. You know we do a lot of shit together, and if he can't be bromantic, then this might not work," Sterling argues. "And before all that...you haven't even fucked Caz yet."

I automatically turn my gaze to Caz to see his reaction.

He glowers at Sterling. "Don't drag me into this. My relationship with Lyric is perfect no matter what."

I move to Caz and drape my arms over his shoulders and kiss his neck, showing him that I appreciate his response. It's not like we've gotten any privacy to take our relationship to a more intimate level.

Sagan leans back in the chair, lacing his fingers to the back of his head. "Maybe you should ask the bastard if he even wants you to claim him, gorgeous," he says, speaking up.

"What kind of question is that? Why wouldn't he?" Dax twines his fingers together and rests on his elbows. It sounds like Sagan's question offends him, as if it's the most ridiculous thing he's ever heard. Now I want to hug him too.

"Sagan makes a good point." Bastien slides his chair closer to Dax and leans in. "Flynn can't even look at Lyric without blushing. I don't think he can handle her." He whispers the words, but we can all hear.

Sterling drops his hands to the table with a thunk and narrows his focus on Flynn, who slumps back in his chair. I think he might've underestimated Sterling and regrets allowing the conversation to go in this direction. "Do you think you can handle her? It is customary to our species to ensure that she orgasms. You've been in the Mortal World. I know there are men there that can't find a damn clit even if a woman spreads those supple meat flaps and sits on his face." Sterling asks Flynn.

"Sterling," I say, reaching over to smack his arm.

Sterling grabs my wrist and drags me across the table before I can react. He nips my earlobe and whispers, "You'll thank me later, blondie."

I bonk my head to his. "You don't have to answer that, Flynn."

Sterling covers my mouth. "Oh, yes you do."

"We do have a bro-code," Bastien adds. "We need to make sure you can follow it. Pack mate rules."

I frown. "What the fuck?"

"Answer the question." Sagan moves closer, and everyone quiets down, waiting for Flynn's response.

Flynn's face deepens in rose color, his muscles flexing on his arms as if he tries with everything in him to resist the question, the sudden interrogation probably worse than he even expected. It's worse than I expected.

"Yes, I think so," Flynn finally says, his Adam's apple bobbing with his words. He releases a small breath through his lips and meets my eyes instead of Sterling's.

"You *think?*" Dax's voice rises with the words. He obviously doesn't like the bit of uncertainty in Flynn's response. "I need more than that for my mate."

Oh. My. Fuck. Can the universe just swallow me whole?

Flynn leans forward and turns his attention to Dax in challenge. His eyes sparkle with his magic, and he tightens his jaw. "I will guarantee it. You have no idea what my magic is capable of."

Oh, man. I now want to find out.

"A magical cock doesn't promise anything when you look as if just touching her scares you." Sterling smiles his cocky-bastard grin and winks at me. "Why are you always so afraid?"

I smack Sterling in the shoulder. "Enough. You're taking things too far."

"Because I'm nervous I could never compete with your experience." Flynn's voice lowers with his words like if he says them quietly enough, none of us will actually hear them.

"Why do you think that?" Caz asks, his voice even. He looks as if he feels badly for the questions Sterling insists on asking.

"I'm a virgin," Flynn says with a groan, slumping forward to hide his face. "I've been in hiding. There was no way I was getting a mortal caught up in my bullshit."

I expect Sterling to laugh and tease Flynn, but none of the guys react at his words. They all turn their attention to me, and I try with everything inside me not to react. I wasn't expecting such an admission. I already know that a few of the competitors have little experience, especially if they never ventured into the Mortal World, but Flynn? It doesn't matter to me. I actually like the idea that he has nothing to compare against.

And shit. Everyone, even Flynn, must've heard my thought.

"Fuck it, fine. I guess I should've expected you'd like that, especially since you can dominate him and teach him a thing or two. Hell, I'll sit in and play teacher, if you want. I'm not against it." He smirks at Flynn this time before turning his eyes back to me. "Go on and claim him, blondie." Sterling nudges me off him and presses his hand to my lower back, pushing me toward Flynn. "Rock his damn world."

Blush burns across my chest and face at his words.

Flynn groans under his breath, just as embarrassed as I am. "It's not about that, so knock it the fuck off. Lyric and I will figure out what we want when we're ready. This is about working together and building a future."

I gape at Flynn's comment to Sterling. I like that he stands up for us.

Dax chuckles, his face lighting up with whatever amusing thought swirls through his mind. "It might not be about it now, but mating season's coming. Lyric doesn't want to have my babies yet, so...you might have to satiate her for a few weeks."

"Or you guys can buy condoms," I suggest, crossing my arms over my chest. "We are in the Mortal World."

"My baby juice will burst through even the strongest protection, so it's best if you let me train your ass, blondie." Sterling licks his lips. "You'll appreciate it later."

I cover my eyes. "This is enough. You guys need to chill out and just give Flynn your answer. Do you agree that we can help each other?"

"Fuck yeah," Sterling says.

"Agree," Bastien and Caz say at the same time.

Sagan drapes his arms over my shoulders. "I want whatever Lyric wants."

Dax stands up and extends his hand to Flynn. "Looks like you get what you want. Welcome to the Lunar Crest pack."

7

New Pack Mate

"DO YOU THINK THEY'RE GOING to remain in their wolf forms more often than not now?" Flynn whispers, plopping down at the kitchen table across from me. He managed to furnish the small apartment pretty quickly over the course of the day with the help of magic.

Tilting my head, I stare at Dax and Bastien curled up together, finally asleep, in front of the door. Sagan and Sterling remain sprawled out in front of the glass slider to the enclosed patio, Sterling's big, furry head resting on Sagan's back. Caz sleeps with his snout buried between his paws in the spot in front of the window.

"Maybe when they get horny enough they'll transform. Probably in the morning," I say, bonking my head on the table. I say it playfully, but I'm totally serious. If I would turn into a wolf and also allowed that kind of intimacy in that form, they might not change back for days. "They won't resist their needs as much since you've been welcomed in as a pack mate."

Flynn chuckles at my comment. "Fucking fates. They were resisting before? I would've never guessed."

I smile and bite my lip. "I can't help giving in, so yeah. They have to be the ones to control themselves. It's kind of weird and embarrassing to explain myself and what my upcoming season does to my body. If it bothers you, I can try—"

"I'm not. I promise. Far from it, actually." Scooting his chair closer to mine, Flynn leans into me, his minty scent mingling with the fragrance of the fruity shampoo I used in the shower. I can't help taking a deep breath to fill my lungs. His scent is intoxicating. I try not to make it obvious that I'm sniffing him, but if he notices, he doesn't call my ass out on it. "I'm a bit jealous, if anything. You all are so comfortable with each other."

"And you're not." It's not a question. This is new for all of us. Only hours have passed since we've come to an agreement that I'm excited to explore, yet nervous, because Flynn is far from forward like the others. I feel like I'm going to constantly have to guess.

"I didn't mean it like that. I'm not uncomfortable...mostly. I'm just thinking about where I fit in. Maybe it would be better and easier if you took the bedroom to get any privacy you want. I hadn't expected everyone to pick places out here, anyway. I was planning on sleeping on the couch, not making you do it."

His comment makes me grin even wider. It's strange yet exciting to know that he cares about me in the way I wanted, and we can actually explore our feelings. It's tempting to rush things, experience his mouth on mine and discover how his fingers would feel caressing my body, touching my breasts and between my legs, slipping inside me...

I shudder a breath and squirm in my seat, pushing my dirty thoughts away. "I might take you up on that later. The guys feel the most powerful as wolves, and I feel it in this form, so sleeping together isn't exactly easy. They practically smother me in bed." Resting my chin on the top of my hand, I meet his gaze. "But then again, I've realized that I don't like sleeping alone."

Flynn rubs his hand through his hair, his lavender eyes roving over my face, the smile on his lips fading. "I'll keep you company if that's what you need to sleep."

Damn it, do I love the offer. But me and Flynn sharing a bed in a room alone? I won't be able to fall asleep with him either. I won't be able to resist snuggling him. And with cuddles, comes kisses. And kisses lead to…

"Someone should really watch the place, though." I push myself upright and cross my legs under the table. Sterling thinks he's the one with boner radar, but fuck. My clit tingles and twitches with the intense look Flynn gives me with his offering. Lady boners are real, and my clit is ready to prove it. "It should be me. I'm the pack leader and all."

"But you have a whole bunch of beasts ready to fight on your behalf." Reaching out, Flynn rests his hand on top of mine. His lavender eyes bore into me, penetrating my soul. He's trying to convince me, but I feel a bit clueless with him. Is this an innocent offering? Does he want more? Fuck me. Where is Sterling's interpretation when I need it?

"I know. It's just…I don't know. I feel their nerves. It keeps me on guard," I manage to say. "It's hard to relax."

"I had hoped you all would trust me and my shield enough to move past this. I'll do anything to keep you safe, Lyric. I hope you know that. I care about you and the guys. Sterling's enthusiasm over the first date thing has already grown on me."

I release a breathless laugh and rest my head on my folded arms. "It's not really necessary, but I appreciate you accepting that. And I'm sure they'll warm up to trusting your magic again. It's our first night in another new place, remember. You haven't let them explore the area yet."

"I promise I will tomorrow. I'm a bit worn out from today. I need to recharge before expanding the shield and tailoring it to all of us. I want to be absolutely certain I can protect you all better than I have been." Flynn rubs his hands together, sending sparks across the table.

"Anything I can do to help?" I link my fingers through his, feeling the spark of his magic on my palm.

His chestnut hair veils across his forehead as he hangs his head, staring at our interlocked fingers. "Rest is sufficient enough to replenish the strength of my magic."

"But there is something," I say, savoring the sensation of his thumb caressing the outside of my thumb. Flynn doesn't have to tell me to know there is something I can do to help. "You know, as your leader, I will do whatever it takes to make sure you're at your best."

Flynn graces me with a sexy smile. "I couldn't ask anything of you. Your guys—"

I surprise him by pressing my index finger to his mouth. "What happened with helping each other? Right now, it feels one-sided, with you only helping us. So tell me what I can do. I mean it. It'll help with my nerves. Maybe after, I can get some sleep."

"Why does it feel like you won't take no for an answer?" Flynn raises an eyebrow in amusement.

"You should tell me why it feels as if you might question my authority as your leader, warlock." My voice comes out teasing, almost daringly, as I goad Flynn to deny me this opportunity. He's been honest about his worry over whether or not my guys truly think of me as their leader or if they're pretending like the leaders' alpha-mates, and I know I shouldn't push him like this, but I'm suddenly desperate to discover where he thinks his place is.

Flynn shoves back in his chair and stands up, tugging me to my feet with him. Holding a finger up to me, he gets me to stay in place while he lowers to kneel on one knee in front of me. "I see you're testing me, she-wolf, so here I am, bowing before you and swearing my loyalty."

I narrow my eyes with a fake-glare. "Are you teasing me?"

"I'm only showing that I don't question your authority. I also don't feel as if this is one-sided either. You stood up for me. Accepted me into your pack. I'm no longer alone because of you..." His voice grows into a whisper. If the guys hear us, none of them react, giving us privacy.

"Exactly." Reaching out, I grab him by the front of his shirt and pull him to his feet. "Which is why you should let me help you. Now no more arguing. My mind is set."

"Just let her, man," Caz murmurs telepathically. "You don't want the others to wake up because you didn't give our mate what she wanted."

I peek over Flynn's shoulder at Caz, still lying under the window. He nuzzles his nose between his paws, looking so cuddly that it nearly distracts me from Flynn.

"Please," I ask, turning my gaze back to Flynn's. "Don't

make me beg."

He groans lowly and smirks as I excessively bat my eyelashes. I swing his hand and bounce on my feet, wondering exactly what I'm getting myself into. The unknowing is exciting and thrilling, and I want him to hurry up and explain what to expect.

"Just a small siphoning spell," Flynn responds, hearing my thoughts as I remain open to him. "If you allow it, I can tap into the magic within you. It's not something permanent, but it will help momentarily strengthen my abilities until I can replenish naturally."

"And then you'll be able to expand your shield?" I ask, breaking my gaze from his to look around the small apartment.

He nods. "I'll be able to do some surveillance too. This place isn't that far from the portal to Lunar Crest or that fucking man-eating lycan."

My eyes widen. "Damn, I had no idea. Now, this isn't a suggestion. It's a command. Use me. Take what you need, so I can see too...please."

My voice comes out all breathy with my words, and Flynn's eyes turn heavy with lust. I want him to use me for more than his magic, but I don't say it. Instead I raise my chin and smirk, daring him to deny me.

Flynn shifts on his feet, finally breaking his stare to look at my guys all still sound asleep except for Caz. I'm nearly certain that he's been put on watch, which allows the others to rest completely. Moving from his spot under the window, Caz pads his way to me and weaves between my legs. Flynn surprises the hell out of me by bending slightly to run his hand through Caz's fur.

He squats down and gets at Caz's eye level. "I promise to proceed with care. Lyric is safe."

Caz nudges his big wolfie body against Flynn's side and silently returns to his spot guarding the window. I blow a kiss at him and turn back to Flynn, who now watches me intently. He grabs my hand and guides me to the bedroom. My heart races with each of our steps, and he whispers something I don't quite make out, sending a strange glow illuminating from the bed.

I spot a glowing ribbon—or I should say, a glowing crystal attached to a ribbon—resting on a pillow. It's like my soul is drawn to it, and I stride across the room, practically dragging Flynn with me.

"Be careful when you touch it," Flynn murmurs. "That's part of my soul made tangible."

I hesitate for only a second before carefully scooping up the stone in my hand. Sitting on the edge of the bed, I cradle it in my palm, the heat of the stone surprising yet inviting. The subtle scent of mint wafts through the air, and I lift it closer to my face, enamored by how extraordinary the lavender stone is. It's the most ethereal, beautiful thing I've ever laid my eyes on.

"It's incredible," I whisper, stroking my thumb over the smooth surface.

"You're the first one I've ever let touch it since my High Priestess created it for me." Flynn eases onto the bed next to me. Our legs press together, and he rests his arm behind me, his body fitting perfectly around mine.

"Thank you for trusting me." I continue to stroke my thumb over it, the sensation tingling through my entire body. "It's so...magical."

"Not as magical as you. As you can see, it's lighting up for you. Magic attracts magic, which is why and how I could feel you when you entered my shield the night we met." Flynn slides his hand beneath mine and uses his thumb to curl my fingers around his soul stone.

I gasp at the electric magic shocking my hand and jerk my attention to him. "Whoa. What was that?"

Flynn chuckles, his face lighting up. "I think the fates approve."

I have no idea what he means by that, but I don't ask. I'm too engrossed with the stone and his closeness. My whole body buzzes in anticipation, and I'm suddenly afraid he's going to ask for the part of his soul back. I can't help but want it. I don't want to let it go...ever. I want it to be mine.

Flynn touches my shoulder, brushing my blond hair to my back. "For the spell to work properly, I'm going to need you to wear it, if that's okay with you."

Excitement rushes through me, and I bob my head. The idea of lacing the pretty ribbon around my neck to let the stone settle between my breasts and near my heart stirs something wild and possessive inside me.

"I want you to do it so badly that it nearly hurts that you haven't done so already," I say, the words sounding odd now that I admit it out loud. I mean, what the hell? I blink a few times and uncurl my fingers to stare at the glowing stone. "Why do I feel this way, Flynn? I—I don't know about doing this. I have this urge to shout that your stone is mine, and you probably don't want that."

Shifting on the bed, I turn away from him and hang my head. Flynn doesn't allow me to veil myself with my hair for long. He combs his fingers through my tresses and gathers my hair, holding it off of my neck. I stiffen in anticipation as he gently uses his free hand to grab the end of the ribbon from my grasp.

My heart races, my skin buzzing. He's going to fasten it onto me despite knowing that he might have to fight me or some shit to get it back. He trusts me enough to wear something of his so significant that I feel as if he thinks I'm just as important.

"Because you are. If you want to help me protect my soul stone, I would gladly let you keep it. It'll ensure I keep you safe." Flynn finishes tying the magical ribbon around my neck, and he adjusts the stone until it thumps between my breasts. I suck in a breath at the shock of it against my skin.

"Really? I can have it? Are you sure?" I ask in surprise.

Flynn smiles at me. "Absolutely. Now if you'll allow me, I'd like to tap into your essence to recharge mine."

I bob my head and return his smile. Leaning closer, my body drawn to his, I whisper. "Whatever you need."

"Luos eim era uoy, Lyric. Reverof sa eno." Flynn caresses his cool fingers around my neck with his spell, and the stone heats up as it glows a brilliant lavender light. "It looks stunning on you. How does it feel? Is it okay?"

I lick my lips and reach my hand up to caress the stone with my fingertips. "It feels as if it completes me." I know it's a cheesy thing to say, but it doesn't make it any less true. Flynn's stone radiates with the same energy I feel when I'm with my mates. It's electric and thrilling and like the stars align to spellbind us together.

Flynn brushes his fingers along my jaw, bending closer, capturing me with his lavender eyes. "That's what I was hoping to hear."

Drawing his gaze to my mouth, Flynn studies my lips. I can't help myself and close the space between us completely. Flynn cups my cheek, sliding his fingers into my hair to guide me to him for a kiss that sends sparks of magic exploding between us. I hum at the intoxicating sensation rippling through my entire body. I don't know what I was expecting, but like the rest of him, his kiss is magical. His lips caress mine tenderly, sweetly almost, like he wants me to know that he'll always give instead of take.

I slip my tongue into his mouth, wanting to set him off and experience the imaginary wild beast I know lives inside him despite him not being a wolf. Savoring the taste of his cool minty mouth, I kiss him deeper, harder, more desperately until he can't resist pulling me onto his lap.

I straddle him with my knees on the mattress, my fingers linked through his while I use my free hand to explore the planes of his chest through his shirt, working my way down to the tight muscles of his stomach.

Hooking my fingers to the hem of his shirt, I yank it off him, my body yearning to feel what his skin is like against mine. He breaks from my mouth and kisses my jaw to the sensitive skin of my neck. He follows my lead and memorizes the curves of my breasts through my baggy shirt.

I take it off for him and gasp as he lifts me higher to kiss each of my hard nipples. He whispers something under his breath, maybe a spell, and my panties rip away with a flash of his magic.

Oh. My. Fuck.

I shift in his arms and reach between us. Stroking my hand over the hard bulge pressing against his pants, I wonder exactly what it'd be like to unbutton them and slide his cock out. I wonder if he'd let me fuck him right here on the edge of the bed with the door open. If my guys would wake up from the noise or if Flynn would cast a muting spell. Or maybe even freeze the world.

Flynn releases my hand and reaches between my legs from behind, sliding his fingers into the warm wetness of my lust for him. I gasp and moan at the sensation as he discovers what I like best from his hand. I bounce a bit on my knees, riding his hand, imagining what more he could do with it. My chest heaves with my panting breath, and I hold onto his shoulder and meet his gaze. His lust lines his face, his power burning across his irises.

"You are so enthralling," he murmurs, puffing his lip out with his own quick breathing. "So perfect. My familiar and soul mate. I want to give you the world. Esiosa erusaelp, Lyric."

Tingles explode between my legs with my sudden orgasm, and I throw myself forward into him, knocking him on his back. My muscles tense and release, my toes curling, and I moan so fucking loud, I'm afraid the competitors in Lulupoterra will hear me.

But silence greets us, not even my guys stirring.

My heart crashes against Flynn's chest, his soul stone squished between us. He smiles and kisses me again, this moment feeling so incredibly important as we give in to our desire and need to be together.

I ease upright and stare down at Flynn, his muscles flexing as his tattoos shift and move. The markings on his body come to life before my eyes, and I watch as the heart tattoo on his pec splits apart, sending geometric shapes to the other side of his chest to form a wolf. It glows for a few moments, drawing my hand to it like a moth to a flame.

I graze my fingers over it, tracing the outline. "What just happened?" I ask, automatically grabbing for the stone on my neck.

"The fates have answered my prayers in the most unexpected way. They've given you to me, and this gift proves it. You're my familiar, something nearly unfathomable. I've only heard stories of familiars from my High Priestess. The High Council has been messing with the fates for so long that they're impossible to find...but you..." Flynn's voice trails off as he loses himself to his thoughts.

A million questions of my own flit through my mind as I try to process what all of this means. The only things I know about familiars are from the Mortal World TV. "I hope this doesn't mean you think I'm some sort of pet or servant."

He shakes his head, pushing up on his arm to meet my gaze. Touching my cheek, he captures me with his gaze. "Never. The best way to explain it is like how you've claimed your pack and they've claimed you, except this...we were fated. You—"

A strange noise hums through the room, and Flynn tenses, squeezing his eyes shut. I don't have time to react before he grabs his shirt and shrugs it over my head. He stands up with me in his arms and carries me across the room.

"What's wrong?" I ask, a blip of fear coursing through me.

"It's the man-eater." Flynn waves his hand, sending a burst

of light through the room. My guys startle awake at the energy quivering through the air like an invisible, tangible wave. "The lycan returned."

I wiggle and pat Flynn's chest until he sets me on my feet. Caz transforms first and comes to our side. Reaching out my arm, I slide it around Caz's back and take a spot under his arm as he drapes it over my shoulders.

Flynn slaps the dining room table, and his magic sizzles across the top of it, turning the wood glass-like and reflective.

The stone between my breasts glows under Flynn's shirt, and his magic tingles over my skin. I automatically reach up and press my hand over it. Bastien circles us, remaining in his wolf form. I run my fingers through his fur, getting him to settle and sit at my feet.

"He's not alone." Dax's warmth caresses my back as he comes up behind me.

"It's his next victim," Flynn comments, resting his palms to the table.

I swallow the lump in my throat, watching two figures materialize outside the cabin. Todd laughs and smiles at a woman, swinging her arm with his. Seeing him as I remember unnerves me, because I know a killer beast waits beneath his skin.

"Shit. Is he stripping?" Sterling asks through our mental link. He stands on his hind legs with his paws on the table, remaining in his wolf form just as Bastien and Sagan do.

Sagan joins him. "Preparing to transform."

"He still has a cock." I can't stop my thought from coming from my mouth, my eyes already being little bitches and directing their attention to his junk. Lycan anatomy confuses the hell out of me because in their lycan forms, they have no genitals. Of course, I hadn't realized they could transform into a human form until recently.

"Not for long. He's going beastly," Caz says, tightening his jaw.

Dax grumbles deep in his throat. "Flynn, shut the looking glass. I don't want Lyric to see this."

Flynn chants something under his breath, breaking the connection.

The visual of Todd disappears. My heart races out of control. What the fuck. I know exactly what Dax doesn't want me to see. He thinks Todd's going to devour the mortal. If that's the case, we can't just stand here and pretend everything is fine.

"Flynn, take me to that asshole. Now," I command, meeting his gaze while feeling Dax stiffen behind me, ready to protest.

"I'd have to leave you there alone to return with your mates." Flynn doesn't agree or disagree, but his words almost sound like he's trying to convince me not to go while also not trying to control me.

Dax links his fingers around my forearm. "He's right—"

"I'll go first and intervene," Caz says, interrupting Dax. He slides his arm off my shoulders, turning to look at the two of us. "This could be our one opportunity to get to him before his witch returns."

"It'll take too long to transport all of you there and back. I'll take Caz and Lyric, but the rest of you need to hang tight." Flynn grabs Caz, chants his spell, and the two of them disappear into the flash of blue light.

Dax spins me around to face him. "I'll go for you. There is no need—"

Another pop of light illuminates the world. Flynn rests his two hands on my shoulders and pulls me into him too fast for anyone to react. My stomach twists with the morphing world. Light blinds me, stealing my senses.

A lycan roars.

8

THE COVENS

ELECTRICITY ERUPTS THROUGH THE DARK night, shocking Todd in his lycan form. Caz launches from the ground in his wolf form. He knocks Todd onto his stomach and bites his shoulder, ripping away a mouthful of coarse fur and flesh. With a screech, Todd swings his dagger claws at Caz. He misses him by inches as Caz pounces off him and out of the way.

I don't give Todd a chance to get up and kick him hard in the side. Flynn blasts him with another bolt of magic, flipping him onto his stomach. I dash forward and tackle him to the ground, sandwiching his arms behind his back to stop him from pushing up. Caz growls and bites his leg hard enough to make Todd shriek.

"Eci ekil ezeerf!" Flynn shouts, circling the three of us. "Eci ekil ezeerf! Don't fight it, or I'll allow my pack to rip you apart piece-by-piece until you give us the answers we need."

Todd releases a guttural noise from his mouth, and I shove the back of my hand to his neck, pressing into it with all my weight. If I maneuver my body just right, I will kill him. I want to kill him. He would deserve it for invading Lunar Crest and attacking me and my pack on several occasions.

"Niap eht leef, beast," Flynn says, stopping in front of me. It's now that I realize he's drawn a circle in the dirt around us.

Todd hollers, his human voice breaking through his monster exterior, and he thrashes for a few seconds, nearly throwing me off. "You fucker! They don't belong to you. I'll give you one chance to leave before I call for my master. If you don't—"

"Eci ekil ezeerf!" Flynn shouts again, his voice booming through the air, cutting Todd off.

He slackens beneath me, though I feel the vibration of his low growl on my palm. Caz slinks next to me and nips at my shirt, trying to tug me off the beast. Flynn motions for me to listen to Caz, and pulls me from the circle.

Todd's body convulses and cracks, his bones shifting as he transforms into a human. I link my fingers into Caz's fur, bracing against his sturdy wolf form. He stands in front of me protectively, growling and snarling, ready to launch forward to attack Todd again upon my command.

"Cross the barrier and see what happens. You might call another witch your master, but you are our prisoner. You will pay for your crimes against these mortals." Flynn waves his hand at Todd, sending power at the line encircling him. A translucent wall of power erupts to form a cage, creating a magical barrier between us and him.

"My crimes? What crimes? It was this bitch who was responsible for this damned curse." Todd glowers at me, his body trembling as if his lycan form lingers just below his skin, waiting to burst free. "This is your fault, number twelve. My life was great before you ruined it."

His comment burns through me, reminding me of my life before my pack came to break the spell my dad had witches cast over me. Guilt rises to the forefront of my mind, and in a way, he's right. It is my fault that witches came and cursed him. I was their target. But it still doesn't make up for the rest of the bullshit. He's eaten people. He was going to eat the poor woman.

With my thought, I swivel and peer around the bone-filled yard. I spot the woman from the looking glass hunkered down and hiding the best she can by the porch. Flynn follows my gaze and whispers a spell I can't hear. Snapping his fingers, he enchants the woman with his magic, sending her falling sideways with sleep.

"Now let me the hell go. I'll let this fucking slide," Todd adds, toeing the barrier like his intimidation will work on us.

Caz turns his body and kicks dirt at Todd. Growling, Todd smacks his hands into the barrier. Sparks crackle, shocking him. He flares his nostrils and looks ready to try to break it down, but Flynn steps in front of me, morphing his features into the monstrous fanged version of himself that creeps even me out. He grows in height, towering over Todd, probably even taller and broader than Dax now. It's enough to get Todd to back down.

"I'd love for you to call upon your master, beast," Flynn says, his voice deepening. "I'm dying to meet them."

"It'd be the biggest mistake of your life," Todd responds. He shifts on his feet, his wannabe badass behavior slipping away under Flynn's intimidation. He's all talk. I know it. Flynn and Caz know it. And I'm really fucking sure Todd knows it and is silently praying that we don't call him out on it.

"Call your master," Flynn says, curling his hands into fists.

Todd's eyes dart to mine, an indecipherable expression crossing his face. "I—"

"He's too afraid." I place my hand on my hip, keeping my other one on Caz. "Admit it, Todd. You don't want to summon your witch. You were probably hoping they'd have come for me by now, and you could carry on with your life as if you're some innocent guy. But look around you. You're a twisted murderer."

"You made me this way!" he yells, baring his teeth. "I can't help it. It's the curse."

"Yes, you fucking can. Do not speak to us as if we're naïve. You might be bound to serve, but no coven would command you to blatantly kill and collect the bones of your victims. It draws too much attention from the Mortal Authority. It will alert the High Council of Magaelorum."

Todd's face morphs with his anger, hair sprouting from his cheeks. He winces and reverts back to normal, unable to transform because of the spell Flynn uses on him to control his ability. Waving his hand, he smacks the barrier, motioning toward the bones. "But all this wasn't me! It was Martin! I just bring people back. He bites them and if they don't turn…"

I scowl at the sound of Mr. Remington's name. "It doesn't matter if you're just an accomplice." Turning to Flynn, I say, "I don't think he'll be of any use to us. End him."

"Are you sure?" Flynn asks, catching my thought about using the fear of death to get Todd to comply without having to ask. He nods subtly, and gathers electric energy in his palms. "Would your pack prefer to handle it over the merciful death I can provide?"

Caz lunges toward the barrier and snaps his fangs.

"My mate would prefer to seek justice." I step forward and scratch my fingers into Caz's furry head. "Slow and painfully, so hold him in place."

Flynn grins a wicked smile and flexes his muscles, gathering more magic. "All right—"

"Wait! Wait!" Todd hollers, once again trying to transform into his monstrous self. "Tell me what you want to know. I'll work with you if you can guarantee me protection from my master. That's something you can do, right?"

Flynn and I look at each other. "What do you think, Lyric?" His voice comes to me telepathically. He joins me in touching Caz on the back, getting him to settle down. "Caz? I can offer some protection to him with a shield, but it's up to you."

I rub my lips together and turn my attention back to Todd. "How can I trust you? You're probably wasting time in hopes that Remington comes home."

"I'm not. I swear." Todd's voice rises with his words, his eyes widening in panic, his breathing quickening. "Please, number twelve."

I know he uses my old apartment number in an attempt to tease my humanity and the woman I used to be before everything changed. But that woman doesn't care about Todd. I always found him an asshole.

"Tell us where Martin is," Flynn says, standing tall next to me. With him and Caz by my side, I feel utterly powerful.

"I don't know exactly. He was going to take the new lycans to meet our master. He usually returns by morning." Todd rubs his hands together and bounces on his feet. He peers around anxiously like he expects someone to show up at any second. It makes me nervous.

I stiffen and grab Flynn's hand. "Caz, sweep the area. Something's wrong."

Caz bolts away without hesitation. I watch him disappear into the dense trees surrounding the property. Flynn tightens his fingers around mine, pulling me into his side protectively. Todd's face scrunches in anger, and he yowls, his guttural monster voice ripping through the air.

The ground shakes as something heavy thuds through the forest. I recognize the lycan disturbance without even having to see the beasts. Caz releases a long howl, his call piercing my soul.

"Get out of there!" Caz's thoughts explode through my mind. "You're being surrounded."

"Shit." Flynn lifts me into his arms, not giving into my desire to stick around to fight for answers.

The deep-seated need of my she-wolf rises inside me, but my human rationale reminds me that I'm without most of my pack. If we fight, we fight together. They're probably going crazy as it is, knowing I'm out here with only Caz and Flynn. I'm sure we'll get an earful when we return.

The world spins and light engulfs us as Flynn relocates us in front of the sleeping woman. He adjusts me in his arms and locks his fingers to the back of her dress, hoisting her up just enough to bring her with us. Todd roars, breaking through

Flynn's shield, but magic swallows us and the woman before Todd can get within reach.

The world jerks to a stop, and I cling onto Flynn, trying to orient myself to the sudden relocation. Heavy paws thump against my side as Caz stands on his hind legs and licks my cheek, whimpering like he will die if Flynn doesn't let me go so that he can assure himself that I'm really okay.

Flynn sets me on my feet. "Guard her with your life. I need to get this mortal out of here."

Caz barks his agreement, and Flynn disappears with the woman. I hug Caz to me, not letting him drop on all fours. His large body towers over me in this position, and I inhale a calming breath of his scent, letting his wild deliciousness fill me up with the strength and determination he radiates.

"We should move," Caz says into my mind, his voice deep with caution. "We're not far from the cabin."

I release Caz and swivel on the balls of my feet to peer around. "Where are the lycans?"

"They were headed toward the cabin. At least three, all coming from different directions. They didn't see me, but I know they could hear you." Caz nudges me with his big head, herding me toward a few trees with low hanging branches.

Bending down, I duck under the branches and squat by the tree trunk, allowing Caz to block me protectively. He plants himself between my legs, his soft fur tickling my bare thighs. I brace on him to keep my ass off the ground and absently scratch my fingers across his chest. Despite his worry over everything, he manages to enjoy my affection, sending a wave of happiness to me through our link.

A bright flash of light erupts in the dark forest, followed by another and another. Caz's body tenses at the realization that none of the portal lights belong to Flynn. Fear prickles down my back, and I hold tighter onto Caz.

"Don't make a sound," I whisper into his mind, afraid that if I even think too loud that one of the witches will discover us hiding here.

"Nightstar needs to control their damn pets," a woman says, traipsing through the forest with a man. "They'll be responsible for the High Council's arrival. It could mess everything up."

"How many do you suspect now?" the man says, stopping in front of the woman. "I will gladly thin their servants to send them a message."

"Oh, Lazlo. Allegra. Don't be so wasteful." Another feminine voice sounds through the forest. "I'm far less concerned over the lycans than I am over the fact that some of our access portals to Lulupoterra have been unexpectedly sealed."

"It was probably Fire Mountain, Evelyn," the man says. From my place, I spot long white hair tied neatly with a ribbon. I can't see his face, but he wears a suit. "McKayla has been quite vocal in her disagreement toward the plan."

The plan? Fire Mountain? Fuck. These witches must be a

part of the covens that helped isolate Lulupoterra in an attempt to re-populate the werewolf species. And now that they've brought up Fire Mountain, it takes everything in me not to charge from my hiding spot to demand answers.

"I guess we'll see, Lazlo," Evelyn responds. She bends down and touches the ground, scooping up a handful of dirt. Her black bob veils the side of her face, but I recognize her to be the woman who collared Antone.

Caz recognizes her too, his body bristling under my hands. It's now me locking him in place instead of the other way around.

"I'm afraid we might be too late with our intervention. The she-wolf is gone. Whichever coven that has been helping her knows High Council level magic. We must proceed with caution," Evelyn adds.

The other witch, Allegra, gathers green magic in her palms. "Indeed. Something is off here. Perhaps taking one of the lycans will benefit us to risk a war."

So many questions swirl through my mind. Do they not know that Nightstar and Fire Mountain have been messing around with the packs the last few weeks? Or that they declared war against the leaders? It sounds like they already don't trust either coven. What if this could mean getting help from them for Lulupoterra?

"Help always comes at a cost," Caz whispers telepathically. "I recognize Lazlo from The Great Sacrifice. The Infinity Coven was there."

Fuck.

The three witches continue to head in the direction of the lycan's cabin, their voices fading with them. I shift on the balls of my feet to twist myself to meet Caz's gaze. He nuzzles his nose to my cheek as I hug him, just taking a few deep breaths to settle my nerves. It feels as if Flynn has been gone forever, and I worry he might not come back.

"I will always come back for you, she-wolf," Flynn says, his voice low but audible as it drifts to me through the trees. "You two can come out now. It's safe."

Caz slinks his way out of our hiding place and transforms into a man. He helps me to my feet, standing naked and tall, so hot in his tense state of protectiveness that I can't help gravitating toward him until he pulls me into his side and hugs me close.

Flynn's eyes flash lavender as he studies the two of us for a second. I can't tell if he's ensuring we're okay or if he just can't help himself. He's been nervous about my pack since we've met, and even though he knows that Caz saw us not that long ago, he almost looks guilty for our intimate moment.

I touch his soul stone, dangling on the ribbon around my neck. "Did you see them? The witches? They were talking about Nightstar and Fire Mountain."

Flynn draws his gaze from my hand on my chest and peers in the direction the witches left. "I did, and I only recognize

Lazlo of the Infinity Coven. He was there. I mean, at the execution of my coven." Flynn's face darkens with his words, and it feels as if my heart sinks into my stomach. "He has ties to the Lioht Coven." The coven his family was accused of killing the High Priestess of.

"Fuck," Caz mutters under his breath. "I'm sorry, man. Go get our pack. We'll take care of this now."

Flynn's face softens at Caz's words, and he shakes his head. "We need more than brute force and a surprise attack to handle this. I can't endanger any of you like this."

I reach out and take Flynn's hand, pulling him closer to me and Caz. "Then what do you want to d—"

A wail rips through the air, cutting off my words. Blinding light explodes through the night like someone magically forces the sun to rise. I shield my eyes, my muscles tensing. Flynn gathers power while Caz morphs back into a wolf.

Flynn holds his glowing hands up. "Stay here. I'll—"

The ground rumbles, shaking beneath my feet. Flynn shoves into me, knocking me over. Caz bites the back of Flynn's shirt and drags both of us toward the shelter within the low branches of the trees. I wince, the rough ground scratching the backs of my bare legs. Flynn hugs me protectively as the ground shakes again. From over his shoulder, I glimpse a black-coated lycan running on all fours.

"Tnelis drlow," Flynn whispers in my ear.

My heart pounds, racing with my rising fear.

Flynn reaches between us and locks his fingers around his soul stone. "Tnelis drlow," he repeats.

A roar rips through the night again.

I tense at the lycan skidding across the forest.

It erupts in magical light.

9

Invidia Nightstar

"WE'RE OKAY. TRUST ME. NO one will know we're here." Flynn eases himself off me and onto the hard dirt. "I've shielded us."

Caz spins in his place and sniffs my hair before gliding his tongue over my cheek. " You okay, Lyric? I smell blood."

I kiss his cool snout, clutching my fingers into his furry neck to hold him still. If he had it his way, he'd poke the rest of my body with his nose until he found my wounds. I wouldn't put it past him to try to lick them, either.

"I'm just a bit scratched up," I say, speaking out loud instead of through our telepathic link. "I'll be okay."

Caz whimpers and paws Flynn. "Can you get us out of here? She needs Bastien."

Flynn's jaw twitches, hearing Caz as clearly as I do. "Not yet. Relocating will disturb the magic they're using. I was fortunate to get an opening when they got the beast."

"Our pack is going to flip their shit if we're much longer." Caz slumps to his belly, getting ultra-close to me. "Maybe you and Lyric can go. I'll be okay."

I frown. "We're not separating."

"She's right." Flynn props himself up and leans against the tree trunk. "We can't. But what I can do is open a looking glass when I get the chance. I have to wait until—"

A holler cuts through the air, the guttural sound sinking into my bones.

"Fuck. Take my hand. Quick." Flynn grabs my wrist and pulls me to him.

He tightens his hold on my fingers and smacks his hand to the tree trunk, sending power sizzling across the bark. Another yell echoes in the forest behind us with red sparks of magic from another witch.

Flynn whispers a spell under his breath, and the bark wavers and shifts, turning reflective. I spot Sagan pacing around Dax, Sterling, and Bastien in their human forms, huddled together. All three of their hands bleed as if they were trying to break down the door, and I realize Flynn must've locked them in.

Like they all sense us looking, the four of them turn their attention in our direction. Sagan bows and stretches, turning into a man, and Sterling beats Dax and Bastien to rush to the looking glass.

"Before you all start yelling, I want you to know we're fine. We're just trapped for a bit," I say, giving Dax a long look. His anxious emotions are hot and palpable, even though we're apart.

"Trapped?" Bastien asks, pushing into Sterling, who nearly takes up the whole view. "Are you hurt?"

"Let us out of here, and we will come," Dax says, looming behind Sterling and Bastien. "It'll only take us a few minutes to find you."

"It's too dangerous," I say, knowing that it'll be less infuriating coming from me than having Flynn deny them the chance to be our knights in shining armor. "There are four lycans and three witches here. They're fighting."

A guttural howl drags my attention to the forest. The white-haired warlock traps one of the lycans in a web of energy. Caz backs into me, sandwiching me to Flynn. I flick my attention from our pack and back to the fight unfolding before us. Dax's eyes widen and Sterling swears. Sagan and Bastien shove close together to get a better view through the looking glass, seeing what I see.

"Gorgeous, please. It's more dangerous if you don't let us. We can help fight them off." Sagan's eyes narrow, and he looks ready to try to dive through the magical looking glass to get to me.

"We're going to wait it out. It'll give us a chance to eavesdrop on the witches here investigating the lycans. They say the Nightstar Coven is responsible for them. Not Fire Mountain. This might be my only chance to learn something that can help my dad." I hug my arm around Caz and lean into Flynn. "Please trust that we'll be okay. We won't disconnect the line. You can watch too."

No one has a chance to respond because a loud crack snaps through the air. The ground trembles as a tree falls. I startle at the loud noise and dig my fingers into Caz's fur. He releases a rumbling, nearly silent growl, and it vibrates across my palm.

"What are they doing?" I whisper, shifting onto all fours to crawl a bit forward for a better view.

"Invidia! Invidia, we summon you," Allegra yells, raising her hands into the sky. "Nommus eth ew lali vekki High Priestess of Nightstar!"

Flynn's hands grab the back of my legs and pull me back. I nearly elbow him in the gut by accident, but Caz expects my defensive move and knocks my arm upward with his head. I force myself to relax as Flynn wraps his arm around me and Caz in preparation to transport if he needs to.

"They're forcing the Nightstar High Priestess to come

here. Be prepared. They're going to make a sacrifice." Flynn's low voice tickles my ear.

"Don't watch, Ma Belle," Bastien says, his voice trickling to me from the looking glass. "Please. I know what seeing what we did to the other lycan tormented you. But this? It'll be worse."

"Way fucking worse," Dax mutters.

"Great. Now, she's going to watch." Sterling growls with his words, sending a shiver through me. "Flynn, whip out your wand. Distract her with your magic dip-stick and show her a damn trick. It'll work. I swear. Do it for our girl."

If I could whack Sterling, I would. But now I also can't help thinking about magic cocks and the kind of show Flynn is capable of.

Unfortunately, my wandering thoughts crash to the ground with my stomach. A black-haired lycan screams an ear-drum-shattering wail as Lazlo blasts the beast with blue magic. Electricity courses over the lycan's body, burning away its fur until a bald, naked man-beast convulses midair. The witches lock the lycan in a twisted spell, chanting something indecipherable, muted by the shrieks of agony coming from the beast.

My stomach twists and turns as I swivel in Flynn's arms, burying my face into Caz's coat the second blood starts to seep from the lycan's eyes. Cupping his hands over my ears, Flynn tries his best to muffle the noise. For the first time, I feel sorry for a lycan. I thought they were the monsters, but they're nothing in comparison to these witches.

I stifle a cry, squeezing my eyes shut. I realize it's more than the torment of this cursed human that has my soul wanting to flee my body. I can't stop thinking about my dad and his current fate in the hands of the Fire Mountain Clan witches. Or Antone. Bastien's brother doesn't deserve such a fate.

My body ripples, my she-wolf begging to break free. "You have to stop them," I plead, feeling the ache of my body transforming without my permission. "Please, Flynn. Do something."

"I'm so sorry, Lyric," he says, stroking his fingers along my back, tugging my shirt off as I uncontrollably transform. "I'm so sorry." With his words, I know there is nothing that he can do. He's not willing to risk our safety, and selfishly, I'm glad for it. But it doesn't make my soul hurt any less.

"It's almost over," Caz says through our mind-link. He licks my snout, nuzzling his head to mine, comforting me the only way he knows how.

An explosion steals my hearing, and the whole world quivers. Panic sends me thrashing in Flynn's hold to see what's happening behind me. The ground quakes and trembles. Leaves and branches cascade from the trembling trees. Haze fills the forest, a strange light zigzagging across the dirt to a centralized spot.

"Nommus eth ew lali vekki High Priestess of Nightstar!"

all three witches yell toward the sky.

The blood of their lycan sacrifice rains down from above, sizzling and popping in the vortex of power, twisting and gathering into a portal of light. Flynn sucks in a breath, his fingers digging into my fur, the sight before us startling even him. If he's afraid, then I know my terror is warranted.

"Get out of there," Dax says through the looking glass. "Get out of there now!"

Light engulfs the world, but it's not Flynn transporting us. The gateway blasts open, sending a shockwave through the forest. My hair blows with the force, and Flynn grips tightly to both me and Caz. Strange noises fill the air, howls and growls and guttural pleas.

The portal vanishes in another blinding flash of light.

Silence falls over the forest.

"Invidia, you've broken our treaty," Allegra says, breaking the silence. "The beasts don't lie."

My body tenses, my mind demanding my she-wolf to release me. I need to be in my most powerful form. I groan with the ache of my transformation back into my human self, but I'm thankful my wolf complies. This is too much. Seeing the witch with the long white hair, watching the others confront her...fuck.

The Nightstar witch, Invidia, remains silent. Her features remain expressionless. She doesn't react to the accusations. She doesn't try to make excuses. All she does is stand tall, her power sparking in her eyes.

"Explain yourself," Lazlo commands, his features morphing, revealing his monstrous side with elongated teeth.

Invidia smirks. "Our treaty has long since expired. I'm now only collecting what is mine. Perhaps you should accuse each other of the same. You're not all blameless."

"We had an agreement," Allegra snaps, gathering power in her palms. "Do you want to start a war?"

Invidia's smile widens. "The war is already over. You all have lost." Raising her hands toward the sky, she shouts, "Em flow ill kaw lota!"

None of the witches have time to react as another portal opens behind them. I scramble back into Flynn's arms at the sight of several hulking alpha-mate wolves leaping through the new gateway.

I recognize Dax's uncle, Luke, barreling toward the black-haired witch. She claps her hands and disappears in a flash of red light. Allegra and Lazlo follow her lead and vanish before any of the wolves can attack. My chest heaves with my panting breath, and I suppress my fear, allowing my anger to take control of my emotions. I want so badly to charge out of our hiding place, but I force my need for revenge and justice away. There are too many of them. I'd never win.

"My faithful servants, gather my pets. I must have a word with them." Invidia saunters toward the alpha-mates. Her long white hair blows behind her, and her eyes flicker with power.

She looks ethereal in a world of dark shadows, her pale features hard and cold, yet devastatingly beautiful. It hurts to stare at her glowing essence for too long.

The alpha-mates snarl and grab onto the remaining lycans, dragging them through the make-shift barrier of the fallen tree. Mr. Remington flails and fights against Luke until the alpha-mate traitor releases him at Invidia's feet. Another wolf herds Todd, snapping his sharp fangs. The final lycan crawls forward on her hands and knees, naked and frail and in her human form. Seeing a woman look so defeated gets under my skin, and I can hardly control the rage burning through me.

"Let's make this easy, shall we," Invidia says, gathering energy in her palms. "It will be far worse for all of you if you force me to yank the truth out of you. I will not pay the price for something I can rip from you another way."

Torture. Fuck. I can't think the thought without feeling sick to my stomach. If they resist her, I will intervene. I can't hide and wait for it to end. I don't care if Mr. Remington and Todd are my enemies. No one deserves that fate.

Invidia narrows her eyes at the woman and throws a burst of magic a foot away from her. She screeches and tries to scramble away, and one of the alpha-mates sinks his teeth into her shoulder and hauls her in front of the witch.

"Are you hungry, my servants?" the witch asks the alpha-mates. "Perhaps a little bite will satiate you. Go on. Ensure she can't run again."

Flynn slaps his hand over my mouth and restrains me before I break through his shield. The wolves growl and snap, surrounding the woman like she's their next meal. My stomach twists, my chest heaving. Sweat prickles across my forehead, cooling with the breeze stirring through the trees.

"Please!" the woman yells, clawing at the ground, fighting to transform. "What do you want from me? I will tell you."

Twitching her fingers, Invidia spells the wolves, freezing them in their tracks before they can attack. "Who told the High Rebels that I was your master?"

"It was the bitch," Todd says, pointing at the woman. "She refuses to accept her new power over the Mortal World."

"What?" The woman scrunches her face in disbelief. "You asshole. No it—"

"Ecnelis mucs!" Invidia sends electricity at both Todd and the woman, shutting them up. Turning to Mr. Remington, she curls her finger, getting him to shuffle closer. "You'll tell me the truth, won't you, my pet? Which one of them is lying?"

I bite my lip, holding my breath. I expect Mr. Remington to take Todd's side. I expect them to throw the poor woman to the wolves. I brace for it, preparing to break free from Flynn's grip to burst through his shield. I might be fast enough to intervene. Or at least distract the witch so that Flynn can do something.

"Tell her, Martin," Todd says, his voice turning gruff. "Tell our master who has betrayed her."

"It was...him," Mr. Remington says, surprising the hell out of me. "He has been disobeying your orders. He's not being discrete. He's wasted four potential turns this week to satiate his desire to control."

What. The. Fuck?

Todd said it was Mr. Remington who failed to turn the mortals and then consumed them. But if it was Todd... Damn it. Of course he was lying to save his own ass, just like he was about to lie to the witch.

"You fucker!" Todd hollers, transforming into his monstrous self. "You worthless piece of shit! I've been working my ass off, and this is how you repay me? I fucking even got the damn she-wolf. If you had been here—"

Invidia claps her hands, the booming noise shaking the world around us. Todd drops to the ground, his legs collapsing out from under him. He hits the ground with a thud, and one of the alpha-mates launches from beside Invidia and lands on his back. Growling, the wolf pins Todd down by his neck, lowering his big head to bare his fangs in his distorted face.

"Where is the she-wolf?" Invidia asks, settling the quaking world down. "Take me to her."

I shudder in Flynn's arms, fear tightening my chest.

"You need to get them out of there, Flynn," Dax says, his voice deep and demanding. "If the witch knows Lyric was recently there—"

"She escaped," Todd says, his words cutting off Dax.

"Martin and Kari scared her off. She was with a warlock."

"And he is shielding her." It's not a question. Invidia swivels on the balls of her feet and peers around the forest. Her long skirt sweeps around her ankles. "Which means I will need a little help."

"Shit," Flynn says, gathering magic in his palms. The lavender light sparkles in his palms in front of me. He keeps me and Caz locked in his arms, like they're the only things protecting us. And who knows? Maybe they are.

"Come here, my servant. Show me how loyal you truly are," Invidia tells Todd, coaxing him to step closer to her. "Help me find the she-wolf."

Todd bobs his head. "I'll do anything."

Caressing her hand to his cheek, Invidia smiles at Todd. "Good. You have served me well. Your sacrifice will bring bounty to your soul. Your life will give me what I need for my summons."

Invidia captures Todd in a strange magical rope, binding him before he can run. He growls and thrashes. Nothing he does breaks him free from the magic. He is at the witch's mercy. The alpha-mates howl, surrounding Invidia and Todd. Mr. Remington grabs the female lycan by her hand and drags her back.

"Flynn, get our mate out of there. Now!" Sagan yells, his voice trickling through the portal.

Tensing, Flynn shifts me in his arms, giving me one more

glimpse at the rest of my pack through the looking glass before slapping his hand over it, shattering the spell. The tree branches overhead rattle and send leaves raining down around us.

"Close your eyes, she-wolf. Hold on tight to Caz," Flynn says, freeing one of his arms.

I grip Caz as hard as I can, afraid if I don't, he'll somehow get left behind. My breathing quickens as the witch chants something low, inaudible over the discordant racket the alpha-mates create, their howls and calls loud enough to make my ears ring.

"Close your eyes," Flynn repeats. "Do it now."

But it's too late.

Blood sprays through the air, catching on a magic breeze as the witch sacrifices Todd for her spell to find me. Light erupts in my vision, stealing my senses away. I clench my jaw, clutching Caz as he whimpers in my ear. My stomach flips, and I tense.

This is it. Flynn didn't work fast enough. The witch out-matched him, and now she's taking me.

My back hits the ground, and I automatically kick my leg, preparing to fight for my life. A hot hand grabs my ankle and hoists me off my feet. Dax's familiar scent engulfs me with the strength of his arms, and Sagan's soon follows. Sterling and Bastien join us, encasing me between their bodies in what I can only describe as feeling like the safest place in the world.

"We got you, gorgeous," Sagan murmurs, kissing the side

of my quivering lips.

"Caz? Flynn?" I ask, pressing my forehead to Dax's shoulder.

Caz's gentle hand strokes my forehead. "We're here. We're all safe."

I ease my head back to look at him before meeting everyone else's gaze. "But for how long? The witch—"

"I won't let her take you," Flynn says, speaking up.

"None of us will, blondie," Sterling adds.

"We now know what we're dealing with. We can strategize. We can fight." Dax hugs me tightly, squeezing the trembles from me. "You saw it for yourself. The witches are no longer allies."

"And it looks as if Nightstar might've taken control of Lulupoterra. The wolves aren't our greatest threat. They will see the truth." Bastien crowds close, stretching to nuzzle his nose into my hair to take a breath of my scent. "We can use this to our advantage."

"How?" I ask, my mind swirling with dozens of thoughts. Just because the witches aren't allies, doesn't make any of them less of our enemies. "The alpha-mates were the witch's servants."

"My brother. The others. If we find the witch who took him, we can get answers," Bastien responds. "We can free them and increase our numbers."

"We can use the witch to find your father. You heard them

talking. They know Fire Mountain." Flynn steps behind Dax to get a better look at me. "I think you might've had it wrong about that coven. Something feels off, and I want to find out what."

"So what now?" I ask.

Flynn licks his lips. "We catch a witch."

If only it was that easy.

10

New Adventure

"HOW MUCH LONGER?" I ASK, tapping my fingers to the table. "They've been gone forever."

"It's been twenty minutes. There is a lot of ground to cover." Sterling offers me another bite of the chocolate cake Flynn summoned in an attempt to cheer me up.

I let him feed me the forkful and savor the sweet flavor of one of my favorite desserts. Leaning in, he kisses me, sucking my bottom lip into his mouth. I sigh at the softness of his mouth caressing mine, knowing he just wants to distract me the best he can.

"Is it working?" he thinks, responding to my thought silently.

I shift from my seat and onto his lap, straddling him in the chair. "No," I say, clutching his face between my palms. "We should all be out there."

Sliding his arms around my waist, he lifts me up with him, carrying me across the small living room and to the bedroom. "No, we should be here. You've been through a lot, and we all agreed that you need to re-charge, catch your breath, enjoy some fun, get a little tender love and care, and also...reward me for my efforts."

I pull away from him and laugh. "You are not suggesting what I think you're suggesting."

Sterling shrugs, offering me a wicked hot grin. "What? I can't think of a better way to get your mind off things."

I wiggle in his arms until he sets me on my feet. "I can," I say, sauntering away from him. I grab the hem of my dirty shirt and tug it over my head. "Flynn mentioned there was a tub here."

"A bubble bath, huh?" Sterling says, quickening his pace behind me. "What about a massage?"

"Oh, you think this is an offering for you to join me? I think I'd prefer you watch me from over there," I tease, peering over my shoulder to smile at him. "I had planned to use this time to strategize how I'm going to get you all on your knees and obeying my commands as your leader. I can't have anyone out of line, not with a war on our hands."

Sterling hesitates in the doorway, watching me start the water to fill the tub. Drinking me in, he waits without a word. I can tell it's taking everything in him to do so, but he's trying to prove to me that he can and will do what I ask of him, even if I'm joking.

I seductively bend over the tub, sticking my hand into the water, playing with the bubbles. "I mean, that bitch witch today did give me a bit of inspiration, and I now have my very own warlock to—"

"All right, blondie. That naughty mouth of yours is going to get you in trouble." Sterling closes the bathroom door and drops his pants. "Unless you're about to suggest Mr. Magic Cock tie me to a bed for you to have your way with me or give me double dicks to double peen you without assistance—"

I laugh in exasperation and sweep my hand across the bubbly water. My wave of bathwater splashes across his face, cutting off his kinky-ass fantasy now imprinted in my mind. Play-growling, Sterling rushes me, trying to bear hug me, but I trip him, sending him sliding across the wet floor.

"Getting you on your knees is far easier than it should be. You're not even putting up a fight." I grin as I step into the bubble bath as Sterling lies flat on his back, butt-ass naked, with his raging boner aimed at the ceiling.

He groans, catching his breath and trying to orient himself. I don't think he was expecting me to use a counter attack and just let him sweep me off my feet.

"I thought you were tougher than this. You obviously don't want me as much as I thought." I bite my bottom lip and sink deeper into the tub, loving his shocked expression at my teasing.

Slapping his hands to the tiles, he hops to his feet and claps his hands together. "You're in so much trouble, blondie. That ass is mine. Get ready for me to spank the naughty right out of you."

I lift an eyebrow. "Only spank, huh? I thought you'd beg for your reward."

Sterling's muscles flex with my comment, and he unashamedly strokes his hand over his cock. "I'm not against begging, blondie. If that's what it takes to experience the tunnel to heaven. I haven't been able to think about anything else besides that teensy glory hole between those sexy, spankable, sweet cheeks."

I tip my head back and laugh, my voice echoing through the room. Alone time with Sterling was exactly what I needed to get out of my mood and push thoughts of the horrible world outside this apartment away. "I seem to recall I had some stipulations before forging on that kind of adventure."

He closes the space completely and sits on the edge of the tub. "I've done everything you've asked already. Got rid of all the others to ensure no interruptions or whimpering to watch.

Have my strategy to guarantee at least five orgasms."

I scoop up a handful of bubbles from my bath and splatter them across his bare chest. "You're so prepared...and utterly ridiculous."

"Why? I love that round, delicious peach of yours." He pretends to squeeze the air like he can already imagine my ass bent over in front of him. "You have no idea."

"Oh, I think I do. I can feel how excited you are, and I hate to kill your boner, but you forgot about something. You're missing the lube." I twist my mouth to the side, smirking. "My ass won't accept your damn spit no matter how much you think you can just lick it and stick it."

He tips his head back and laughs. "Don't be so negative, blondie. It's going to be fucking awesome."

I smirk. "If that's the case, maybe you should let me mount you and let that be a determining factor. You know I've been practicing." It takes everything in me to keep a straight face as I remind him of our game of surprise hump.

I feel his light-hearted, amused reaction a moment before he graces me with a smile capable of melting any and all future panties I'd wear. It's in this moment, I know I'm going to give in. It's hard not to be curious about this ass-venture with how excited he is.

"You're so kinky. I love it. Who knew my pleasure pipe could get any harder, but now listening to you thinking about humping the hell out of me? How could I say no? Your desires and needs are important to me." The little shit. He damn well knows I'd prefer to get mounted by him and that I'm full of shit. He totally just beat me at my own game.

I narrow my eyes at him. "You're so bad."

Sterling grins wider, leans over, and kisses me. "I'm going to prove to you that I can make you cream no matter what hole on your body I slip my man-meat in. You can thank our claim for that. My pleasure is all yours, blondie."

I rub my lips together, knowing he's right. I refuse to admit it, though. "I highly doubt that's true. I'm pretty sure neither of us will get anything out of you trying to screw me in the ear. With the way you guys all talk about mating season, it feels like you might try to get creative." I toss another handful of bubbles at him, splashing them right across his raging boner.

He uses the suds to rub himself again, knowing how much I like watching him get off. "Well, perhaps you should have thought about that before staking your claim on Flynn. We were all set for five, but now there's a six..."

An image of taking care of all my guys at once flicks through my mind. Two hands. My mouth. Fucking double dicks. That's five.

What am I even thinking?

Sterling reaches out and combs my damp hair behind my ear. "Don't worry. I'd prefer not to turn my need to fuck your brains out so literal, blondie."

I crack up and sink lower in the bath, letting the bubbles

blanket my body up to my neck. I had no idea this was where the conversation would lead, but I'll admit, I had thought about it a bunch of times, despite not even sleeping with all my pack mates yet.

"I mean, maybe if I was a sapiosexual like Bastien. You might have to watch out for him. I'm just a Lyric-sexual. I can't even look at you without being turned on. And your scent? Fucking forget about it. I'm done for. I hope you know if I had it my way, we'd never do anything but stay in bed, maybe go to the couch. The shower will work too. I can prop you up on that ledge...damn, the dining room table. Seeing you all hot over a little spanking—" He purrs deep in his throat, sounding more feline than wolf.

His dirty thoughts continue to fill my mind, and I squirm in the tub, my body getting turned on. I'm tempted to touch myself while he just continues to fantasize about me, because now he's taking too long. He doesn't have to convince me of anything. It's not even a reward at this point. The smooth bastard has me fully on board.

I sit up higher in the tub, exposing my hard nipples to Sterling. Rubbing my fingers over my boobs, I dip my hands under the bubbles, teasing him with a soft moan as I imagine him joining me in the tub. I'm so fucking hot and bothered for him. The fact that he doesn't drag me out of the tub, bend me over the counter, and screw me from behind this second leaves me aching. Desperate.

He hums under his breath and strokes the length of his erection again, slow and seductively, loving every bit of my reaction. The gesture sends an explosion of tingles between my legs, and I think about getting out of the tub to throw myself at him. He might get to experience me mounting his sexy ass after all if he doesn't stop teasing my wild, insatiable nature.

"I want to see," he murmurs, strolling the two feet it takes to get to the sink. Sterling blindly pops open the medicine cabinet and snatches a clear bottle from the top shelf like he already knew what to expect. He air-pumps his fist and grins at me. "That warlock's already my best friend, blondie." Shaking the bottle, he flicks up the cap and sniffs the liquid. "This lube is perfect. I bet it's magical even."

"You're joking," I say, watching him pour a stream of it into his palm.

Desire lights his gray eyes, and he rubs the lube across his cock and shakes his head. "Not if you don't want me to be joking. I can feel your curiosity, but I respect your hesitation. I'll do whatever you want, Lyric."

"I know," I tease. "And right now, I just want you to watch me."

Pulling myself from the warm water, I sit on the wide ledge of the tube against the wall. Sterling moans under his breath, his gaze devouring my soapy body as the bubbles drip down my breasts and stomach. He continues to stroke his cock, now slippery with lube, and I curl and uncurl my finger to get him to move a bit closer.

I trail my hand down my stomach and massage my fingers between my legs, drawing slow circles over my tingling clit. Sterling groans, his eyes following the motion of my hand and he climbs into the tub like it's torture just to watch me pleasure myself.

"It is," he murmurs, sinking to his knees in the tub, settling between my legs to rub his hands over my knees. "But I still enjoy it. I just want to help. I like to be the reason you cum."

He doesn't stop me from masturbating, but instead, he spreads my legs wider and kisses my thigh. His hand joins mine, and he slips a finger inside me, stroking me from the inside, creating enough pressure to make me moan as he finds my G-spot. And fuck. The touch of his finger sends pleasure crashing through me, and I comb my fingers through his hair and pull his head toward my body.

He hums his enjoyment, linking his free hand with mine, so he can take over and kiss my clit, twirling his tongue over my buzzing skin. I moan and roll my hips, savoring the pleasure he elicits inside me.

"It feels so good," I murmur, rubbing his soft hair with my free hand.

"Yeah?" Sterling's voice sounds so breathy and sexy I want to hear him say more. I want to feel the sensation of his rumbly voice on my body, how the vibration increases my pleasure, bringing me close to my peak. "You're incredible, Lyric. The taste of your body intoxicates me. I could have you like this for breakfast, lunch, and dinner and be the most satisfied man in the universe."

"Mmm-hmm," I say, chewing my lip through another wave of pleasure. "It's what I want for you. To give you whatever you want and need."

"Is that so?" The thought comes into my head as he continues to flick his tongue over and over again while stroking my G-spot, making me moan so incredibly loud that I'm sure the rest of our pack can hear us, probably feel my excitement too. I bet it won't be long until they ask for me to let them all participate...

Sterling picks up his pace, adding more and more pressure until my body explodes with my orgasm, and I automatically clench his head between my thighs, rolling my hips as I ride through the intense sensation that I'm certain is responsible for the clear fluid splashing across his face. A wave of pride rises inside me, trickling from him to me, and he eases away from my body and drags his hand across his pouty lips and pops his finger into his mouth with a moan of contentment.

"Fuck, I want more of that," he says, his lips puffing with his quickening breathing.

My breasts rise and fall as I try to catch my breath, the pleasure from my orgasm lingering in every cell on my body, the intensity enough to trigger something deep in my soul that sends me sliding into Sterling's arms. He tangles his hands through my wet hair and kisses me passionately, drawing his hand down my back to lift me out of the tub by my ass cheeks. I curl my body around his and let him carry me to the small bedroom with a bed only big enough for the two of us. I half-expect someone to peek in from the living room, tempted to return by the feeling of my ecstasy, but Sterling locked the door.

"Sometimes we need a little uninterrupted alone time," he murmurs through another deep kiss as he lowers my dripping body onto the blankets.

Sterling joins me on the bed, and I lace my fingers around his cock, feeling his hardness throb and flex against my fingers. His desire cascades over me, and he squeezes my ass in his hands, messing with my ass cheeks, his mind already thinking about the one thing he's been obsessed with for at least a week or two.

"Not the only thing," he says, responding to my thoughts. "I'm obsessed with all of you. And like I said, whatever you want to do, I'm good with. I love being with you regardless."

I smile and tip my head back to meet his gaze. "I love you, Sterling."

His face lights up with my admission. "I love you more, blondie. Borderline obsessed with you, like you said. You complete me."

I laugh and nuzzle my nose to his. "It's impossible for you

to love me more. You know why?"

"Why?" His handsome face remains soft and amused, his eyes wide with his excitement.

"Because I'm about to give you exactly what you want." I poke his bottom lip with my index finger. "And I'm not even going to make you work for it by asking you to give me four more orgasms. But grab the lube. That's one thing I'm serious about. I've seen enough porn, you horn-dog."

He chuckles and rolls to the edge of the bed, pulling open the top drawer of the nightstand. Waving another bottle of lube, he says, "My new best friend has my back...and your ass. I begged him for a couple of options." He inspects the bottle and squeezes some onto his fingers. "This one is definitely magical. I can feel the tingles already."

I laugh, my voice ringing through the air, his damn excitement over this so incredibly contagious I'm starting to think I might crave anal sex just to experience his pleasure alone. Sterling kisses me again, working his mouth down my neck. He flips me onto my stomach, surprising the hell out of me. I moan into the pillow as his tongue slides down the length of my spine.

I can't believe I'm about to have anal sex with Sterling. It's not exactly something I've ever thought about before he brought it up, but hearing and feeling his excitement of trying something new, determined to ensure my comfort and pleasure while playing out his own fantasy has me anxious in a good way.

"Relax, Lyric," he murmurs, repositioning himself and me, lifting my body up by my hips to curl my legs under me. "Don't be nervous."

"You're about to lick my ass," I murmur into my pillow. It's one thing to have him do it while I'm sitting on his face, and he's enjoying the rest of me, but he's just going right for it now. I'm fucking nervous.

He chuckles and grazes his tongue over my ass cheek. "And you're going to love every second of it."

I press my face against the pillow and squeeze my eyes shut, shuddering through the sensation of Sterling's tongue exploring my body. Smacking my ass cheek, he licks my body in a way that makes me moan despite my mind whirling with a dozen thoughts. The anticipation is torturous in the best way. He's really all in, taking his time, treating me with respect and gentleness.

"Relax," Sterling repeats, his voice trickling into my mind. "I love every damn inch of your body. Your ass is so perfect like the rest of you. I want you to enjoy this as much as I do. I love you."

I suck in a slow breath, losing myself to the sensation his mouth creates on my body. Sterling eases away, and he drips the cool lube onto me and gently rubs his finger down the middle of my ass cheeks, testing my reaction as he slips one finger in to work me up to him while touching my clit with his other hand. I gasp in a good way, the slight pressure not as bad as I expected. Actually, it's not bad at all. The lube Sterling uses really is magic, sending an indescribable pleasure through my body that I can feel in my soul. The two different sensations burst tingles through my body and I moan, stretching my arms in front of me, arching my back.

"How does this feel?" he asks, his voice husky and full of lust. I love that he asks me, despite knowing I'm loving every second of his attention. "I need to hear it out loud."

I turn my head, pressing my cheek to the pillow. "It's different...good. Better than I expected. I want more."

He moans at my words and taps his hard cock to the split between my ass cheeks. I gasp a breath in anticipation, the buildup so fucking amazing that I can't wait to feel his reaction to fucking me how he's been fantasizing about. I've never wanted to please someone so much in my life.

Sterling digs his fingers into my side, bracing on me while squeezing lube onto his cock. I shift and wiggle my ass, peering behind me to watch him. He sucks in his top lip, his bottom lip now so pouty and kissable, his lust and desire prominent in his sexy, heavy-lidded expression.

Aligning his body to mine, he rubs his tip from my clit, working his way up. "You're so slick and hot. Are you ready for me?" His breathy, velvety voice turns me on, and all I can think about is how much he's going to enjoy this. How much I'll enjoy the pleasure he gets from me.

My vagina tingles in anticipation even though I try to tell it not to get too damn excited. Being so open and connected blurs the lines between my feelings and his, and I have to remind myself that this might not feel as good for me. What if it hurts? He's not exactly small.

Sterling's heavy weight eases onto me as he bends forward and on top of me. He kisses my shoulder. "Don't be afraid to speak up. I want this to be fun. If you'd prefer, I'll give you everything you want instead. You're important to me."

"I do want this. I had no idea I would, but that doesn't matter. I want this to be about you. You're always so obsessed with taking care of me," I murmur, swaying my hips to rub my ass against the length of his shaft. "Let this be all for you."

He hums his disagreement. "It's about both of us, blondie. My pleasure is yours and yours is mine."

"I suppose that's a perk," I say, my voice light and breathy, my need and excitement pushing away all my hesitation.

"Damn straight."

Smacking my ass again, he massages his fingers into my ass cheeks and spreads my body wider, dripping more lube onto me. The cool sensation makes me shiver, and I gather the blankets in my hands, feeling Sterling tap his hard cock on the line between my ass cheeks.

"Try not to tense. I want your sweet star to welcome me in. If your body resists, I won't push you." He aligns his cock with my body, squirting even more lube to ensure he can slip inside me.

I inhale a few deep breaths, the pressure strange yet thrilling, my body so turned on that I'm more excited than I expected. Maybe it's Sterling's emotions tangling with me, or maybe they're really mine. Either way, I want to hear him moan. I want to hear how good my ass feels. How much he savors my body.

Sterling releases a sexy rumble from his throat, sending a burst of sizzling pleasure zinging from my groin and to the rest of me. Hooking one hand to my hip, he moans, easing his tip into my ass without thrusting, just letting me get used to the pressure and pleasure coursing from him to me.

"Lyric," he murmurs, my name a breath of hot ecstasy I can feel deep inside me. "You're so perfect. Tight. Sexy. I already feel like I'm going to cum."

I laugh breathlessly as he slowly pushes deeper, letting me get used to the feeling. "That good, huh?"

He groans and eases his hips back, just rocking his body into mine without getting carried away. I moan along with him, closing my eyes, losing myself in the pleasure and love rolling through me from him in wave after wave.

Sterling whispers my name over and over again, his sexy moans sending explosions through me. He reaches around and rubs his fingers to my clit, adding more pleasure until my mind feels as if it turns to mush, the only thing I can think and feel and crave is the ecstasy of our passion.

Sterling whispers he's going to cum and picks up the speed and pressure of his hand until I scream with intense pleasure. I orgasm at the same time he cums, my muscles tightening and releasing, my body clenching his, every inch of me bursting with incredible sensations I want to savor forever.

"My beautiful, bombshell blondie and your tight, sexy, amazing ass. I'll never forget this moment." Sterling slides out of me and rolls me over, sinking his weight onto me as he cuddles me close. "Was it okay for you? I didn't hurt you any?"

Snuggling my nose into the crook of his neck, I say, "It was unexpectedly good."

"You have no idea what kind of fun is in store for us." Kissing my temple, Sterling takes a moment to sniff the scent of my hair, his wild desire still prominent.

I laugh against his shoulder. "Oh, boy. I swear if you say double the peen—"

He hums deep in his throat. "Just imagine. It'll be so fun."

I shiver at his excitement and hug him close, sucking the sensitive skin of his throat, leaving a hickey, loving my mark on his skin. Sterling lifts me off the bed with him, taking me to the bathroom to clean up.

Talk about a new level of closeness.

A knock on the bedroom door draws my attention away from Sterling, soaping up in the shower. I grab a towel and wrap it around me, wiggling my fingers at Sterling to get him to stay put. I saunter across the bedroom and crack the door open, meeting Sagan's gaze. A smile crosses his face, and he sweeps his gaze down my body and back up again. Reaching out, he tucks the wet strands of my hair behind my ear and kisses me sweetly.

"Did you have a good time?" he asks, his mind open to me, his curiosity getting the best of him. He can't help thinking about my moment of passion with his brother. I'm sure Sterling told him and all of them his plan. There aren't many secrets between us.

"I did," I say, smirking. I automatically think about Sterling's joke about double the peen, and now I visualize such an adventure with the two of them. Sagan's growing hard-on grazes my hip as he listens to my thoughts, and I can't help wondering how the hell it would work. Would I be in the middle of their sexy muscle sandwich? Could one of them hold me up while the other pleasures me from behind?

"Fuck, blondie, I'll do whatever the hell in whatever the hell position you want. Just drag that asshole in here and lock the door before Dax, Bastien, Caz, and even fucking Flynn come sniffing around here, asking to join in on the fun. This bed is too damn small, and I doubt the innocent little warlock wants to jump into the hot wolf sex scene in an orgy."

Oh, fuck.

Sagan chuckles and nudges me back in the room, kicking the door closed. I don't have time to dodge out of the way before he scoops me up and tosses me onto the bed. Sterling high-fives him, and I cover my eyes with a groan, knowing they're totally having a conversation about me. The bastards.

"Hey now," I call, wagging my finger. "Don't you think I'm the one who deserves the high-five?"

Both of them laugh harder, and for fuck's sake, I'm nearly certain I hear Dax laugh from the living room.

If this is how life's going to be when the world isn't trying to explode around us, I'm not sure my burning cheeks will ever recover. Their excitement and closeness is a whole other level of bonding. I can't stop thinking about the coming weeks. They say it's going to get worse and worse, and I'll be even hornier. If that's the case, I might as well just ask them to go pick up a vibrator to give my body a rest from all their dicks.

"Damn," Sagan says, commenting on my thoughts. "That sounds fun."

I snatch the pillow off the bed and chuck it at him. He dodges it and jumps onto the mattress beside me. Sterling dives next to me, pulls me on top of him and grabs my legs, giving Sagan a view of my body that leaves him licking his lips, his erection as hard as the rest of his bulging muscles on display. He obviously just got back with the others and hadn't even dressed.

"Ready to ravish our mate, brother?" Sterling teases, nipping my shoulder.

And damn it. I'm so ready to be ravished and fucked and pleasured by the two of them. I want Sagan to flip me over and spank my ass again like he did as Flynn was prepping the truth serum. I want to feel the tingles blossom across my heated skin, how turned on and wet my body gets where I wonder if it's possible to drip my excitement across Sterling's eager face. I—

"Holy-fucking-hell, I think we're all going to need cold showers," Sterling says, kissing my throat. "I was only teasing you, blondie, but that sexy, utterly filthy, naughty mind of yours is about to get the three of us in trouble."

I frown. "What are you talking about?"

Sagan groans and flops next to us. "We have what we need, and Flynn's working on the tracking spell to locate the witch who collared Antone and the others. There's only one thing missing now, so you're up, gorgeous."

"Me?" I crinkle my brows. "Why does he need me?"

"Come on and get dressed. Flynn will explain everything." Sagan pulls me away from his brother and helps me to my feet. "But save your intoxicating fantasy for later. I want to fulfill your every need."

I place my hands on my hips. "Why do I have a feeling I'm not going to like what Flynn has in mind?"

Sagan's smile disappears. "He needs some bait."

"Bait?" Great. This is exactly what I wanted. "How do the others feel about me being the bait?"

"It's not exactly what you think." Sagan smirks and kisses me. "Flynn will explain. Don't worry. None of us will be put in any danger. We will finally get answers, remember?"

"But then what?" I ask, rubbing my arms. "I need to make sure we have a solid plan."

"Double dick sounds pretty solid to me," Sterling teases.

Sagan punches him in the arm. "We'll prepare our search for Levi. Flynn is confident that this witch will know where to locate the Fire Mountain witches. With them on guard against Nightstar, we'll have a better chance."

My heart flutters at his comment. "Really? Are you sure?" I had almost given up hope on finding my dad. But now, it suddenly doesn't seem so impossible.

If only my racing heart didn't sink into my stomach. A bad feeling swells inside me, my instincts begging me to leave things alone. To worry about my life and taking care of my pack. That my dad made his choices, and he has to live with them.

If only things didn't feel like they were about to seriously change in a bad way.

Or that one of us will get hurt or worse. I'm afraid I'm about to lose everything I managed to salvage. I'm afraid that no matter what we do, the world will be against us and the witches will win.

I fucking hope with everything in me that I'm wrong, and that my instincts are off.

But what if I'm right?

11

BAIT

"YOU'RE FUCKING JOKING," I SAY, crossing my arms over my chest. I knew I was going to be used as the bait to lure in the black-haired bitch witch but damn it. This is a bit humiliating. Like sure, okay, I'm naked like eighty-five percent of the time and just let Sterling stick his cock in my ass, but I'm not on the same level with everyone.

"I don't even see what the big deal is. It's not like you haven't pissed in front of me before. We're a pack. We've all bonded. You can't possibly be shy." Dax adjusts the front of his shorts, arranging his cock. "Hell, I'll whip it out and piss with you if it'll make you more comfortable."

"Hell-fucking-yes I can be shy. I'm not you guys. I have no desire to get into pissing matches. And plus, Flynn said I have to transform." I peer over my shoulder at Flynn, who looks at me from over Bastien's shoulder as they quietly talk about something I can't hear. The others stand on guard in wait, and I can just hear them plotting to gang up on me at any second.

Flicking my fingers, I motion for Flynn to turn the hell away. Sure, I'm supposedly his familiar, and he's bonded to me, but this is all new. I definitely close the door in front of all of them most of the time, and especially in front of Flynn, so I don't care if we're in this for life. I will pee in front of them when I'm ready. Right now, my wolf is not.

"I've never gone pee in my wolf form," I add, huffing a breath.

"Why the hell not? You should be one with nature." He tries to keep a straight face, but breaks into a huge smile and laughs at his own comment.

I glower, step closer, and cup his bulge through his pants. "Says the bastard with a damn hose."

"Haven't you ever popped a squat?" he questions, searching my eyes like I'll suddenly reveal the answer to him.

"No, never." Even if I had, it wouldn't make a difference. Just the thought of urinating out here in my wolf form weirds me out. I'm pretty sure if I couldn't transform back into a human, I'd still figure out how to get my ass onto a toilet. I have great balance.

He puckers his brows. "What the hell do you do during the games? I could've sworn I've smell—"

I give his cock a squeeze through his shorts, cutting off his words. "I hold it, thank you very much, though now I'm a bit grossed out knowing you've stuck your nose in either Harlow or Emerson's piss. I've kissed that damn snout of yours."

Dax laughs again and cups my face, leaning down to kiss the tip of my nose. "It's all part of tracking that sexy ass of yours, and I'm sorry if you're jealous."

"I am so, so, so not jealous of you sniffing another she-wolf's piss," I mutter against his lips as he continues to kiss me, grazing his lips to mine just lightly, sensually, without getting carried away.

"Mmm-hmm," he teases, sliding his hands lower down my back. "Maybe that's the reason you need to pop a squat. Let me imprint your scent in my brain, so I never make the tragic mistake again."

I groan and smack my hands against his chest, playfully pushing him away. "You're so gross."

"You still love me." Dax swats my ass as I walk away.

Tugging my tank top off, I toss it over my shoulder, hitting him in the face with it. I traipse a bit farther into the vegetation overgrowth on the side of the road, leading into a shallow ravine. I slip out of my short-shorts, throwing them at Dax next as he continues to follow me. I give him a small show, swaying my hips with my movements.

He hums deep in his throat at the sight of my ass in my thong, and I tease him by snapping the stretchy fabric against my skin. Reaching behind my back, I unclasp my bra and let it drop to the ground. I bend over in front of him, loving the sound of his deep moan as I give him a different view of my body, teasing the hell out of him.

"Careful, Lyric. I might want to test to see if that sexy ass of yours is as amazing as Sterling claims," he says, his voice going all deep and rumbly.

I flush and clench at his words. "Yeah, that's not going to happen unless Flynn gives you magic lube that shrinks your cock so it's no longer like a third leg."

Dax comes up behind me and links his fingers to my hips, pressing his now hard erection against me. "Not happening. And to be honest, I've never seen much of the appeal."

"Probably because it would be like trying to tee off with a basketball in a game of golf. That ball will never fucking fit." I hook my fingers into the waistband of my panties and shimmy them down right in front of him, wiggling my ass in the process. "It barely fits in the place it's intended to."

"We were made for each other, you know. I fit as I should." Dax tests the strength of the fabric of his shorts to rub the length of his boner against me, turning me on in the process. Teasing the hell out of him helps me not think about the fact that Flynn needs me to pee in the woods to hopefully draw the bitch witch to us, where we can be ready and waiting to capture her and get what we need. I've tried hard not to think about what's happening to the kidnapped competitors under the witch's collars, but I know it must be awful. I can't even imagine. I just want to get them back.

Dax groans and hugs me from behind. "They are strong, Lyric. They can survive until we break them free."

"What if we can't?" I hate to even think it, but it's a very real possibility.

"That's why this is important. Now please, hurry up and piss so I can throw you over my shoulder, carry you back to the apartment, and fuck Sterling from your mind. The cocky asshole won't stop gloating that you've finally started fantasizing about him and his damn wicked tongue."

Fuck. Me. I'm nearly certain I'll never get used to the fact that my pack totally and unashamedly discusses everything I do with them. It's like they compare notes, working together to see how long it'll take before I just decide I'm never leaving the bed again. And right now? That doesn't seem like such a bad idea.

I push the thought from my mind, hoping none of them hear it swirling through my head. Arching my back, I bend forward, teasing Dax one more time. I transform into a wolf and swing my torso, shaking off my nerves the best I can. It's weird to even think about peeing in this state, because it still feels unnatural, but I have to suck it up. It technically is natural, and I know I might be making a bigger deal than it is. I'm sure it's probably not as embarrassing as it would be if I dropped my pants as a human. At least this way, I don't have to worry about peeing all over my legs and clothes since I don't have the luxury of a man-hose. Lucky bastards.

Dax nudges his big wolf head between my back legs, lifting my hindquarters into the air. I yip and growl, flailing off of him. Launching away, I try to put space between us. Dax is fast and determined, chasing after me just like he used to during the games.

Pouncing toward me, he cuts me off and nips me on the collar. "Don't make me call for backup, Lyric. I think Bastien knows exactly how to express your bladder for you."

"You have to be kidding me," I think to him, releasing a pathetic whimper. "That sounds so...much more uncomfortable."

He noses my backend again. "Then pop a squat already. Here. I'll go first."

I dash away and hide behind a tree instead of watching him lift his damn leg next me. I mean, come on. I know this is natural to him, but I'd like to keep as much of my mortal world humanity as possible. And peeing in the outdoors? Easier for guys, damn it. Totally unfair.

"Five seconds, Lyric," Dax calls into my mind, giving me

space.

"The pressure is making it harder," I respond, circling in place, sniffing the ground to see if my wolf nature will let me get over myself.

"Four." Fucking Dax.

I reluctantly comply and do my business. Rushing back to him, I barrel into him, knocking him sideways as I attempt to pin him down. He releases a playful growl and nips the fur on my neck, trying to flip me. I make a mad dash in the direction we've left the guys. Bastien struts into view a dozen feet away like he was about to find me to do exactly what Dax warned me against if I didn't suck up my shyness and just accept my nature. Weaving around a tree, I sneak my way around to pop up on him from behind.

Dax howls, sending a call through the air, drawing Bastien's attention, and I pounce on him from behind, hooking my front paws around his waist. I yip and bark, laughter filling my mind as I surprise hump Bastien like I usually now save for Sterling.

He chuckles and grabs me, flipping my wolf body over his shoulder and into his arms. He buries his face into the fur on my chest. "You good, Ma Belle?" Bastien asks. "I told Dax I should've been the one to mark with you."

I lick his chin. "Why? So you could make me piss if I was suffering from a shy bladder?"

He chuckles. "I'd never. Is that what Dax said would happen?"

I release a growl, wiggling in Bastien's arms. "Among a lot of other things."

Setting me down, Bastien continues to scrub his fingers into my fur, giving me a rub down to show his affection for me, even in this form. "Want me to hold him, so you can put him in his place?"

I yip and bow, wagging my tail in the air. "What kind of question is that? You already know my ans—"

Two strong hands lock around me and lift me from the ground. Dax's familiar scent engulfs me, and he strokes his fingers over my snout. "Transform, Lyric. Now."

The sudden command in his voice sets me off, and I close my eyes, willing my transformation to grab a hold of me. A blip of panic seizes my heart, and I clutch onto Dax as if a pack of monstrous lycans will burst through the trees.

But it doesn't happen.

An eerie quiet stills the forest.

And then I hear it. A howl.

What the hell? I thought after everything that the competitors would've given up on their search. Invidia obviously reigns over them, and I figured she wouldn't risk leaving Lulupoterra because of the summons by the witches.

But I guess she finds me worth it. I can see how she would force the alpha-mates to risk getting collared, and they'd gladly accept it for the chance to turn me into their damn submissive omega.

"Flynn," Dax calls, his voice echoing through my head. "They're competitors."

"They're not alpha-mates?" I ask him, surprise washing through me. I would've sworn...I guess the black-haired witch bitch isn't taking chances. Shit.

Bastien turns into a wolf in front of us, his white coat gleaming in the sunlight streaming in through the bare branches of the trees. I inhale a few breaths. My heart races out of control. Tension tightens my muscles, and I search around. I can't see the wolves, but I can hear them. They're coming fast.

The witch can try to use the captured competitors to kidnap me and hurt my pack, but she'll be sorely disappointed when she fails. I have something on my side that she doesn't suspect—Flynn—and he's our ultimate weapon just like we are his.

"They're coming from the north," Dax says, thinking the words into my mind. "Sterling and Sagan, I need you two to split up and try sneaking up on them from behind."

"Will do," Sagan says, answering for him and Sterling.

"Caz, stay with Flynn. Guard him as if you would Lyric. We're going to get her out of here." Dax tightens his arms around me. "How much time do you need, Flynn? I don't want us to stay apart long."

"Just five more minutes," Flynn says, his voice trickling into my mind. Because I remain receptive to him, all of my mates can hear him in their minds like I can. It's a strangely handy spell, and something I'm utterly thankful for in this moment.

"We're coming up to her marking now," Caz says, his voice turning a bit weird in my mind. A wave of his lust nearly steals my breath away.

"Ah, yeah. I feel you, Caz. Her scent makes me want to learn how to knot myself to her so that my cock will never be away from her sweet slice of grapefruit." Sterling chuckles, though his wolf remains quiet.

"Focus, Sterling," I snap, sending my thoughts only to him. "I don't want anything to happen to you because of your sex-obsessed brain."

"Not my brain, blondie. My cock. It loves you as much as I do."

I inwardly groan and snuggle my cheek to Dax's hard pec, choosing to accept his need to carry me around like I can't walk on my own. It's not worth the argument, and he obviously needs it more than I do. I can feel his protective streak flaring even more with the sound of another howl.

"They're getting closer, but I still can't pinpoint their location," Sagan says, his voice swirling through my mind.

"Fuck. Something's up. I think we need to fall back. You done, bestie?" Sterling asks Flynn. "My desire just died."

Sagan calls out a howl. "He's right. It sounds like they're coming up on us, but I can't see—"

Snarls rip through the air, a sudden fight breaking out

stabbing me straight in the heart. I expect the ground to shake with the roar not unlike the ones of lycans, but the guys are right. Something is definitely wrong. My human rationale sets off my fear instincts, and I squirm in Dax's arms to get down. He needs to be able to fight with Bastien, and I need to watch their backs to ensure nothing happens to them.

An ear-piercing shriek cuts over the sounds of the wolves attacking each other, and I clutch my chest, feeling as if my heart will hammer its way through my ribcage. Because fuck. I've never heard shrill agony like this before. Even when the Stargaze Hill pack sentenced one of their own to death.

"Sterling? Sagan?" I ask, sending my thought to them through our mental link. "What the hell is happening?"

Sagan howls again, the echoing noise drawing my attention in what I think might be somewhere north. "It's the collared ones!" His voice shouts through my mind, freezing my soul. "They're being cloaked. We can only see them when they attack."

"Fuck, the shield is open to them." A bright flash of light streaks through the forest, exploding against a tree. "Head this way. Keep moving. Don't let them draw your blood. I'm coming." Flynn's electric power ignites another tree in purple flames.

"They're fast as hell. Creepy. Get Lyric out of here because they keep saying her damn name." Sagan's growl reverberates through my bones, and I can sense him getting closer.

Dax transforms into his huge mahogany form and shoves his head between my legs, lifting me off my feet. I have to bow forward and clutch onto him or risk smacking the ground face-first. I squeeze his soft, furry body with my thighs and clutch onto the scruff on the back of his neck.

"I can't believe I'm riding you like a damn horse," I mutter into his ear, the sensation of his fur caressing all of my sensitive naked spots weird as fuck.

He chuckles despite the fear crashing through me. "It's not like this is the first time."

This bastard.

I don't get a chance to respond as a blur of pitch darkness crosses the path in front of us. Bastien bolts past us at the familiar figure, flickering in and out of existence. Antone's howl penetrates deep in my soul, the sound full of such agony that my eyes well up with tears. I've never heard something so sad that I could feel it as if it's tangible, tightening around me to steal my breath. If misery could be summoned into physical form, it would look like Antone in this moment, spelled with red magic that sizzles across his black fur as he appears a foot in front of us.

Dax tries to skid to a halt, but he can't stop fast enough. We collide into Antone, and I jerk forward, flying off of Dax. I tumble across the compacted dirt, my skin burning with road rash as I can't do anything to protect myself. Snarls snap through the air as Dax and Antone roll across the ground together. And fuck. Antone looks as if he can't change into his wolf-form completely, his front paws long with his fingers yet his nails are narrow and sharp like he can now extend them like the claws of a cat.

"Brother, stop," Bastien says, his voice swirling through his mind. He circles and barks, looking for an opening to intervene. "You don't want to do this."

Flynn materializes a few feet away. "Frigi eht og!"

Antone screams, his voice rising to a pitch I never knew possible coming from a man with such a deep, rich voice. He convulses under Flynn's spell, flopping away from Dax. His body smashes into the ground, writhing and moving on his back, fighting whatever spell Flynn casts over him. He sheds his black fur with his movements. The fur falling off of his grotesque body shows the extent of the freaky-ass mutation from whatever the witch who collared him has done.

Antone's bare back glows with streaks of red slashes like he's been whipped over and over again only to have his wounds filled with lava. Tattoos unlike anything I've ever seen shift and move across his arms, winding around his wrists like unbreakable chains. And his eyes...oh, shit, his eyes. They glow red, sending an eerie blood-like haze across his cheeks and beard. He bares his fangs, now glistening with black froth, the gross fluid sizzling as it splashes across the ground.

"Kill me," Antone says, his guttural voice sending a shudder through me. "Kill me."

Bastien howls and circles Antone, a rush of panic and heartache splitting me wide open as he listens to his brother's pleas for death. Dax snatches Bastien by the tail and drags him back, and the two of them scuffle until Dax manages to pin Bastien.

"We have to," Bastien snaps, his voice sinking deep into my soul. "Ma Belle, please. He can't live like this. He's in so much pain."

I clutch my hands together, unable to take my eyes off Antone as Flynn shouts another spell, holding out his palms to shoot a burst of lavender light over Bastien's brother. Antone yelps and shrieks, his agony so intense that it steals my breath, sending me dropping to my knees.

"Frigi eht og!" Flynn yells again, repeating the words over and over. But all his spell does is twist Antone's body into impossible positions, the sound of his bones cracking and breaking leaving me dry heaving.

"Kill me," Antone begs, his voice trickling into my mind. "Please, Cherie. It hurts too bad. I can't take it. Kill me-e-e-e." Releasing a pitiful howl, Antone stretches his back, exposing his belly to me like he hopes I'll gut him.

Bastien whimpers in his wolf form, flailing underneath Dax as he refuses to let him go. Pulling my shit together, I push my aching hands into the dirt and get to my feet. My whole body trembles, my heart crashing around in my chest, every nerve on my body burning with despair. I can't stand this. I can't bear to see Antone in this state. I don't care if he was an asshole to me. He doesn't deserve such a fate. This is Bastien's brother after all.

"Lyric, stay back," Flynn says, his voice calling over the howls of Antone's agony.

I ignore him and meander forward, my body gliding me slow and cautiously toward the beast before me. My toes sink into the tufts of Antone's black fur now scattered across the ground, and I tighten my mouth to keep my lips from trembling.

"Antone," I whisper, my voice barely able to escape my lips. "I'm so sorry. I'm so, so sorry you've had to experience this."

"Kill me," he says again, his voice wet and gurgly with his half transformation. "I don't want to live like this."

I kneel on the ground beside him, and he snaps his teeth at me, snarling, like he can't tame the wild beast yearning to devour me.

"Lyric," Flynn says, the sound of my name on his lips as desperate as I feel to end Antone's suffering.

But how can I kill him, even out of mercy? How can I live with myself? Will doing so put a wedge between Bastien and me? Could he look at me the same if I take his brother from him?

A dozen more questions whirl through my mind, my heart and soul at war with each other about what to do. I wish the world would just stop for a damn minute. I need a moment to think and process everything before I do something I know I'll regret.

I lick my lips and extend my palm out to Antone despite everyone's warnings. Caz, Sterling, and Sagan slink closer through the trees until it's me and my pack, my guys surrounding me with their strength and support.

"Antone, you bastard," I say, my words coming hoarse as uncontrollable tears burn my eyes. "Why couldn't you just continue to be the bane of my existence? Why did you have to show me such loyalty?"

"Cherie, please. Show me mercy." Antone's voice trickles through my mind with a strange sensation that fills up my entire soul with his presence. "I will bow to you for such a thing. I just can't bear this."

I test his reaction and stroke the back of my hand across his red cheek, burning with the light of his red eyes. Tears trickle down my face, and I continue to pet his warm body, opening myself up completely to soothe his torment the best I can. It's the least I can do. My sudden need to protect Antone, to take care of him and bear his pain so he doesn't have to, consumes my entire being.

His eyes flicker from red to black, a part of his humanity peeking through the spell of the witch. "Cherie..."

"You're going to be okay. Just let me in. Open up to me. I'm here for you, Antone." My voice swirls from my mind to his, and he exhales a breath, his tense muscles relaxing. "I got you."

A strange, overwhelming need locks around me.

Mine. He's mine.

Gasping at my claim, Antone arches his back, his whole body rippling through spasms that leave him frozen and whimpering and curling in on himself. I stroke my hand along his back, waiting for his body to stop trembling.

"Lyric," Flynn says softly. "What have you done?"

I crinkle my brows, staring at Antone's handsome face, his features identical to his brother's. "I don't know. Whatever it was...it feels right for our pack."

Dax growls, the noise vibrating across my skin. "Fuck."

"Oh, shit," Sagan says, crawling closer in his wolf form.

"Blondie, you claimed *him*?" Sterling asks, joining Sagan's side.

I shrug my shoulders, pulling Antone's head onto my lap, staring at him as peace sends him into a quiet slumber, his body needing to rest as I break the invisible collar choking his humanity.

"I guess I did. I don't know. It was strange," I say.

"Ma Belle, I had no idea you felt this way," Bastien says.

I lick my lips and glance at him as he kneels beside me in his human form. "He's your brother, Bastien. Family. I couldn't let him die...it's really confusing."

"Frigi eht og!" Flynn suddenly shouts, making me tense.

"Someone grab her!"

Growls echo through the air as my pack reacts to his words.

"What? What's wrong?" Dax asks, his voice sounding through the air with his transformation.

"His collar." Flynn steps forward and surprises the hell out of me by locking his fingers into my hair to pull it from my neck. "Her claim transferred it from him to her."

"Oh, fuck," Sterling snaps.

A musical, feminine voice drifts through the air, drawing my attention to the forest around me.

I stiffen at the strange tightening sensation around my neck. "What's happening...?" I try to clear my throat, but nothing works.

And then fire explodes through me.

"Grab her now!" Flynn roars, gathering electric light in his palms. "Frigi eht og!"

Bastien locks his fingers around my wrist. "Lyric, fight. Fight it! Don't let her take you!"

If only the world didn't shimmer around me.

I feel as if I'm already gone.

12

STOLEN

"WHO'S A PRETTY GIRL? COME here, you sweet thing. Let me get a look at you." A man stands in the doorway to the dank room, snapping his fingers at me. "Fates, has it been a long time. You have grown into a beautiful beast. Will you come to me if I loosen your collar? It's not so bad if you don't fight it. I've been looking everywhere for you."

I release a low growl, shoving my body into the corner of the room. I snap my jowls, my she-wolf in complete control over my existence. Anger and confusion wind around me like a leash of unbreakable chains. I can barely think.

"Frigi eht og!" Flynn's voice explodes through my mind, dragging my attention to a strange light growing in front of me. "Lyric, fight! Yoque bavito lotuessa! They can't have you. You're my familiar. Now fight!"

The air blurs in front of me as if fire lights the floor, the heatwave shimmering across my vision. Every molecule on my body buzzes. Flynn's presence swells in my mind, the urgency and determination combating my panic. The magic collar on my neck loosens enough to breathe freely, and the weight of Flynn's soul stone sinks against my fur. I imagine lacing my fingers around the most precious gem in existence to hold it close. Light blasts from me, illuminating the room.

"What the hell? No!" Clapping his hands, the strange warlock sends red sparks shooting through the air. He rushes into the room toward me. "Devante anula vite! Sisters! The spell is breaking! He's taking her back."

I growl and snap, threatening the man the best I can. I'm afraid if he touches me, Flynn won't be able to transport me back. I'll be trapped like an animal with these evil witches, collared and forced into submission.

"Yoque bavito lotuessa! My soul, return to me!" With Flynn's words, light erupts in my vision, shaking the concrete floor.

My humanity breaks free in a ripple of agonizing pain. Fire burns from my throat and over the rest of me. It lasts only a few seconds, but it's the most painful thing I've ever experienced. My stomach smacks the cold concrete floor and a blast of power crackles straight for me. Rolling, I get my shit together and catapult to my feet.

"Yoque bavito lotuessa!" Flynn shouts again, calling me and the part of his soul I keep back to him. The world shimmers. Seven figures materialize in front of me, blurring with the warlock as he tries to shout a counter spell.

He launches at me in an attempt to tackle me to the floor. I screech and dodge out of the way. Jerking my leg up, I kick the fucker in his balls. He snarls as his teeth elongate into fangs. My muscles spasm again as he tries to force me to transform back. I heave and clutch my knees, my mind unable to process what's going on as magic sparkles through the air.

"Grab her and don't let go." Flynn's words tie around my very being, dragging me away from the man.

The agony stealing my breath cuts off and darkness consumes my vision. Another streak of light crashes into me, lighting my soul with molten magic. The power sizzles through me and eats away at my soul until there is nothing left but a single thought.

I'm a dead wolf.

Because there is no way I'm living like this in this world absent of everything I love.

"Yoque bavito lotuessa," Flynn says, his voice echoing through the nothingness. Cool relief chills the smoldering, suffocating void imprisoning me. "Lyric, my soul, you're safe. You're home."

"Fuck yeah, bestie! You're the fucking man." Sterling's voice is like a sweet melody, playing my heartstrings. Hot, muscular arms wrap around me, but it's not my horn-dog. My fuzzy senses struggle to recognize who holds me. Fingers caress my cheek, and Sterling adds, "Antone, give her here. I'm sure she's not going to want to open her eyes and see your bastardly ass. Her thoughts call to me. I'll take over."

"You're not a doctor," Antone says with a growl. The muscular arms, Antone's embrace, tighten around me. "I will ensure she is okay. She needs me. It's my fault she went through that hell."

"Brother, please. You need to rest too. I got her. I know you're feeling the effects of her claim, but you're going to freak her out. She hasn't bonded to you yet." Bastien's familiar touch grazes across my forehead.

I struggle to open my eyes, my body just wanting to be held. I don't care who does it as long as I'm with my pack, in my human form, and not with those witches. I dig my fingers into Antone's shoulder, pressing my head to his chest, trying to gather my strength.

He inhales a deep breath of my hair. "She won't be. I'm hers. She relies on me to protect her right now. Can't you feel her emotions? Cherie craves my strength. Her soul is weary of the constant pressure of command. I will act as her—"

Ah, hell. All it takes is to feel the sudden rise in his dominant attitude, feeling how he thinks because I'm incapacitated, that he can speak and act on my behalf. I shoot upright and flail my arms, bucking away from Antone. The heat of his hug vanishes, and my body feels as if I freefall in a pit of darkness. My vision dances with streaks of red and lavender light, making it hard to see anything except for the blurry figures around me. My back hits the floor, and I gasp in a breath and cough. The world jumpstarts, my body, mind, and soul coming together at once in a seemingly haphazard mess.

I cover my mouth, my stomach wanting nothing more than to expel my insides.

"You both need to back up," Flynn says, his shadow towering over me. "Give me some space. She's been ripped from dark magic. As my familiar, she needs to realign her soul to mine. Just give her breathing room for a minute."

Antone swings his fist at Flynn, missing his knee by an inch. "Who the fuck do you think you are, warlock?"

"Enough! All of you except Bastien, out. He and Flynn will care for Lyric. We need to circle the area and make sure none of those damn witches managed to snag something of hers to track us down. We cannot risk them trying to steal her away from us when we least expect it." Dax's rumbly voice hums through the air. Bending down, he gets in my face and clutches my cheeks, drawing my focus to him. "We got you, Lyric. Take a breath. You're safe. You were so incredibly brave and fierce, fighting those bastards' magic. I'm proud to be your mate." Kissing me softly, he soaks me with his affection until the tiny room clears out. He eases away and puffs out his bottom lip with his frown. Even though he suppresses his stress and fear from me, it's written all over his brooding face.

"We all are," Bastien adds, kneeling next to Dax. "I've never seen anything like it."

"Because that kind of magic comes with a costly price. The Dark Ones luckily did not expect our soul bond." Flynn finishes off their small circle. "Lyric is...extraordinary."

Dax nods. "Which is why you need to guarantee she is safe." A threat lingers in his gruff voice, but he doesn't say the words out loud. He doesn't have to.

Flynn tightens his jaw in recognition and stretches his shirt collar to reveal the wolf tattoo on his chest. "See this? It's your guarantee. Lyric's soul imprinted with mine, and our lives now intertwine. And right now, you should help the others settle down for her sake. I need to focus on ensuring there are no residual effects on her. Her soul was ripped from powerful magic unlike anything I've ever seen. She needs to rest, and too many people wanting to take care of her might become overwhelming."

Lacing his fingers through mine, Dax tugs my hand to his chest. He touches my cheek and tucks the strands of my hair behind my ear. "Is that okay, Lyric?"

I bob my head, my body automatically responding without discussing it with my mind. I'm so confused. What the hell happened to me? Now that Flynn mentions the dark magic, I can't stop thinking about the collar that transferred from Antone to me. How the witches used it to capture me. How Flynn pulled me back.

Fucking hell.

I reach up and touch my neck, the ache in my throat increasing the more I think about it. "I—I—" I can't form even a sentence. Did the collar steal my ability to talk normally?

"Here, let me help you." Bastien holds up a cup of water to my lips. "Drink this. It'll cool the burning and help you speak."

Dax kisses the top of my head and quietly exits the room. I spot the others all gathered around the door in anticipation to barge back in. A part of me hopes they disobey Dax to do so, because I want nothing more than to be smothered with their endless affection to remind my soul that I'm okay. I'm not actually trapped in a cage with powerful witches. I'm not so sure I ever was. My mind and body feel a strange disconnect that I can't seem to sort out.

"Drink, Ma Belle. Nice and slow," Bastien says, offering me the drink.

He tips the glass forward to my lips until sugary-sweet liquid coats my tongue and washes away the horrible, fiery taste in my mouth. The heat crackling over my skin subsides, and I inhale a small breath and sink against Bastien's chest while staring at Flynn kneeling in front of me.

"Why don't we move her to the bed?" Bastien asks, curling his arms under me to cradle me against him. I snuggle my face to the crook of his neck and just breathe in his familiarity. He hums, totally enjoying it, so I kiss his throat. "I want to give her a thorough exam."

"I'm not injured," I murmur, my voice hoarse.

Bastien meets my gaze. "I know you're tough, Ma Belle, and I know you minimize any pain you experience, but what you went through—it was traumatic on your mind and body. Forced transformations aren't easy on you. So please, let me double check."

I close my eyes, deciding against arguing. "Whatever will make you feel better."

"It'll make you feel more yourself, too. Bastien will assist me with rubbing in the cleansing lotion. The faster we apply it, the better it will be." Flynn scoops up a stone bowl and gets to his feet, following Bastien as he carries me to the bed. "It'll help you relax, and maybe then you'll be stable enough to talk."

Talk? My throat hurts, yeah, but I can talk.

Bastien shifts me in his arms. "There are some things that will be a lot to take in."

Oh. Flynn didn't mean I'm incapable of speaking. He has something to discuss.

Now I'm nervous.

"It's going to be okay," they both say in unison, hearing

my thought. "Just relax the best you can. I'll do everything in my power to make this enjoyable," Flynn adds.

Setting me on the bed, Bastien slowly runs a damp cloth across my cheeks, wiping away the sticky streaks. The fabric turns pink as he cleans my skin. Blood. I was bleeding? What the hell? I feel like I was out of my body for only a minute or two, trapped in the strange cell with the witches, but then...fuck. I don't even know. Maybe the forced change literally ripped me apart.

I shiver at the thought, trying my best to suppress it. I don't ask about it because I really don't want to know.

"Does anything hurt?" Bastien asks, keeping his voice soft like if he speaks even a teensy bit louder, I might react and try to fight or something.

I rub my lips together, my throat aching. Bastien dabs my cracked lips with the wet washcloth, and I can't stop my tongue from darting out to taste the fresh liquid. The bed shifts as Flynn sits on the edge by my feet and lifts my leg on his lap to cradle my foot.

I moan so embarrassingly loud as Flynn puts pressure on my arch with his cool fingers. He begins rubbing in the strange lotion, and I can't control my damn body's reaction. The relief he brings to my aches has me shifting and stretching my back. It feels incredible, mind-blowing even, that I need his hands everywhere. I ache for it more than I knew I could.

Bastien chuckles and traces my jawline, his eyes sparkling

with an expression I can only describe as mischievous—tight closed-lip smile and lowered brows. "I think I know exactly what you need, Ma Belle. Give your voice a rest and we'll see if you can talk without pain in a minute. Let us just take care of you."

I bob my head and lie back on the pillows, my eyes flicking between Bastien and Flynn. My body tingles in anticipation, yearning for the touch of their hands to smooth away the goosebumps prickling across my skin.

Bastien scoops up a handful of cleansing cream from the bowl Flynn hands him, and I bite my lip to muffle another moan as he starts applying it to my arm. The two of them rub and massage every inch of my body, leaving an ache for more of their affection in their wake. I've never experienced the kind of touch arisen from tender love and desire to ensure I'm the best I can be. Their fingers knead across me in a sensual way, the tranquil air around us soothing my soul. I can feel every part of me—my mind, body, and soul—realign and merge, making me feel myself again.

I shift on the bed, rubbing my legs together. "I think I'm good," I say, my voice escaping me in a soft breath. "Thank you both. I don't know what I'd do without you or our pack." Because it's true. I can only imagine what my life would've been like had the wolf packs never come for me.

"You gave me a scare, she-wolf," Flynn murmurs, scooting closer to rest his cool hand on my bent knee. He remains cautious in handling me in front of Bastien, and I can't help wondering what wanders through his mind. I'm so used to my guys being all in. They're beyond their worry and uncertainty with Flynn. My soul proved it to them.

"Do you think I should give you your soul stone back? You almost lost it." I try to remain expressionless, but it pains me even to say the words.

"I almost lost *you.*" Flynn scoots closer, drawn to me like it hurts him to have even a foot of space between us. Maybe it's the fact that I wear his soul stone or something, but I don't question it. I welcome it, regardless of why.

"I've never seen a spell transfer like that before." Flynn summons his bravery and takes my hand, tracing his thumb over mine.

"I'm still confused by what happened. Did I disappear? Was I really in a cell?" I ask, the memory of the concrete room flitting through my mind.

"What do you remember?" Bastien caresses my shoulder with the back of his hand, responding to my question with his own. He has as many questions as I do.

"A man—a warlock. He was tightening the collar around my neck. He...I think he knew me. He said I had grown." I shiver at the memory, my brain wanting to push his image away. "I felt so helpless. What if it was someone from Fire Mountain?"

"I don't think it was," Bastien says. "What do you think,

Flynn?"

"No, they took her from the Mortal World. Fire Mountain doesn't live in Magaelorum." Flynn's eyes light with his lavender presence.

"I was in Magaelorum?" I ask in surprise.

"At least partially. They couldn't hold you for long. Not with you possessing a piece of my soul." He shifts his gaze to Bastien for a second. "Thank the fates for that."

Bastien nods in agreement. "What else, Ma Belle? Did you see any of the other wolves?"

I shake my head. "Just the warlock. Not even that witch Evelyn was with him."

"Did he hurt you?" Flynn groans at even the thought. "Touch you?"

"I wouldn't let him." Glaring at my bare legs, I try to calm myself as my mind wants to get worked up all over again.

He puffs a breath through his lips. "I'm relieved to hear that. I think my spell should hold up then. They shouldn't be able to activate the collar to fight for control over you."

Touching my throat, I feel for this supposed collar but only feel the ethereal sensation of the ribbon. It's so light and airy, I'm not even sure if it's really tangible or if it's just made of magic and part of Flynn's soul. "What is that supposed to mean?" I manage to ask. I sit up and look around for a mirror, but the room only has a bed and a nightstand.

Bastien clears his throat and stands. "Are you hungry, Ma

Belle? Why don't I make you something to eat? You're probably starving."

"Are you avoiding my questions?" I frown in confusion as he blatantly refrains from telling me what Flynn means. "Why does it feel like you're trying to escape me, Bastien?"

Leaning closer, Bastien presses a kiss to my forehead. "I'm sorry. I'd never try, but..."

"Bastien feels your emotions on a level I can't, and your reaction might complicate our relationship as a pack. If you're upset, he will react. It's just part of your nature as wolves. So, we've already discussed how to handle things when you came to, and it's best if the growly protective beasts keep a bit of distance in case." Flynn turns his gaze to Bastien. "I'll call for you when I need you again."

I furrow my brows. "When you call them that—"

"I called myself that." Bastien smirks and playfully punches Flynn in the shoulder. "And I expect you to care for our pack leader in any way she needs. I can feel her desire for your affection."

He did not just say that.

Bastien winks at me. "I did," he says into my mind. "Let him take care of you. Doctor's orders."

Flynn remains expressionless as Bastien exits the bedroom, and I catch sight of the others still in the living room. Knowing that they're still so close, all antsy as fuck and wanting to be with me gets under my skin a bit. But I understand their reason for keeping their space. They can get a bit wild.

Flicking his hand, Flynn closes the door and remains in his spot beside me, holding my hand. Silence falls between us, and I stare at him, waiting for him to say something. His eyes sparkle with magic and a dozen indecipherable thoughts morph his expression into a series of lines, sharpening his handsome features. Nerves build in my stomach at his prolonging telling me whatever it is on his mind that makes the rest of my pack incapable of hanging around because they think I'm going to turn bat-shit crazy or something.

"Flynn," I say, clearing my throat. I shift and scoot forward until I sit on the edge of the bed next to him and dangle my legs off. "Please spit it out already. If it's that bad, it's not going to matter how you tell me and the wait feels like utter torture."

He turns his head to meet my eyes. "I'm sorry, Lyric. I'm still trying to understand all of this. You shouldn't have been able to take a collaring spell onto yourself. And now...the only way I could save you and keep them from trying to break our soul bond was to bind you to me completely. You wear my soul stone, but...now I have a part of your soul. You are bound to me in a way I never intended, but I promise. I will never control you."

"So you've leashed me?" The idea of wearing a magical collar, no matter who holds the leash, explodes a wave of despair through me.

"You can say that," he murmurs. "But I swear to you that I will do everything in my power to figure out how to free you from the magic. I just need more time. If my High Priestess was still alive..." Flynn's voice trails off and he hunches forward with a groan. "I need the strength of a coven to provide me with support."

"What about a pack of wolves? You said that we were magical. Can't you use us?" I pull his hand up to my chest, wanting to feel the sensation of his touch close to my heart. "We agreed to help each other, remember?"

Flynn scrubs his free hand over his forehead, pushing his chestnut hair out of the way. "I was supposed to be the one to give you hope and comfort, not the other way around."

"Well, perhaps it was never me who needed it. I know everyone is still familiarizing themselves with me, but you have to understand one thing. I've been alone ever since the Fire Mountain Clan stole my dad from me. I felt hopeless and deserted and scared for my future. But then things changed. I know the She-Wolf Games are fucked up as hell, and my dad obviously knew it as well, and that's why he entrusted my future with my intendeds. But what he didn't realize was that he taught me well. He gave me the resources and confidence I needed." I squeeze his hand, savoring the touch of our hands intertwined. "He also taught me how to teach others."

"It's more than that. You don't just teach others, you change them." Flynn tugs our hands from my chest to his and presses them to his heart. The melodious beating of his heart soothes my very essence, making me want to press my ear to his body and curl in bed with him. "I don't know what kind of spell your father had the Fire Mountain witches cast, but it's powerful enough to change everything. The price of something like this—it'd cost more than his freedom."

I furrow my brows in confusion. "What do you mean?"

"Magic of this proportion would require several lives, maybe more. The coven had to have not only changed the fates, but they would've also had to break whatever spell the supposed five High Priestesses had cast to bring the packs together. We need to find out." Flynn shifts on the bed and rests his knees against mine. "But I can't ask you to help me. There must be another way."

"You don't have to ask me. I'll help you regardless. This is my life and pack we're talking about. Whatever we have to do to figure shit out to take care of all my fucking enemies...I'm going to do it. Just tell me how." I lick my lips and touch his chin. "That's an order, warlock."

His jaw twitches at my attempt to command him, and he cocks an eyebrow, somehow managing to keep a straight face. "What if I told you it requires a whole different kind of mental link?"

"I already have five—I mean, six—of those. What's the problem with one more?" I offer him a smile. "It can't be any worse than feeling Sterling's constant lust for me."

Flynn chuckles and shakes his head, his face lighting up with a smile. "The problem isn't my emotions. It's my magic and constantly tapping into yours. If you thought it was invasive before...especially because..." His voice trails off with his words.

"Not invasive. Intimate. And you don't have to be nervous. I'll behave. I know we're still getting to know each other," I say, a teasing smile crossing my lips. I can't help it.

He lifts and drops his shoulders. "It's not that exactly. I just worry this might all be...a fluke. You might resent me."

I startle at his admission, surprise stealing my ability to keep things casual. Because I need to show him that his fears are unwarranted. I can't resent him. It feels impossible. We're all doing the best we can in a crappy situation. I'm not perfect and neither are my guys. What's important is we all know that and recognize it.

I cup his face, getting him to look at me. "Flynn, I won't resent you. You've saved me on so many occasions. You never abandoned me, even when my pack wanted to murder you. You said it yourself. I'm your familiar. The fates gave us each other for a reason, and it wasn't to implode our lives."

I don't know what the hell comes over me, but I feel like I need to grab hold of Flynn's reserve and worry and kiss it the hell out of him. I want him to realize that resentment is the last thing on my mind. But at the same time, I'm afraid to push him. He's always been cautious, yet so adorably curious that I kind of want to claim him right here and now and show him he's mine.

"Blondie, you're so, so bad." Sterling's voice interrupts my thought, a wave of his lust washing through me. It does nothing to settle my body down. "I'm getting so fucking jealous right now, and not of my warlock bestie. I just—damn. I wish you could've been around to teach me a thing or sixty-nine."

This bastard.

I jerk my attention to the closed door and call, "Get the hell out of my mind, Sterling. I don't need your commentary. Weren't you all supposed to go scout the area. Ensure I'm safe?"

He laughs through the door. "Sounds like we need to be here to back up Flynn. He has no idea what he's in for."

Heat floods my face. "Sterling! You're in so much trouble for listening. You just wait."

"Ma Belle, you're projecting your thoughts to us and not the other way around." Bastien says loud enough for Flynn to hear through the door.

Sterling huffs. "Shut up. I want her to punish me."

"Just fuck him already, Cherie. I want to be next." Antone hums with his words, his fresh mind-link to me sending a crazy-intense zing right to my vagina. Like damn. "I have to show you my appreciation and thanks to you. You will love me being on my knees. It might be the only time I allow you to tell me what to do," he adds.

Oh my fucking-fuck.

"Everyone, get out. Go take a damn walk. Get some fresh air. Go wrestle in the woods." Because with seven guys, all of them now seemingly eager for my attention... It's a bit over-whelming.

"Just wait for mating season," Antone's voice whispers into my mind, his thought sultry and seductive. "You will beg me to bend you over. Hearing you moan my name will be music to my ears. My cock already throbs with need."

I'm about to punch my own vagina for loving his words way too much. The traitor kinky bitch wanting to submit to Antone like the good girl he wants. She damn well knows that none of my future plans included Antone, and here she goes, getting all excited and wanting to invite him in.

Antone hums a soft moan. "It won't be long."

He says that like I actually want to. But damn it. Why does he have to push all my buttons—good and bad? I'm going to have to fight him into submission, so I won't have him try-ing to question my authority other times.

"It's okay if you want to be my obedient good girl. I know it's exhausting always telling everyone what to do. You especial-ly deserve a little stress relief, and I'd be happy to make you obey if you need the excuse." Antone's presence fills my mind, my claim on him so fresh that it mutes everyone else out. "All you have to do is say, 'Please, sir,' and get on your knees."

My traitor kinky bitch vagina is so on board with this that

I wonder how everyone would act if I crawled toward the door. Fuck. I'm in for some trouble.

"You won't be able to resist your feral need, Cherie," Antone says. "And it's okay. Don't be shy."

Someone growls before something crashes against the wall. "Let's get one thing straight, Antone. Our mate made it clear that she's not down for mating season in the way you want. She won't need to be able to resist. If she says she doesn't want to be with you now, we will make sure her heat doesn't mess with her willpower then," Sagan says, his voice deep with threat. "We've already agreed that we'd stay away if we have to, because she doesn't want to breed with us yet."

Whoa. He makes it sound so...animalistic.

"That's enough," Dax says, his voice commanding attention. "Everyone out. We're going to do as she asked and get some fresh air."

"Going to need a cold shower, too," I mutter under my breath. Because damn. We're going to have to do some serious talking as a pack. Going from four mates to seven is brand new territory for them and practically unimaginable for me. Rules must be set.

I get up from the bed and cross the room, preparing to fling the door open. Another door slams as I touch the doorknob. Shit. I might've just lost my chance. Easing the door open an inch, I peek out into the small living area just to make sure they're actually gone and not faking it to avoid hearing the list of rules I'm already setting in my mind.

I should be freaked out that they actually left and are out of my sight, but something about this apartment and the surrounding area feels even safer than Lunar Crest. It's strange to realize that in this wild moment of racing hearts and desire.

"No one's getting within a mile radius of us," Flynn says from behind me, speaking up for the first time since the guys distracted me from me need to claim him.

I spin on my feet and crash into his chest. Grabbing onto my shoulders, he steadies me, his sudden closeness stirring something wild inside me. His lavender stare penetrates my soul as he captures me with his entire presence, stealing all the thoughts of Antone from my mind. His attention awakens a strange feeling inside me, like I've been starved of his attention, and now that he gives it to me, I can't get enough. Is this what it's going to be like as a familiar? Collared and leashed to his magic. Desperate for every ounce of him?

My hand flies up to touch my throat, and I expect to feel the collar around my neck. Flynn tilts his head without breaking his stare. He gingerly reaches up and brushes his cool fingers across mine and to the sensitive skin of my neck. Tingles crawl from his touch and through the rest of me, igniting me in a way that draws me even closer to him.

"Does it hurt?" he asks, swallowing. "You'll tell me if it does, right? I hate seeing the collar on you like this."

Surprise washes through me. I knew it was there, but if it's visible? Fuck. "You can see it?"

He slowly nods.

I blink a few times and turn toward the bathroom. "I need to look." Jogging across the room, I rush toward the bathroom to look in the mirror. And holy shit. A band of purple glowing magic encircles my neck, mimicking what I can only describe as a magical chain.

"Shit," I mutter, everything finally sinking in. I don't know if it was because my guys distracted me, but now that I see the collar, I have to accept that this happened to me. I'm bound to another in a way intended to serve. And it freaks me the hell out, even if it is Flynn who holds the leash. "It's real. This is really fucking real. I'm wearing a collar. People are going to notice this shit in public. How the hell will we do anything? You can't expect me to stay inside this tiny-ass apartment all the time."

With the words, I have a sudden need to run. To transform and break down the door. To bolt away as fast as I can. My she-wolf craves freedom from this mess. She wants to take control of my body and try to break the bond herself.

Flynn locks his fingers to my shoulder and spins me around to face him. Panic crashes through me, the reality of the magical collar screwing with my head. I didn't think it was that bad, and maybe I didn't believe it, but now? Fuck.

"Take a breath, Lyric," Flynn says softly. He hooks his other hand to my hip, pulling me closer to him. His fingers sink into my bare skin, exposed and vulnerable in a moment I feel out of control. But it doesn't feel as if he restrains me. It feels as if he grounds me, assuring me with his presence that everything will be okay. "Only you and I can see it."

I gasp a few times, my lungs heaving but feeling as if I can't get enough air and now I'm suffocating. My skin ripples, my she-wolf begging me to break free. She doesn't care that I trust Flynn or that we're connected. She just wants out. She wants to fight the magic.

Flynn's eyes widen as blond fur sprouts from my arms. "Please, Lyric. Don't." Flynn clutches my face. "Don't transform. I have a few things I need to do to ensure your safety with the collar. If you transform before I can...just please. Resist it. Fight it."

I groan, my legs wobbling, threatening to send me to the bathroom floor. "I can't stop it. It hurts too bad. I'm out of control."

Scooping me up, Flynn sets me on the counter, positioning his body between my legs to cage me in with his hands pressed against the mirror. He bows forward until he's all I can see. Capturing me with his lavender gaze, he shares my breath, hypnotizing me with the sparks of vibrant, nearly breathtaking, magic, and the world around us fades.

"Kiss me," I say, puffing air through my lips. "Distract me. I'm begging you."

Because if he doesn't do something, anything, I will transform into a wolf. An innate need claws at my insides, my beast on the verge of stealing complete control of me. I'm afraid Flynn's concern is warranted. If I change, I'm not so sure I could come back. I'm afraid the magical collar will steal away the most powerful part of me.

"Lyric—"

A whimpering plea escapes my lips.

Flynn's eyes search mine, something wild igniting in his gaze. Linking his fingers to the back of my head, he yanks me to him with so much passion that I automatically wrap my naked body around his, devouring the softness of his lips, the heat flourishing between us, how sweet and soft his tongue tastes stroking against mine.

My desperation fades with the shock of electricity igniting through our touch. His hand travels from my hair and down my back, pulling me harder into his body like my she-wolf awakens a different kind of beast inside him. I moan at the sensation of his hardening desire pressing right between my legs, sending a thrill through me, the newness of everything feeling like the fresh air my inner wolf craves. I don't need to transform and run with my heart pounding this wildly, my hands mapping down his back until I grab the hem of his shirt and yank it up, my fingers determined to dig into his skin.

Flynn drags his hand from my back to touch my breasts, gliding his fingers over my tight nipples. Explosions shudder across my body in a hot wave that awakens my desire even more. How bad would it be to jump onto him, rip his pants open, and sink my tingly body onto him right here and now like my life depends on it? Would he let me? Is it that crazy to think about knowing his experience or lack thereof?

So I test him for his reaction, summoning my nerve to show him exactly what I want from him in this moment. All I can think about is how his cock will feel thrusting inside me. Reaching between us, I rub the length of his shaft, surprised by the intimidating size of his body. He's larger than I expect, and I bet I'd feel his penetration in every nerve-ending on my body.

"Lyric," he says, moaning with his breath. "You have no idea how much I want you."

"I want you too," I say, popping open the button on his jeans.

"Are you sure?" His question hums with another moan as I pull his hard-on free, preparing to align it with my body.

"Mmm-hmm," I say, sliding his tip against my wetness. "You're mine."

A strange flash of light erupts in the air, startling me. I stiffen in Flynn's arms, the world turning hazy with red glowing light. I gasp and rip my mouth free of Flynn's, smacking my head hard enough on the mirror to shatter it.

"Em nommus flow uoy eht," a feminine voice says, chanting the spell.

My throat tightens, my eyes bulging.

Flynn yells my name, grabbing onto my shoulders, but his

touch disappears. I hit my hands and knees to the muddy ground of an unfamiliar forest. Dozens of howls erupt through the air, and then a whistle blows.

"Lyric, get up. Hurry," Emerson says.

"Transform now. You have to run!" Harlow shouts.

I scramble a few feet forward, my whole body refusing to cooperate. Pushing to my feet, I spin around and catch sight of the alpha-mates sitting on golden thrones with the pack leaders bowed at their feet.

My heart sinks into my stomach. "What the fuck?" How the hell am I here? What happened? I don't understand.

A woman with white hair materializes in front of the rulers of Lulupoterra. My heart stalls at the glimpse of Invidia's sharp features. She rubs her hands together, sending blue light zapping through the air. A bolt of lightning illuminates the dark world and explodes into the ground next to me.

More wolves howl, and Harlow and Emerson dash away from me.

The witch raises her arms toward the sky. "Let the Omega Hunt begin!"

13

The Omega Hunt

THIS IS TOO MUCH.

Confusion threatens to slow me down, but I force my feet to keep up pace with my racing heart. The same questions keep running through my mind over and over again as I try to process. I mean, what the hell is really going on? How did I get here? Which territory in Lulupoterra am I in, anyway? How the hell did the white-haired witch bitch from the Nightstar Coven summon me here, kidnapping me from what I know was Flynn's strongest magic? What kind of price did she pay? I'm afraid to even think about it. It wouldn't be the first time the alpha-mates arranged wolves for sacrifice.

And as for this supposed Omega Hunt? Shit.

It hasn't been that long since we've abandoned this place, and it's like everything just exploded. I knew something was wrong after the confrontation in the forest outside the lycan's cabin, but I had no idea it was this extreme. The she-wolf leaders no longer control the packs, and their alpha-mates bend to the will of the witch as her servants.

What does all of this mean for our species? For me?

I don't get much time to think about it because a heavy body crashes into my back. I skid across the dirt on my stomach, clenching my teeth through the fiery pain. Two heavy paws smash the breath from my lungs as one of the competitors pins me down. Bringing my elbows toward my sides, I use my arms to frame my body. I push my arms into the dirt as hard as I can and roll, throwing the massive wolf off my back.

"Yer still as feisty as ever, lass." Fergus's deep voice erupts in my mind, the intrusion sending my head pounding. "C'mere, sweet thing. Let me get a good sniff of ya."

Fergus stomps his paws into the dirt, the soft thuds drawing closer as he noses the ground. Stretching before me, he transforms into a man and wags his pale ass in the air as if he still has a tail. He pushes to his knees and wiggles his hips again, wagging his flaccid cock next, grinning at me like he expects me to enjoy the show.

"Come any closer, and you'll never have children, you fucker," I say, feeling around the forest ground for something, anything, I can use as a weapon.

I don't like the sadistic look in this asshole's eyes. His gaze roves over me, devouring my body as he lets me hear the disgusting fantasy playing in his mind. It twists my stomach in knots. I'm usually unafraid of pervs, but his thoughts dive into psychopath territory.

"Yer gonna wanna think twice about fighting me. The rules of the games have changed." Fergus licks his lips and risks crawling a bit closer on his hands and knees. "Ya hurt me, and I get yer claim. Bow down, and I get yer claim. No matter what ya do, I will get yer claim. Now let's make things easy. Agree to be mine, and I'll treat ya like my queen. Make it hard, and you can spend the day in chains. Which will it be?"

Panic tightens my chest. What the actual fuck? I thought the games before were barbaric. But now? This is unthinkable. Sick. I'd rather fight and risk death than face a life submitting to Fergus.

I swallow and ease myself down to the ground, faking submission to him. He's fucking out of his mind if he thinks I'll agree to either of those things. If he thinks he's getting his dick anywhere near me, it'll be the last time he'll ever be able to piss standing up. If he thinks he can chain me, he better pray I never escape, because I'll put a damn collar on him and throw him to the lycans.

Releasing a throaty noise of contentment, Fergus pushes to his feet, stroking his damn cock in excitement like I just agreed to let him have his way with me without putting up a fight. I silently count the seconds as he strolls around me, checking out my naked body. He thinks my bow is an offering of my body to him.

I try to calm my wild heart.

I try to suppress my fear.

But as soon as he steps behind me, I break. I can't play this part even for a second. Thrusting my leg back, I swing it up and into his groin hard enough to send him a foot into the air. He howls and drops to the ground, clutching his hopefully bruised cock.

Instead of running away to put space between us, I tackle him and punch him in the face over and over again, sending his blood pouring from his nose. He flails beneath me and manages to punch me in the boob, stealing my breath with the force. I gasp and bow forward, unable to stop myself, and Fergus shoves me off to roll on top of me.

He's too slow to grab my wrists, and I jab my fist into his hairy groin and scratch my fingers deep into his thigh. He hollers in pain, trying to throw himself off of me. I clutch his balls and squeeze, stilling him in place, his fear of me ripping his nuts off turning him into a weak little bastard. And damn it, touching hairy, sweaty balls shouldn't feel so damn satisfying.

"Move and I'll neuter you with my bare hand," I say,

keeping my voice low. I sink my nails into his tender skin and watch the angry, agonizing tears fill his eyes. "Don't think I'm not strong enough."

Fergus releases a low growl as he fails to keep his tough-ass persona. "You're going to regret it."

He sounds like he's going to tattle to his master instead of retaliating. Either way, he will be the only one full of regret. I will never regret putting him in his place and ensuring he can't join a she-wolf pack. Any sort of consequence will be worth it.

"Doubt it, you weak, undeserving witch pet," I snap.

I squeeze his tender skin harder, rolling the two balls together in his nut sack. His chest heaves, his fingers digging into his thighs. This position should gross me out. The fact that my gesture gives him a boner, and his body doesn't fear my touch like his mind does should send me fighting to get far away from his veiny member. All it does is prod at my deep-seated nature as a true leader, my mind and she-wolf unwilling to be anything less than the powerful woman my dad raised me to be, and I feel my muscles tighten and ripple with my oncoming transformation. My fingers release Fergus's balls, and the sensation of my hand shifting into a paw startles me. Because fuck.

Fergus growls and snatches my front leg, trying to bend it in a way it doesn't go. Arching forward with the pain, I bury my wolf head between his thighs. I snap my jowls, sinking my fangs into the tip of his cock. The awkward position doesn't give me enough reach to gobble it like he deserves. Releasing his bleeding boner, I thrash and stretch to bite more of his dick much harder, attempting to stay true to my word. Fergus screams at an impossibly high pitch and tries to throw himself off me. My wild wolf nature plans to tear him apart, even if I have to eat the fucker to do so. I bite his thigh next, pinching his skin with the strength of my jaws. He screams again and punches me in the snout, getting me to release him.

Shadows edge my vision as pain swells through my snout. Fergus doesn't run away like I expect and rushes me, grabbing my back legs to hoist me from the ground. I thrash and growl and snarl, doing everything I can to break free from his hold. The world spins with his quick movements, and he carries me in front of him, facing out, treating me like a wild beast.

Closing my eyes, I try to summon my humanity, knowing that if I change into a woman, I'll stand a better chance. I can use my fighting skills to defend myself and put Fergus in his damn place, which if he tries to do what he wants with me, will be with him gutted and deep in the ground.

I will not stand for this. I will not bow and act as a docile female intended only for breeding. I will fight until my last breath to ensure the other she-wolves don't face this horrifying future. I will blow all of Lulupoterra up and break the shields, even if it means putting my species in danger. Those who haven't been ruined by the alpha-mates will learn to fight. I can't truly believe that every competitor is a monster like Fergus. There have to be others like my pack mates.

Fergus yanks my body higher into the air and presses his face to my back, sucking in a deep breath of my scent. "Breaking ya to be my good little bitch will be sweet, lass."

I growl, the guttural noise vibrating deep in my throat. Swinging my body, I try again to thrash my way free, hating how his hot breath feels warming my coat. I try again to transform, but my muscles don't tighten or anything. My neck burns with fire, and I yelp, bucking my body with the agony from the magical collar igniting.

Fergus loses his hold on me, and I crash into the ground. Stars pepper my vision, and I stumble, my paws giving out on me. I can't get myself up no matter how hard I try. I can't transform. I can't do anything except dig my claws into the dirt and try to drag myself forward. Because fuck. I will not let things end like this. I will not allow Fergus to have power over me. If what he says is true about the competition, if he captures me again, I'll not only be chained, I'm nearly certain the witches will learn about my magical collar. My freedom will be over. Everything my parents and guys have given up to help me rise will have been for nothing.

Fergus snatches me by the fur on my neck and lifts me up, shaking me a few times. With his free hand, he dangles a vine in front of my face. My heart sinks into my stomach. He let me get as far as I had because he was finding something to use against me. I can't even snap my teeth before he drops me to the ground and kicks me onto my back. Straddling me, he locks his big hand around my muzzle and stops me from open-ing my mouth. He pinches the vine between his index and middle finger and winds it around my snout over and over again so tightly that it hurts to even breathe, the air flowing into my nostrils struggling to reach my lungs through the ago-nizing constriction of his make-shift muzzle.

"There we go, lass. Isn't that better?" Fergus says, scratch-ing his fingers into the fur of my chest, petting his way down to my belly.

I whimper and wiggle, refusing to give up on fighting him. "You're a dead man, you asshole," I say, sending my thought into his mind.

"Hold onto those thoughts, lass. Whatever makes you nice and wet for me." Fergus continues to drag his hand lower on my body and reaches between my back legs. I thrash as his fin-gers lace around my tail, and he lifts me up, his slow touch purposefully intended to torment me.

Pain swells in my hindquarters, and I wonder what part of my human body will be affected if he dislocates or breaks the bones in the part of me that disappears with my transfor-mation. Once again, I try to will my wolf to give in and release me, but the magical collar burns once more.

Something is wrong. I can't do it, and I wonder if this is why Flynn was so adamant about trying to prevent me from changing into a she-wolf. Maybe he knew that this would hap-pen.

The thought is enough to send more panic through me, my mind racing with a dozen morbid thoughts. What if this is permanent? What if I never turn into a human again? What if I'm an animal forever, my humanity caged inside me until it starves and withers away? Will it even matter to me? Maybe this is for the best. If I give in to my deep-seated nature, I won't care about the Mortal World or my state. I'll act as the animal these assholes want to treat me as. It might be better than suffering.

A growl reverberates through the air as another wolf stalks Fergus through the forest. He tosses me onto his shoulder to free his hands. I try to tip my head up, but it hurts my snout to move even a little. But whoever approaches isn't my savior. It's just another competitor hell-bent on turning me into their baby-making sex slave that will bow at their feet.

"She's mine, Alonzo. She submitted," Fergus says, his deep voice threatening the tan, gray, and black wolf with a rumble of a growl.

The tri-colored wolf, Alonzo, doesn't let Fergus stop him. His soft footsteps thump against the ground, slow and purposeful, like he cautiously slinks his way closer, strategizing how to take me as his own.

"Alonzo, I mean it," Fergus snaps, digging one of his hands into my fur to ensure Alonzo can't steal me away. "Go find your own she-wolf. Lyric is mine."

"The rules say she is only yours if you cross the finish line with her." Alonzo growls with his words, his voice trickling into my mind. "And she's about to be mine."

Fergus hollers in anger and drops me to the ground. Agony bursts in my back leg, my bone breaking under the force of my fall. I whimper and struggle to get up, limping a few feet until I manage to figure out how to walk only using one back leg.

Snarls echo through the air behind me as Fergus and Alonzo tear into each other, fighting for a chance to claim me. The only few times I've heard such a terrifying fight between wolves was when they were determined to rip each other apart—participating in a fight to the death.

I can't help turning my neck to peer behind me, and I watch in shock as the wolves stand on their back legs and snap and bite at each other, each of them trying to rip the other's throat out. And now I realize that the rules of the games have changed more than I realized. Killing the competition might be the only way to win the Omega Hunt, and both of them look willing to face such a fate.

Getting my shit together, I finally manage to get the nerve to turn my back on them and limp away the best I can. My snout throbs, messing with my sense of smell, the lack of circulation numbing my muzzle. If I don't manage to unwrap the vines soon, the lack of circulation might cause irreparable damage.

I force my mind to focus on my surroundings, and I weave

between two gnarled, low-branch trees, trying to get some-where harder for the competitors to navigate. If I can just find somewhere to hide, so I can rest and lick my wounds, Flynn might find a way to get to me. I'm sure my whole pack will already be on their way, willing to risk a death sentence to bring me home.

If only the risk wasn't so great. It's not even the wolves I'm worried about. It's the Nightstar witch.

I won't be able to live with myself if one of them gets hurt or worse. It is my duty to protect them and to be the fierce leader my dad taught me to be. I'm better than this. I'm not a scared little damsel. I might be trapped in my wolf body, but I'm still the woman from the Mortal World. I'm Lyric Larson, daughter of Levi and one helluva fighter. And not only that. I'm also Lyric of Lunar Crest, daughter of Melody, and the she-wolf who will change things. Not because it's in the fates. Not because my dad gave up his freedom to guarantee it. I will change things because I'm powerful. I'm an alpha, and all these fucking competitors will bow. I'll rule every single one of them. Witches be damned. Like Flynn said, I'm fucking magical.

Pawing at my snout, I work to yank the vine down so that I can tug it off. A small whimper escapes from me. I can't con-trol the damn sounds, but they annoy the hell out me, because I'm afraid someone will hear them and track me. It's bad enough some competitors are great at scent tracking. I feel fucking defenseless, unable to bite or transform. If I make it out of here, I'm going to hunt down the damn witches who did this and devour every single one of them.

A low howl sounds through the air, sending the hackles on my back rising. I limp deeper and deeper into the unfamiliar territory, rubbing my muzzle to every tree trunk that looks rough enough to sand through the tough cord.

Nosing the ground, I push a couple broken branches toward an old gnarled tree, dry and broken, its trunk looking to have been struck by lightning. I build a den the best I can, creating a shelter to wait out the hunt in.

If only I wasn't too nervous to call out to my pack, hoping that maybe they're already here and searching. I don't trust myself to keep everyone else out in this moment, so I lock my mind completely.

Resting my snout on my paws, I flatten myself to the ground and peer out of the small opening of my make-shift den. The forest doesn't glow as brightly as it should in my wolf form, and I wonder if the muzzle is messing with not only my sense of smell but also my vision.

Another howl sounds through the air, the hum growing unnervingly close. I remain utterly still and listen to the forest around me. If a wolf gets near, I will hear them. I picked this spot for a reason. There is no way a competitor can stalk me soundlessly with the dry vegetation littering the ground.

A branch snaps from somewhere in front of me, and I freeze and watch the dark world in front of me. The same tri-colored wolf from earlier slinks through the low branches and crawls his way in my direction like he knew exactly where I'd hide.

I send a silent prayer to the universe that the fucker will keep going and miss me. I hate how easy it is for the competitors to track me, using their sense of smell to pick up whatever hormones and chemicals my body releases as I near my heat.

"Lyric?" a soft, masculine voice says, sounding through my mind. "It's me, Alonzo."

I focus on keeping my mind closed.

"I'm your mate's brother," Alonzo continues, talking to me like he knows I'm here.

I still don't answer him. All of my pack mates have brothers, but that doesn't mean I'm going to just put myself in danger of getting captured. Alonzo could try using that against me, strategizing a way to claim me. It's not like my guys are here. Without them, everyone is free to try to hunt me down. There are no restrictions.

"I'm not going to hurt you. I'm here to help," Alonzo says, padding his way through the overgrowth but not in my direction. He must have picked up some sort of scent, but thankfully, he still can't seem to find me in my hiding spot.

"Caz would never forgive me if I let someone hurt you. Please, I know you struggle to trust me, but I'm against the way things have turned out. This hunt is bullshit. The only reason I'm participating is to hopefully stop one of the assholes who think of the she-wolves as beneath them from winning. I was raised better than that, and frankly, she-wolves aren't my type. I'd give anything to stand up and fight my uncle and help my mother, but she's brainwashed." Alonzo continues to stroll through the forest until he stops somewhere out of my view, growing silent for a couple of my racing heartbeats. "So instead, I want to do what I can to help those against this power shift. I want to help you."

Fuck. He sounds so convincing. I want so badly to believe him, but I can't. I can't leave myself open like that. I can't trust anyone outside of my chosen pack, despite the fact that he's Caz's brother. The only one I can trust here is myself, and my wolf wants nothing to do with Alonzo or anyone for that matter.

"Please, Lyric. What can I do to make you believe me?" Alonzo's voice softens in desperation. "If someone doesn't cross the finish line with you, the High Priestess will kill more of us to summon you with magic like she had to get you here. She will force a few chosen competitors to fight each other to the death. If that happens..." His voice trails off with his words.

And fuck.

A part of me really, truly wants to believe him. But a more dominant part of me doesn't give a shit. Let all the asshole competitors fight to the death. That's fewer jerks to worry about.

"Lyric," Alonzo says again, my name soft and pleading on

his voice, like if he says my name enough, I'll finally give in and respond to him. "Please. Please, please, please. I'm begging you. What can I do to make you believe me? I'll do anything. I don't want you to get captured by one of the monsters. I don't want my brother's mate to face a fate of chains or to be abused and beaten into submission."

I huff a breath through my nostrils, the sudden force stirring up dirt. And fuck. My. Life. I sneeze, the exertion sending shooting pain right to my brain. I yelp and jerk my head up. My make-shift den crashes down on me. I lie under the branches without moving, knowing that at least half of me gets exposed. But I hope if I don't move, maybe Alonzo won't notice.

Two big paws thump the ground in front of me, and Alonzo drops to his belly and rests his snout on the tops of his paws. His brown eyes meet mine, and he releases a quiet whimper, sounding sad as fuck. Those damn puppy-dog eyes work even better as a wolf, and he crawls forward and nudges his nose to mine.

I whimper, the pain of the vine muzzle hurting worse with the gesture, and I try to back away. Alonzo sniffs me and then licks the side of my snout like he can somehow make things better.

"That looks painful," he thinks to me, licking me again, but not in a weird way. It feels natural, my wolf appreciating his concern and attempt to help ease the pain. "Why don't you transform and pull it off?"

I whine and paw at my snout. "You don't think I've tried?" I don't mean to snap at him, but my annoyance grows to uncontainable levels. His question makes me feel like I'm missing the obvious.

"Here, I'll help you." I expect Alonzo to turn into a man, but he remains a wolf and gently chews at the end of the vine sticking out from the wrap. Pulling it with his teeth, he manages to break it free and unravel the make-shift muzzle.

I release another whimper and nuzzle my snout to my paws, trying to rub away the pain, my skin tender. Scooting closer, Alonzo licks my snout again, the cool sensation of the breeze caressing my damp fur and tender skin helping with the ache.

"Thank you," I think to him, resting my head to the ground without moving from my spot. I lock my gaze to his, trying to see beyond what's in front of me. I can see his similarity to Caz, and it helps calm the wild beats of my heart.

"Whatever I can do to help," Alonzo says, nuzzling his nose to mine, mirroring my position. "I'll do whatever it takes to prove to you that I honestly just want to do what's right. We're not all terrible alpha-mates like those under the witch's control."

I continue to gaze at Alonzo, and he stills under my scrutiny, not pressuring me with pleas but instead choosing to support me with his presence until I'm ready to speak. I shift on the ground, the ache in my snout dulling. Silence blankets the world around us, and I wonder how long it'll be before another competitor sneaks up for a chance to get me. I wonder what my pack mates would want me to do in this moment. Would they want me to put up a fight to test Alonzo? I mean, if he has ill-intent, he'll try to force me into compliance regardless. He'll only act as nice as he does now until he realizes that it gets him nowhere.

On the other hand, I'm so fucking tired and confused. I shouldn't be here. The witch shouldn't have been able to summon me like she did. I was supposed to be safe and well protected in Flynn's apartment.

And now that I think about Flynn...fuck. I'm angry. The witch interrupted a moment I wanted more than anything. How dare she force me into these nightmare games. I'm going to kill her. I'll make her regret ever messing with me.

"Okay, I'll let you cross the finish line with me," I finally think to Alonzo, my body buzzing with my need for retaliation and revenge toward the bitch witch.

Alonzo pushes a breath of relief through his nostrils. "I swear to the fates that I won't let you down. I'll keep you safe from the other competitors until we can figure something out."

I scoot forward and out of my den. The branches collapse, tangling with my fur and scraping the pads of my paws, but I ignore the aches and shake the debris free. Alonzo stands and nips at a few sticks, dropping them to the dirt. He circles me, rubbing the length of his bulky body against mine in an affectionate way I'm only used to receiving from my pack...but then again, I've never let anyone else get so close.

Alonzo licks my snout again. "I know this is going to sound fucked up, but I need to drag you across the finish line and pin you in front of everyone to win your claim."

I jerk my muzzle back and growl. "You need to what?"

He whimpers, sounding like I just punched his snout with my reaction. "It's how the new rules work. If the witches or alpha-mates think we've rigged anything, they have the power to hand you over to someone else within the Meadow View pack, and my uncle will automatically award you to his son."

"This is fucking bullshit," I mutter through my mind. "What if they try to do so anyway? It sounds like you all are competing for your pack and not for yourselves. What happens to the territories that were given to the she-wolves?"

"You belong to your territory, so winning you means winning the territory." Alonzo nudges me with his head. "We even get to spend the day there."

My heart flutters with his words. "We do?"

He bobs his wolf head. "I have to choose three guardians and potential allies from other packs, but I'm confident in my chosen ones. We can handle anyone we need to if there are any problems." He says the words softly, lovingly, and I wonder if there is more to it.

My excitement stops me from asking. Because, fuck yeah,

I can help them too. Especially in my home territory. If I can get to Lunar Crest, I will have the advantage. I know where the gateway to the Mortal World is, and if that fails, I have access to the one place only members of my pack can go...my mother's den.

"Are you sure you can trust them not to betray us? This fucking hunt seems like it would be the perfect chance to kill the competition," I ask.

Alonzo nods. "They're who I desire to be pack mates with. We'll figure this out and help you. We can help each other."

I tip my head to stare at the moon in the sky. "I'm trusting you, Alonzo. I hope you realize how hard that is for me to do."

"You won't regret it. We just need to make it through the games. Once they are over, we can figure the rest of this out. Find my brother and your chosen ones."

I yip at him. "I'm not waiting that long. I know they're on their way, and I have a plan to get us out of here."

He tilts his big head like he's not sure whether to believe me. "You do?"

Rubbing my body to his, I nudge him to move. "What kind of she-wolf would I be if I didn't? I'm the Lunar Crest pack leader, after all."

14

SUBMIT

I GROWL AND SNAP MY teeth, fighting against Alonzo as he carries me by the scruff of my neck near the finish line. Howls and cheers sound through the air, the other competitors enjoying the fight I put up against Alonzo. And damn it. It pisses me off that these bastards get off on seeing him man-handle me. If it were still the She-Wolf Games and not this twisted competition to earn a damn sex slave for the rest of their life, I might not hold it against them and plan to murder them.

"I'll bite your damn balls off!" I shout through my mind, using the gross energy of the horny bastards starting to circle us like they plan to try to intervene. Who knows? They might try. It keeps me on guard and more dangerous than ever. I've already bit one cock tonight, and my wolf-self isn't afraid to sink my teeth into another two or five or ten.

Looks like the fucker alpha-mate followers aren't the only sadists. Because I will savor all these bastards' agony and be the ultimate pain in their dicks. They'll learn quickly as hell that none of them could ever break me. I'll punch, bite, bend, slap, and sprain a thousand boners before I lie docile and allow any of them get in line to train bang me. That's only something I'd consider with my pack. Weird? Totally. True? Damn straight.

Alonzo loses his focus, probably hearing my dirty thoughts as I try to suppress the crazy world around me by twisting my fears into hot fantasies to include my guys. I don't know how else to deal with the ickiness of knowing that some of these assholes are the type that should spend the rest of their lives locked up and castrated for their beliefs of where women stand.

"Lyric, watch out," Alonzo says, releasing me as a hulking sandy-brown and tan wolf launches from the crowd.

Pain edges my vision as my injured leg tries to break my fall. My adrenaline isn't enough to numb the pain, and I brace for someone else to snatch me.

"She's mine!" Alonzo yells, staying true to his promise to protect me.

Getting in the asshole's path, Alonzo cuts off the wolf and attacks. He grabs the wolf with his bare hands and tosses him toward a couple wolves, who then take over and try to rip the fucker apart and put him in his place.

I stare in shock at the madness. It's like they've been spelled to be ruthless, violent beasts. Teeth latch onto my tail and drag me back a few feet, my focus on the fight leaving me open. Because I hadn't seen another competitor sneaking up on me, I don't have much time to react. My fighting reflexes aren't as fast for me as a wolf. My injury doesn't help. Jerking my head, I snarl, snapping my jowls in an attempt to bite one of the bastards from Stargaze Hill. My chest tightens, my mind panicking, stealing my ability to recall who this wolf is.

"She's mine!" Alonzo repeats. He stretches his body and bows, transforming into his wolf.

Growling, he plows into me instead of the fuck-head. The heavy weight of his wolf body is enough to knock me away from the wolf and get on top of me. I growl and fight, my instincts to protect myself going crazy. Cheers echo through the night, and I manage to break away from Alonzo's loose grip. He wants to give the audience a show, so we're giving them a damn show.

"I'll neuter you!" I scream through my mind, letting everyone hear. "You can't do this. I will never bow down to you."

Alonzo releases a deep, throaty snarl, the noise reverberating in my soul. If I didn't know any better, I'd think he had changed his mind about acting our way through this to really force me into submission. I scramble away from him as he transforms back into a man once more, the competitors around us no longer wanting to try to steal me and instead savoring this damn moment for their twisted spank banks later.

"I mean it!" I yell, my wolf barking with the thought. "I will never bow."

Alonzo launches at me, risking his naked body as I growl and try to snap my teeth to show that even acting, I'm not going to just give up on my fight. Crashing into me, he locks his arms around my wolf body and rolls with me a couple times as I thrash, pushing through the pain of my injuries. People laugh and clap, some of the competitors returning to their human forms to show off their damn boners for this moment.

Latching his hand to the back of my neck, Alonzo flips me to my side and pins me down, ramming his knee into my ribs and his large palm against the side of my wolf head. I growl and try to fight, but his strength is too much. My body doesn't want to continue, my humanity counting on Alonzo's promise to be my ally.

A whimper escapes my mouth, my body relaxing as I finally give up my fight.

Something dark sneaks into my heart, a sorrow unlike anything I've ever felt cascading over me. Despite knowing that I agreed to put on this show with Caz's brother, I can't help wondering if this is the exact feeling I'd have if it were someone else forcing me into submission. It's like a part of my soul shatters, the pieces turning to dust to scatter across all the territories.

Grabbing my snout, Alonzo forces me to look at him. He leans forward and gets in my space, sharing my breath. "Lyric of Lunar Crest, you're mine."

I whimper again, my emotions spinning with my racing heart. Shifting beneath Alonzo, I spread my body out, exposing my belly to him. My chest heaves with my breaths, and a strange sensation crosses my skin, my body prickling.

"Congratulations, Alonzo of the Meadow View pack. You have won the Omega Hunt." The musically sweet voice of a woman echoes through the air, drawing my attention from Alonzo as he stands above me. "Bring your she-wolf to me. I will ensure you're heavily rewarded for your outstanding efforts to prove your capability."

I blink a few times at Invidia's words. She's so close that if I gather the last bit of my strength, I could launch at her. I could knock her down and rip her throat out. She's one witch, without her coven present, and there are dozens of wolves here. Why no one has tried...? Alonzo mentioned wolves died for her to summon me here. Perhaps they were the ones who stood up against her.

Alonzo scoops me off the ground and cradles me protectively in his arms. "I have her handled."

Invidia clicks her tongue, sauntering even closer. I tense in

Alonzo's arms as my fear and panic try to get my she-wolf to flee. It's like my soul will take flight and free me from this nightmare at any second.

Blue light crackles in Invidia's palms. "I'm sure you do, but it is my job to align the fates for you tonight. You no longer have to wait for the breeding season. The ultimate proof of your worth to lead a territory will be proven in the form of producing an offspring for me. Your firstborn will serve me well."

What. The. Fuck. Is. She. Talking. About?

Alonzo, and everyone else for that matter, looks as confused as I do.

"I don't understand," he says, speaking up. His fingers sink into my coat as he tightens his hold on me, anxious by the witch's words and looming presence. "She's not in heat."

The witch saunters forward and rubs her hands together, sending more blue magic sparkling through the air. A strange stone materializes from her electric power, and she closes the space to Alonzo and stares at me in his arms.

"My beautiful she-wolf. You will thank me later," she murmurs, leaning into my face. It takes everything in me not to bite her face off. I'm not sure I'd survive this if I did. "You will no longer have to rely on the fates to be blessed. I will help you like it was intended. You will do great things for your species."

Her words stab me through my heart. I can't believe what

I'm hearing.

Snarling at her, I flare my nostrils. This is it. I'm going to die fighting. My prickling body and screaming soul won't allow anything else. "Stay back," I think, hoping she heeds my warning.

She doesn't.

Snatching my snout, she forces my mouth open before either Alonzo or I can react. She shoves the strange stone down my throat with her fingers and tightens her hands around my muzzle until I can't do anything except for swallow.

"Beb luv tof alionzo veta," she murmurs, a wicked, unsettling smile crossing her face. "She will be fertile, completely healed, and ready for you within a few hours, Alonzo of Meadow View. May the fates be in your favor." She releases my snout and scratches my ear. "And if they're not, we will find someone else, Lyric. Your first born will be mine."

I have to get out of here.

I have to run and fight and escape. If I don't, then this is the end for me.

Because this is the most fucked up thing I have ever faced in my life. I thought the beginning of the She-Wolf Games was bad, and then I thought having a death sentence issued to my pack was even worse.

But being forced by a witch into my heat? Killing Alonzo or any of the competitors if they don't knock me up after a night? Taking my first born child? What kind of horror movie is this?

Oh, right. Not a movie.

This is my fucking life.

And I can't even do anything about it. I'm trapped as a wolf with the brother of one of my mates, and now we're going to go into a damn mating frenzy all because of a spell. I thought I'd have more time. I thought we'd get a plan in place. But now? Fuck.

"We have to get out of here," a masculine voice says, drawing my attention away from my reflection in the mirror of my pink room in Lunar Crest. "I would rather die than betray our species. This isn't right. My dad would be ashamed."

"But how do we get out of here? All access portals have been closed." Another competitor paces right outside my door.

"Alonzo, you need to let us talk to her. I doubt she will want you to die. Caz is your brother." This comes from the last man Alonzo had chosen to be one of my guardians.

"I have thought about it. Even if we mate, it will not guarantee anything. I will not ask her to do this for me. It isn't right. No she-wolf should ever be put in this position." Alonzo growls with his words.

"Please, we don't want to lose you," the first guy says. "You're our mate. Please, let's just run it by her. We can all try if she lets us. We just need to buy time."

Whoa. I don't even know how the hell I feel about the

conversation taking place between them. I mean, I don't want anyone to die, but...fucking fuck. This sucks.

Padding to the door, I scratch my nails against it, wishing Alonzo hadn't shut it on me while I took a quick nap. I couldn't help myself. I'm so damn exhausted, and I worry that whatever spell the witch cast on me will only make things worse...well, actually, I know they will. I'm going to be coming into my fucking heat.

"Alonzo, why don't you guys just come in here?" I ask, sending my thought through the air. "I want you to introduce me to...your mates?" He mentioned them being men he wanted as pack mates, and now I know why.

The door cracks open and Alonzo meets my gaze. "Yeah, sure. I'm sorry, Lyric. I thought you were still sleeping." Flaring his nostrils, he gives me a once over and surprises me by slamming the door in my face. "Better yet, maybe I should lock the door."

"Shit," one of the other guys says. "I need to run. I can't stay here with her like this. It confuses the hell out of me."

I spin around and put space between myself and the door, realizing that most of these guys probably have never been around a female in heat. And fuck. If they're anything like Sterling...if *I'm* anything like Sterling...

My womb is doomed.

I can already feel my body tingling like I'm in desperate need for relief. I wonder how long my she-wolf self can hold off before I start bumping my damn backend to the door. Because being stuck in this form makes me feel even more out of control. I can't exactly masturbate. I also know that it doesn't matter which form I'm in. The guys will probably be unable to resist giving into their innate mating needs as wolves as I lift my tail and invite them to breed with me. Fuck. I never thought I'd have sex like this...at least not with guys that aren't mine.

I whimper and flop on the floor. "Are you guys certain all the portals have been closed?" I roll on my back, my body humming, my damn wolf vagina tingling with an all-consuming sensation that makes my soul anxious.

Alonzo thunks his head to the door. "I've tried. We're trapped."

A whine escapes my mouth and I get up and pace the room. This is nuts. I thought my guys were exaggerating about the coming season, but damn. This is worse than I imagined. It's like I have an itch that I can't reach. A hunger that nothing will satisfy. It's like—

I howl, a strange electrical current zinging from my groin and to the rest of me. Whimpering, I lose control of my body, my innate nature stealing control. I rush and jump on the door, trying to break it down. An overwhelming scent steals my attention, and all I want to do is break out of here, lift my tail, and let—

Guttural growls echo through the air, the familiar sound of my pack sending my heart soaring. I knew they'd come for me. I knew it. But now that they're here...fuck. I'm terrified for what will happen next.

"Get out of my way before I disembowel you." Dax's voice rings through my ears. "Lyric is ours."

I yap and bark, jumping on the door. "Dax! Dax! Don't hurt them. They're our allies."

Lavender light explodes through the pink room, and Flynn materializes in front of me. His eyes widen, and he rushes to close the space, a dozen indecipherable emotions flickering through his gaze.

"Shit, you transformed," he says, dropping to his knees.

I launch forward and pounce on him, sending him to his back. "I couldn't help it. Nightstar invaded Lulupoterra. The witches have changed the games. She even—"

The door to the room flies open, and Dax enters first. His eyes sweep across the room until they land on me, sitting on Flynn in my wolf form with my ass in the air. Flaring his nostrils, he inhales a deep breath. Sterling and Sagan push him inside and freeze behind him. I spot Caz and Bastien in the open-air hallway outside, along with Antone, Alonzo and the other three guys.

And fuck.

They all look at me like I'm the best damn thing they've ever seen in their lives.

I pant a breath, my whole body buzzing with an all-consuming need. If Flynn didn't roll over and tackle me, I'm pretty sure I'd hump the hell out of all of them, my body going wild, my desperation to get it on worse than I've ever felt it in my life.

"Shit," Flynn mutters, gathering power in his hand. "Stay back. All of you. It's a spell."

Sterling ignores Flynn's warning. "I don't fucking care. Our girl is in heat. She's dying for me. Can't you hear her thoughts?"

I whimper again. "I just want it to go away. He can help me."

"I will fix this," Flynn says, clutching my fur, trying to get me to stop squirming. "Just stay back, everyone. I need a minute."

Growls reverberate through the air, every one of the damn horny wolves challenging Flynn to even try to do anything.

"Lyric, focus," he says, giving me a shake.

I realize I'm growling the loudest of all.

Flynn can't even brace himself as I thrash, breaking free of his hold. I dart away from him and use the wall to catapult over him on the floor to rush toward Sterling as he stretches and turns into his silver wolf.

My mind tries to fight my body.

I can't believe I'm spinning around and lifting my tail.

I can't believe I'm going to let whoever reaches me first in wolf form mate with me. That I want them to.

My whole body buzzes, and I whimper again as Sterling

mounts me from behind.

Dax growls and shoves into him, knocking him off. The two of them start fighting, their wolves stealing away their humanity. Bastien approaches me next and circles, waiting for me to expose my body to him. Once again, I lift my tail and whimper.

Bastien locks his paws around my body, climbing on top of me. My whole body sings in anticipation, the need turning me into a true animal.

"Fuck, stop!" Flynn shouts, sending a spark of magic across the floor. "Get a hold of yourselves."

"Fuck off, warlock," Caz says, circling around me and Bastien, looking ready to intercept him.

"Elisava pret eht guisa!" Flynn shouts.

Bastien falls away from me, and silence hangs heavy in the room. I spin around and whine, seeing all of the wolves knocked out and lying on the floor.

"What have you done?" I ask, baring my teeth.

"Lyric, we have to go. The witches are coming," Flynn says, his words snapping me out of my lust-filled haze. Waving his hands, he uses magic to drag Dax, Bastien, Sagan, Sterling, Caz, and Antone closer to us, leaving the other competitors on the floor.

"What about them?" I ask, shifting on my paws.

"I can't take them into the one place that can shield us here. You haven't claimed them." Flynn summons a tornado of sparkling light through the room. "I'm sorry, Lyric. We have to go."

Clapping his hands, he drenches the world in lavender light. A wave of fear crashes into me, and I spot a blur of darkness break into Flynn's light.

I squeeze my eyes shut and brace to be taken. I brace for the world to end under the blast of magic.

But Flynn's light consumes the darkness.

A veil of tranquility blankets over me.

"Lyric, we're safe," Flynn says.

If only it felt that way.

15

Mating Season

"DRINK THIS," FLYNN SAYS, SETTING a bowl on the stone floor in front of me. "It'll hopefully break your she-wolf's control over your state."

I sniff the strange glowing liquid, the rancid smell twisting my stomach. "You can't sweeten it or something?"

"Do you want to remain a wolf forever?" he retorts, sitting on the floor next to me. "I don't know about you, but I miss your smile. I know your pack couldn't care less about which form you take, especially with you wagging your damn tail at them...but it's just not my thing. I mean, unless you'll accept some damn belly rubs."

Hooking his arm around my side, he drags me to him and flips me onto my back. He cradles me and scratches his hand into my belly fur, making me growl. "Such a good girl. Who's a good girl? Not Lyric. Lyric's a naughty girl. She's so bad and won't get anything she truly wants." Flynn chuckles at his own damn teasing, gripping me tighter so that I can't flail away. "But you, pretty she-wolf, you get all the belly rubs. Where's the spot? Show me the spot. Just a little leg kick. You won't be so grumpy."

This fucker.

Flynn tips his head back and laughs. "Just admit it. You love this."

I squirm and nip him, hating that he might be a little bit right. It's more about his playfulness and not the petting, though. With the lightness in his voice, things don't feel as heavy or twisted. I feel some relief. "I can think of a dozen other things I'd love."

"If you drink the elixir, I'll let you pick one of them." Flynn continues to ruffle my fur, grinning at me with a teasing smile.

"Only one?" I say, wiggling free only because he lets me.

His smile widens, and the bastard puckers his lips, making kissing sounds at me. "Okay, maybe two. Don't make me have to wait for your mates to wake up. They're a bit useless right now."

I play-growl. "I wouldn't call them useless. They know how to satiate my every need. And right now. Fuck."

Flynn's eyes darken, and he quietly pushes the bowl to me once more. I watch his smile fade as he taps his finger to the liquid to drip it onto my nose. I automatically lick the drop and flop over dramatically, playing dead. His hand wanders back to my belly, and he combs his fingers through my coat over and over again in silence, the weight of his stare getting me to roll to my stomach and force myself to drink his gross concoction.

My muscles spasm, and I arch my back, my body burning as my she-wolf fights for control. I want so badly to be myself again, to have hands and smooth skin, to take on the form Flynn desires. His cool hand presses into the small of my back, stroking up the length of my spine as I complete my transformation. I rest on my hands and knees, panting a few deep breaths as everything finally catches up with me.

"How do you feel?" Flynn murmurs, combing my hair from my shoulder to stop it from veiling my face. "Anything hurt?"

I lick my lips and push up until I sit on the cold stone floor in front of him. "I had broken my leg, but the witch healed it with the same spell that forced this bullshit on me. Now, I only ache..." It sounds so good to hear my voice humming in my ears. With my admission, tingles burst from my groin to travel through the rest of me. I might no longer be a wolf, but fuck. Transforming has done nothing for my out-of-control libido.

"Where? Let me see what I can grab to help you." Flynn stops short from digging his hand into the black bag at the edge of the bed. His muscles flex, and he stills.

I lick my lips, a strange wildness cascading over me in a hot wave. "You might want to summon a leash or something. This uncontrollable feeling..."

"Is temporary," he murmurs, reaching out to caress my bare knee.

I lick my lips and cover his hand. "I'm not so sure."

"If you give me a minute, I can cast a counter spell to hopefully ensure that your mates shoot blanks, and they can help you..." His face reddens at his thoughts. "Fuck, I'm sorry. This is awkward. I'm not used to feeling this way."

I can't stop my hand from gliding up his leg to stop at his thigh. "What way?"

"I'm jealous, Lyric. Not of your mates, but just—I can't explain it. I—"

Lifting my hand, I cut off his words by touching his lips. "I was told only another wolf could truly help, but you're different than a mortal. My soul wants you as much as my body. I think you can help me just fine."

Surprising Flynn, I slide onto his lap and kiss him, slipping my tongue into his mouth. He's all I want to taste and experience, our near moment of passion rekindling my need to be with him since I never got the chance. He moans deep in his throat, reacting to my affection with crazy intense passion that prods at my wild desire exploding through me. My fingers drag down his shirt until I link them to the hem and yank it off him, my skin craving the sensation of his against mine.

Rolling my hips, I dry-hump him through his jeans, the hardness of his cock pressing against the sturdy fabric doing nothing but making me crave more of him. I want to find out what kind of pleasure he can arouse in me, his desperation to give me everything and anything I want humming through with his panting breaths.

"Can I take you to the bed?" he asks me, sliding his hand down my ass and between my legs from behind. His fingers caress the warmth of my desire, making me clutch him harder.

I moan at the pressure of his exploration, his finger slipping in and out of me as he tests my body, using my reaction to push him forward. Any reserve he had before melts away the second I land on the mattress.

Grabbing the front of his jeans, I unfasten the button and drag the zipper down, desperately wanting to touch and taste him, my desire to ensure I'm the only thing he'll ever think and dream and fantasize about ever again turning all-consuming. He's mine, and I want to take care of him how he needs and wants and craves. It's all I can think about, my tongue sliding across my lips as I grab his hard-on and lace my fingers around it. With my other hand, I drag his pants down his hips until he kicks out of them.

He bends to kiss me, brushing his sweet lips to mine, trying to ease me onto my back, but I break away and shake my head. I want to savor everything about this moment.

Is it crazy that I can't stop thinking about wanting to destroy all future moments of passion he could ever consider having with anyone else? Because if this doesn't work out, if my pack becomes too much, I want him to always think that no one could ever stand up to me.

Grabbing his hips, I graze my fingers over his ass to pull his body to my mouth. He moans and tangles his fingers through my hair, his desperate touch begging me to give him what he desires.

"We don't have to do anything you don't want to," I murmur, stroking the length of his hard shaft. "I know this situation is weird for you."

"It's not," he says, playing with my hair.

I smile and lick my lips. "Good."

Licking my tongue across his tip, I tease him before sucking his erection into my mouth. His moan sends my body screaming with pleasure as intense as it would be if it were my moan. I don't understand it, but I don't question it either. I know deep down, we're connected just as intensely as I am with the others. His soul stone proves it. And now, I want nothing more than to lick him until he cums for me. And then after? I want more. I want him over and over again. I want to ache for him, because of him. I want to consume his every thought, so he aches for me too.

Tracing my free hand lower, I cup his balls, listening to the sound of his moans grow louder as I suck him off. His muscles ripple with my bobbing motion, and he feels ready to pull away to toss me on the bed to give me what I need.

Mumbling something under his breath, Flynn spins my world with his magic, and I land on top of him like a reverse cowgirl. He grabs my hips and drags my body to his face, the sensation of his tongue rolling across my clit unlike anything I've ever felt in my life. Like magic. I'm nearly certain he uses magic to get me off, and I scream my pleasure at the pulsing vibration that makes me explode with an orgasm.

And holy fuck.

"Flynn," I gasp, every inch of my body trembling, my ecstasy making it hard to think about anything else. "Whoa. Oh, fuck."

"Was that good?" he asks, his voice husky and deep, humming against my body as he kisses between my legs again.

I pant, my body still trembling. "Good? It was amazing. How did you do that?" I stroke his hard cock, thinking of a few ways I want to see him cum. "I'm afraid I won't be as good. I can't summon magic."

He rubs the smooth skin of my ass. "You *are* magic, remember? Everything you do is perfect."

I bow forward, grabbing his cock again to suck him as desperately as he makes me feel. Sweetness builds across his tip, the addictive flavor coating my tongue, and my mouth waters. Just the teensy taste of his excitement awakens a hunger inside me that prods at my very nature. Flynn moans and reciprocates, kissing and licking and sucking my body while teasing me with his fingers. He sounds as if he enjoys me as much as I enjoy him, our lust and pleasure tangling, igniting an unforgettable passion that steals my breath, bringing me to completion all over again.

"Lyric, I'm going to cum," he murmurs, his words encouraging me to continue. I want nothing more than to see this through, experience his orgasm, to discover if it tastes as delectable as his excitement.

He moans and arches his back, his muscles tightening as he cums in my mouth. The burst of delicious flavor, like white chocolate drizzling over my tongue, makes me hum as I swallow. I enjoy giving head to my pack, but this is crazy and sweet, and I want to blow him all over again.

He chuckles at my thought, rolling me over only to get to his knees and nestle himself between my legs to kiss me again, his passion still hot and wild, his mind opening to me in an unexpected twist of the fates he holds dear. He intakes a small breath against my mouth, letting the connection consume him, his thoughts racing with a dozen different ways he wants to make love to me.

His cock hardens again, already throbbing with his need, reacting to my own, and I reach between us and align our bodies. He shudders with his moan, caressing his lips to mine. I gasp at the pressure of his hard-on, teasing my body with his tip. Puffing his lips with his fast breathing, he stretches upright like he wants the best view of me as he uses his magic to levitate my body high enough to push into me.

"Lyric," he says, my name so incredibly sexy coming from his mouth. He closes his eyes, scrunching his face, savoring the feeling of our bodies connecting. "You feel even more incredible than I could've dreamed of."

He guides my levitating body to his, the sensation unlike anything I've ever experienced. His gentle touch manages to send an explosion of pleasure through my insides like he can touch every single nerve-ending at once.

Opening my body wider while gripping my bent knees, I gasp and moan with each of Flynn's thrusts. His tattoos swirl and move over his chest like I've awakened his magic with his pleasure. He locks his gaze to mine, his eyes flashing with his lavender light, and he touches my clit with his fingers, pressing it hard enough that my whole body sings with the sudden vibrations created from his magic.

I arch, practically hanging upside down, my muscles tensing with another orgasm that makes me scream in ecstasy that I'm sure the whole universe can hear. Flynn moans and traces his hand up my stomach to rub my nipples. I gasp at another round of explosive pleasure, his magic tingling over me, zinging across my body. I can't catch my breath, his fast thrusts hitting me just right that he makes me cum so hard that my excitement gets him wet.

He moans, his nostrils flaring, and he grips my hips, holding me tight as he pounds his body to mine exactly how I want and crave—rough with passion and desperation, our bodies connecting so furiously that it's like my ass gets spanked by his balls. I grab for him, wanting to taste his lips and tongue. I want to feel the vibration of my name escaping his lips.

Dropping me to the bed, Flynn bows and kisses me, nipping my lip to stretch it before kissing me deeper. I scream in short bursts through his passionate kiss, my body going wild with every new and intense sensation igniting a pleasure so intense that I scratch my nails into his back. He thrusts into me with his orgasm, the sudden weight of his body pressing me into the bed feeling so perfect and protective. I hug and cling onto him, my body begging for more. I want it so badly. I want him to satisfy my very nature.

I roll him off me to get on top, but he sits up and clutches my face. "The need won't stop. I'm not a wolf."

"I don't care," I say, caressing my lips to his. "You're amazing. I honestly didn't know what to expect...but I can't believe you were a virgin. I want more. I need more." Fuck, did I just whimper? Fuck yeah, I did. I never considered ever feeling the need to beg, but my wolf isn't against it. "Your cock is magical. Is that normal?"

He arches up to kiss me with a smile. "I might've felt the need to ensure I could compete with the others. I...I didn't want to disappoint you." Chuckling, he laughs at his admission.

"That's impossible," I say, reaching for him, the ache in my body turning nearly feral. I'm out of fucking control. My lust before was nothing compared to this. "I can't get enough." I rock my body across his, still so turned on that I could probably orgasm just dry humping him.

He eases away from my fervent kiss to meet my gaze. "You're incredibly hard to resist, my beautiful she-wolf, but the others will wake up soon. I'm a bit nervous how they might react to...us, like this, when they're going to be a bit more wild. Probably aggressive. They have their pack bonds, and I'm...fuck. They're going to tear me apart. We never fully discussed any of this."

"They know I've bonded with you. It's not going to be how you think. Plus, I plan to have them too. I can't stop thinking about it. I'm so..." My words trail off with my admission. I can't believe I just said that, but the thought crosses my mind. Just the idea of each of them ravishing the hell out of me any way they want makes me moan in excitement. Double the peen suddenly doesn't sound so out there.

Flynn's eyes widen, and I'm positive he heard my thought. His gaze drops to look at me straddling him naked and exposed, and I can almost feel his questions and his slight bit of concern penetrating me as deeply as my mates would.

"Fuck, I'm sorry," I whisper, forcing myself to flop off of him and onto my back. Covering my face with my hands, I try to suppress my urge to satisfy my entire pack at once, the thrill and excitement coursing through me at even the thought enough to send slick excitement dampening my thighs. "You...have to fix this. The way you're looking at me—why do you look like you feel bad?"

Now that I ask the question, I can't stop the annoyance from stealing this perfect moment between me and Flynn to shoo it away. I grab the blanket, flicking my attention to the archway leading to where my pack remains asleep. They'd never make me question if what I want should be shameful. They'd—

"Lyric, wait." Flynn grabs my hand, trying to stop me from bolting across the room. "Please, you're misunderstanding my expression. I never want you to feel ashamed of your fantasies."

His words put a stop to my escape, and he tugs me to him, engulfs me in a hug, and flips me onto my back. Surprising me, Flynn tickles my very nature, stretching my arms over my head while straddling me. My chest heaves with my panting breath, and instead of feeling weak in this state of submission, I feel strangely empowered. Because we both know I can easily flip him off and dominate him. The only way he could ever truly make me submit is with magic, but he'd never do it. Even now, I'm in complete control.

"There is absolutely no shame in your desires or your needs and wants from the relationships you have with your chosen ones," Flynn says, sliding both his hands through mine as I spread my legs enough for him to lie between them. "It's just—my species is monogamous. Who we choose to grow relationships with stems from one's power and not the tangling of fates you feel."

I frown, worry gripping my chest. Now that he says as much, I can't stop thinking that he'll leave me, because I can't give him the life he thought he'd get with someone. I don't come alone. I come with those who I've claimed as mine. And I want Flynn to be mine too. But...fuck. I can't, no I won't, give up the men I have chosen.

"Maybe this was a mistake," I say, my heart crashing wildly with my words. Now that they're out there, I can't take them back. "I know I'm your familiar, but I should've never put you in this position." My eyes prickle, and I blink a dozen times. Fuck. Fuck! I can't cry.

Flynn releases one of my hands, and swipes his finger under my eye before a tear can even fall. "Lyric, no. Please. I didn't intend for you to feel bad. This was not a mistake. Far from it. It was the best damn moment of my life. Being with you—I want this. I want to make it work. I'm just—I'm not ready to participate in something that sounds like a mating frenzy with you. I want to get to know you on my own. I want to build friendships and trust with your pack too."

His words spark happiness inside me, my heartbeat slowing as I process his words. I never expected him to want what he does, and the idea of him wanting more than just me fills my heart with contentment.

And desire.

"You're insatiable," he murmurs, hearing my thought.

"I can't help it. I want you so badly all over again. What you said about me and my pack...let me show you how much it truly means to me." I smile and kiss him, savoring his affection.

His body reacts to mine, and I moan at the light caress of his hard-on against my sensitive skin. I arch my hips, unable to stop myself from rolling my body to see if he'll fuck me again. It's all I can think about with him so close and ready.

He releases a breathy, utterly sexy noise at my attempt to silently seduce him, but he doesn't give in to me. "Lyric." He moans my name, his desire to experience me again pressing to my heated flesh. If I wiggle enough, he'll slip in. I know it. I can hear the thought cross through his mind. I can nearly feel his anticipation.

A sharp intake of breath drags my attention from Flynn and to the doorway to the heated pool of my mom's den. Dax rubs his eyes with the heels of his hands like he needs to see things more clearly. Flynn stiffens, his nerves getting the best of him. Scrambling off me, he gets to his feet, clutching a pillow to his groin like Dax has never seen a naked cock.

Dax growls, but the sound isn't threatening and more like just his wolf recognizing what it means that I'm in this situation.

"You smell irresistible," he murmurs, ignoring Flynn completely like he's not even here. Dax's body hardens, his dick throbbing as it points in my direction. "I need you. I can't think about anything else."

His voice sets me off, and I rub my legs together in anticipation, my whole body buzzing.

Slowly spreading my legs, I expose my body to him, the thrill and excitement of seeing his lust cloud his eyes driving me crazy.

"Dax, hurry. Give her what she wants. I can't stand seeing her begging for you." Sagan's soft voice whispers in my mind, his own lust hazing his stare.

"Fuck, blondie. I can't wait. Let me join you." Sterling dodges past Sagan, looking fully prepared to push Dax onto the bed to throw me on top only to mount me from behind to show me exactly what it means to be in my sexy mate sandwich.

Bastien and Caz devour me with their gazes, their bodies so hard and ready to satiate my every desire.

I can't even stop myself from biting my lip as Antone enters the room, grabbing the wall like it's the only thing preventing him from lunging.

"Fuck," Flynn mutters from his spot. "You need to control yourselves. We have to strategize a plan. The Nightstar Coven put an impenetrable shield in place. The only—"

"I plan on only penetrating our mate and not some damn shields," Sterling says, licking his lips. "Now back up. I can smell your sex all over blondie, and it's driving me crazy. I want nothing more than to make her cum and scream my name. I want to bust my damn nut inside her just how she wants. You can't be the only one to get off."

"They have needs to," I murmur, stretching out my arms. "I want to take care of them."

Flynn groans. "Lyric, you'll have time—"

My lust steals all chance of being able to reason. "I have time now. I mean, look at all those raging boners. They're mine. I want to see them all cum."

"Yeah, you bastard," Dax says, reaching for my ankles to pull me to him.

I arch and moan at even the thought.

And then all of my pack mates tense and moan. Dax cums all over my pelvis, the warm liquid surprising me.

"What the fuck?" Bastien asks, dragging my attention to him.

My mouth drops open in surprise as I stare at streaks of cum splattered across the floor. And what the hell? Every one of my guys just ejaculated, cumming without me even having to touch them.

"Did you do this, Flynn?" Sagan asks, his face twisting in confusion.

Dax growls. "He fucking had to."

"You son-of-a-bitch cock block," Caz mutters, his mind swirling with thoughts of annoyance that I gave myself to Flynn first. Uh-oh.

"Chill out, everyone," Sterling says, raising his hands. His gesture surprises the hell out of me. "You can't be pissed off. You know Lyric doesn't want to get knocked up. You should thank my bestie for the waste of all your damn baby paste."

I gasp and laugh at his joke, the ridiculousness of it snapping me out of my horny, heat-triggered haze. Everyone turns their attention to me, my cheeks now burning with warmth. I cannot believe Flynn actually did that. And damn it, he totally upped the bar on how to get off my mates in a way I can't.

"Fuck, blondie. If I ever cum that fast for you—fuck that. He has nothing on you," Sterling says, twisting to glower at Flynn.

Flynn opens his mouth to say something, but a familiar whistle cuts through the air. Panic fills my heart, stealing away every ounce of warmth from my body. I can't believe this crazy-ass shit continues on, even without me.

"What's going on?" Sagan asks, twisting to peer out the archway. "They're playing the She-Wolf Games here again?"

I clutch my hands together, the thought of the last games swirling through my mind. "No, they play the Omega Hunt, but I don't know if this is it. I don't know the rules to anything anymore. Invidia is in control."

"We have to find out for sure," Dax says.

"And then what?" Sagan asks.

Bastien flares his nostrils. "We tear all of Lulupoterra down."

16

TRUST

DAX BLOCKS MY WAY TO the river, my emotions running wild as I struggle not to climb him like a tree and straddle his branch until he gives into me. I had no idea that Flynn assisting them with their release would temporarily cool them off.

I giggle at the thought again.

If only it did something for the crazy ache begging for someone to help me rub one out. Dax intakes a breath at my thought, and I jerk my attention to his rippling, muscular body, waiting for his cock to grow to its usual intimidating proportions.

"Nu-uh, blondie. You want his dick, then be prepared for it to go pounding on your back door until it barges in for a hole invasion. Flynn needs a bit of time to disarm our sperm shooters, and as surprisingly delightful as it was to get off at lightning speed by warlock magic, it wasn't as fun as it sounded." Sterling comes up behind me and grabs each of my ass cheeks, spreading me open from behind to nudge his cock against me. "But, if you're desperate..."

I clench my ass cheeks, locking him in place. "Grab the lube."

Dax and Sterling release the most dramatic groans at the same time in response to my comment. Because clearly, I am desperate.

"Flynn, damn it! I told you she'd ask. Summon me that magic slick dick serum now. I'm going in." Sterling hooks his arms around me and drags me away from Dax.

The world spins as he throws me onto the bed. I clutch the blankets in excitement, rubbing my legs together. Playfully growling, he climbs on the bed, dropping on his stomach to crawl towards me. Sterling hooks his hands to my knees and opens my body for his face, practically diving down with his tongue ready to warm me up.

I moan so embarrassingly loud, my whole body buzzing with excitement. I don't even care if my loud noise of passion brings all of my mates to the doorway. Dax clenches his teeth and releases a warning growl, so utterly serious in completing his task to act as a wall to separate the others from me. I guess he underestimated Sterling's obedience, but he remains firm, our eyes locking as I pant and gasp as Sterling flicks his tongue with desperation right against my clit in front of everyone.

A flash of sparkling light erupts through the room, and Flynn uses his power to get past the five-body deep wall of pure muscles and lust to enter the private quarters of my mother's den. He averts his gaze to the rock ceiling at the sight of Sterling with his face buried into the apex of heated, sensitive, buzzing flesh between my legs.

"If you stop him, I'll throw you out of here and into the river," Dax snaps, crossing his arms over his broad chest like it's the only thing stopping him from lifting Flynn off his feet to move him out of the way. "Our mate needs this. Can't you smell it? She hurts otherwise, and I refuse to allow her to suffer."

I comb my fingers through Sterling's light tresses, any sort of reserve long gone as the two of us put on a show. Who knew I wouldn't care? Who knew that with my building release I would have to bite my tongue before I call for Dax to come to me next?

He steps forward at my thought, his body thick and long with his lust and desire to do more than make me scream in pleasure. I don't even care that thoughts of mounting and mating and holding me down to cum inside me flash through his mind. It excites the hell out of me enough that I orgasm and trap Sterling's head between my legs as I arch my back and savor my needs finally getting satiated.

"Everyone, cool off. Now! Revir eci og wot no!" Flynn claps his hands together, and all my guys disappear. A loud splash, followed by groans and swears, echoes from where the icy river laps against the wall leading into the heated pool.

I stare at the empty space where Sterling was, my whole body zinging and aching in his absence. Annoyance rushes through me, and it takes one look from Flynn, standing stiff a few feet away with his face a series of hard lines, to get me to flop over and bury my face into the pillow.

"Lyric, I really fucking hate having to tell you this but get your shit together," Flynn says, cautiously crossing the room. His muscles bulge on his arms, his tattoos moving with the gesture. "I know this is your first heat around your mates, and I can only imagine how...inconvenient and consuming it is—hell, it's probably even more intense than what it naturally would be because of the spell—but I need you to focus. I need you to remind yourself what is at stake. If we stay here, the witches will eventually find us. They will start killing off the competitors they find weak. The she-wolves will live horrifying existences, controlled by those who want them for one damn thing only, and you all are better than this."

Well, shit. When he puts it like that...

I shake my head, suppressing the lust and deep-seated nature of my she-wolf, reminding myself that I'm more than a womb. There is more to life despite the pleasure induced by my horny pack mates with their own desire to lose themselves to the mating frenzy.

My dad wouldn't want this for me. He'd fight my entire pack and put them in their place, so they can be of use by my side and not only between my legs.

"Just think of it as being a reward," Flynn says, risking me launching myself at him to fuck his brains out. "When we destroy the Nightstar Coven's control of your home, get the lycans back in order, find your dad and figure out the magic he changed you with to know exactly how to deal, then you can do whoever the hell you want. Maybe by then, I'll be ready to join and things can be...really fucking magical."

I sit up and grab the pillow, hugging it to my chest. "You sure know how to give a convincing pep-talk, warlock."

He groans with a chuckle and tips his head up to stare at the rock ceiling. "I never thought I'd have to cock block so many wolves. They're going to resent me, you know."

I rub my lips together and scoot toward the end of the bed. Extending my hands out, I wiggle my fingers and motion for Flynn to come closer to help me up. He shuffles my way, his gaze darting up and down my body, lavender magic flickering in his eyes. Stealing himself against my seduction, he finally helps me to my feet.

"They'll get over it," I say, draping my arms on his shoulders. Stretching up on my tip-toes, I caress my lips to his, kissing him sweetly, suppressing my desire to slip my tongue into his mouth. "And I will thank you later. Promise. I know this is awkward as hell."

He chuckles and tightens his hands on my waist. "I'll get over it too."

I smile. "Good."

Voices draw our attention from each other, and Caz strides to the doorway, soaking wet with river water dripping from his hair. Goosebumps prickle his skin, and I ease away from Flynn and grab a towel from a chair. He smiles as I wrap it around his shoulders and run my hands up and down his arms. The simple gesture sends the purest, warmest appreciation I've ever felt washing over me from him. It's in this moment that I feel as if I finally breathe. I don't know what it is, but it's like Caz's feelings for me somehow manage to clear the haze-inducing lust.

"It's because we haven't physically claimed each other," he murmurs, lifting his arms to rest his hands on my bare waist.

I blink a few times in consideration. "I still feel so very attracted to you, Caz, so I don't know if it's that...it's hard to explain."

He caresses his fingers along my jaw. "Like I've told you before. This is different for me. You claimed me on a soul-deep level. I adore everything about you, and I do want to take things to a more intimate level, but it's not all-consuming. At least, when the others bond to you isn't prodding at mine."

"Thank the fates," Flynn murmurs from behind me. "A pack mate with some good sense and control."

I swivel and raise my finger to him. "Says the man who gave in to me without even being capable of being triggered by my body's massive amounts of sex chemicals."

Caz chuckles and stops me from pulling away from him. "Which is why I'm officially your guardian until we get this shit sorted out. Unless you want Antone. He can't promise not to try everything in his power to seduce you, though. The whole twin thing with Bastien might give him a bit more leverage."

I crinkle my nose, pursing my lips. "Yeah, no. I'm going to have to have a talk with the bastard. Just because I claimed him and saved his life..."

"Cherie, you plan to doom me? Every one of these assholes has just as strong of an alpha-streak and desire to see you on all fours. At least with me, you know I'm not bullshitting you into thinking you have control of me."

I flick my glower to Antone. "Yet. All this talk of omegas has opened a position for you in our pack." A smile crosses my face as his eyes darken with a mixture of emotions. He's amused yet annoyed, and most definitely looks like he might try to spank me.

"Not only spank you." Antone winks at me, brushing his fingers through his dripping tresses. "I plan to tie you up and blindfold you. Withhold your orgasm until you beg me for release."

I try to remain expressionless to the fantasy he arouses in my mind. The fucker.

"Every now and again, even the most dominant ones such as yourself crave to submit. You'll be calling me sir and pretending to be my naughty little girl so that I bend you over my knee and spank you until your ass turns the perfect shade of red in no time." Antone licks his lips and drags his hand down his body, knowing my damn eyes will follow his gesture until he strokes his cock.

Caz spins and growls, shoving Antone out of the room and into the rock wall. "Respect our leader, you bastard. If she feels you'll best suit our pack as our omega, then you will fucking accept it."

Antone doesn't fight Caz, keeping his gaze trained on me, his dark eyes drinking me in. "She loves when I talk to her like this. While all of you are bowing and trying to give her the things she needs, I'll be ready and waiting to give her what she really wants. Just say the word, Cherie."

This bastard. He's totally wearing me down, and I have no fucking clue how to deal with it. Maybe I'll give in just once to satiate my curiosity. But not today. Not this fucking week either. I have better, more important shit to do rather than getting my ass spanked into submission and giving in to his need for me to call him master.

Flynn flicks his fingers at Antone, shocking him with a

burst of sparks. He raises his hands in defeat and finally averts his eyes, releasing me from his stare. It's now that I realize everyone else hovers anxiously by the heated pool, awaiting directions. They look ready to do anything for me, whether I ask them to all fuck me one at a time, all together, or you know, the more important stuff like face the damn Nightstar witch who has managed to curse the whole territory and taken control of our species.

"Your priorities are a bit messed up, blondie," Sterling mutters, bouncing anxiously on his feet.

Sagan punches him in the shoulder. "Get it together or you're going back for an ice bath."

Bastien comes up to his other side. "And maybe Flynn can freeze the water and shrink your cock in the process, so you'll stop waving your damn boner around, trying to seduce Lyric. It was bad enough you—"

Sterling spins before Bastien can grab hold of him. "You better not fucking say there was anything bad about pleasuring my blonde bombshell. It's my duty to ensure all the stress relief. If it was about me, I'd have bent her over like I wanted and screwed her from behind."

I groan and cover my eyes. "Enough. I can't focus."

Flynn claps his hands, freezing everyone except for Caz. Caz frowns and glances around, his brows puckering. I want to snap at Flynn to release my mates, because he really shouldn't use his magic against them like this, but it's getting too hot in here. My body buzzes, the ache in my groin growing uncomfortable. I doubt we'll get anything done if I keep feeling the need to have someone assist me in rubbing one out.

"If it gets too intense..." Flynn lets his words trail off, realizing that it might not be the best idea to mention in front of Caz how fast he made me orgasm earlier with his magic.

I know Caz says that he's here for me regardless, but he doesn't have to be here for Flynn, though I'd like us all to get along. Especially now. It's important we stick together and figure things out. Alone, we might be powerless against the Nightstar Coven, but together? The witches are going down. We just need to figure out how to break her spell to get us out of Lulupoterra. I mean, if it's even possible. I'm pretty fucking sure this forced heat of mine was intended to screw me up.

"Whatever you can do to help her," Caz says, surprising me. "But right now, keep your damn cock to yourself like the rest of us. You're obviously capable of providing relief without even touching her."

Am I pouty? Yup. Because that sounds so...medical and not magical. What's the fun in that? The only way to not get pissed off at this forced heat is knowing everyone is willing to make me better.

A dozen thoughts rush through my mind. And damn it, I wish I could keep some things to myself. I'm sure Flynn doesn't want me replaying every detail in my head for everyone to listen in on. But once I get started, it's hard to stop, and now

I can't stop my mouth from watering at the memory of his white-chocolate tasting cum.

The spell over everyone breaks as Flynn loses his concentration. I need to get out of here before I attack him with my mouth to suck him off. I had no idea how true lady-boners were, but I now have a throbbing, massive one for Flynn and his magical cock.

Sterling groans. "Are you fucking kidding me? How the hell am I supposed to compete with magic cocks and dessert cum?"

"At least she won't be wasteful with us. I'd prefer my little guys have a chance to hunt her precious egg down." Oh. My. Fuck. Dax did not just say that.

"He did, Ma Belle. And I must admit. I might feel the same." Bastien's voice trickles through my thoughts.

"I don't care where you want mine," Sagan says, his voice light and playful. "My guys just want to be near you."

I throw my hands up. "This is too damn much! Everyone get back in the river except for Caz." I swivel and narrow my eyes at Flynn. "Including you."

"Yeah, bestie. At least we have a fucking excuse. Literally." Sterling laughs out loud at his lame joke. "So drop your damn pants and let's find out how magical your fucking cock really is. I bet it shrinks just like the rest of ours."

I sigh. "Flynn is not getting naked for you. He needs a couple of dates first." I smile, trying to summon a cocky-bastard grin as I use Sterling's words against him.

"Gorgeous, I'll leash my brother and tie him to a tree for you, if you want." Sagan pops into view, keeping a hell of a lot of painstaking space between us when he's looking too damn cuddly in his wolf form, like the only way he can control himself is if he remains in a form I'm not ready to fuck in. "Flynn, how fast can you summon a collar?"

Flynn doesn't respond, his eyes darting back and forth across the ceiling like he's reading something none of us can see.

"Flynn? Hey, dude. Did you hear me?" Sagan asks.

Again, he doesn't respond.

I step closer and snap him out of his racing thoughts by cupping his scruffy cheeks between my palms. "Are you okay?"

His tongue darts over his bottom lip before he sucks it into his mouth. "Yeah. I just thought of something and am trying to figure it out."

"About the witch?" I ask, now anxious that he doesn't just spill his thoughts.

He nods and turns his attention back to the ceiling. "Sort of. It's about what Sagan said."

"You want him to tie Sterling up?" I question, twisting my lips in amusement. I know it's not what he's actually thinking, but his intensity makes me want to lighten the mood.

Turning his attention back to me, he smirks. "Maybe some other time. What I was thinking about was your collar. I can unleash you and use it to break through the shield." He rubs his hands together, shooting sparks through the room. Flynn reaches up and caresses his fingers to my neck. "Do you trust me, Lyric?"

"With what?" I ask. My question curls his handsome features into a frown, but I can't help asking. It's still hard for me to give my trust blindly without knowing what we'd be getting into.

"Do you trust me?" he repeats, instead of answering. His lavender eyes bore into mine, penetrating my soul. His soul stone warms the skin between my breasts, and he absently picks it up and cradles it between his hands. "Because this might not work if you don't completely trust me, my soul mate." Soul mate. The reminder sends a wave of certainty through me. I carry his magic, and we're tethered together. We're bound like I am to the others.

I bounce on the balls of my feet and glance at Caz, meeting his brown gaze as he stares at the two of us. He discretely nods, encouraging me to answer Flynn honestly, even though we both know that the others might have some trust issues. But is this about the others? I don't think so. It's about me.

"I trust you, Flynn," I finally say, taking his hand to hold the stone together with him. "I'm sorry if I still hesitate about things. I'm learning to open up the best I can. Now tell me what's on your mind."

"I want to let go of your collar. And for this to work out in our favor, you have to trust me to protect you. You must trust me to keep your mates safe while we're gone." Flynn squeezes my fingers and puffs a breath through his lips. "You also have to trust that we will get through this. Unleashing you from me might be the only way to get you out of here."

"Okay, but what's with all the talk about trust?" Nerves bunch my stomach. If it wasn't such a big deal, Flynn would've told me already. He's tiptoeing around what it means for him to let go of the magic that gives him control over me.

"If I unleash your collar..." His words trail off. "You know what? It's too risky."

"Why? You just said you can use it to break through the magical shield locking all of us in Lulupoterra." It sounds as if it's riskier to stay. It sounds like this might be our best option, and I'd rather risk myself than put the rest of my pack in danger.

"It's how I have to do it that worries me. If I unleash you, the witches who tried to take you from us in the Mortal World will know and do it again. They will summon you back to them, and because you carry my soul as my familiar, I can follow. The problem is that they have more power than I do because I have to act alone." Flynn swallows and rubs more sparks between our palms, the sensation buzzing against my soul. "You have to trust me to keep you and your pack safe by putting you in danger."

"I'm not sure I grasp everything you're saying. What kind

of danger are you talking about exactly apart from the witches regaining control of Lyric?" Caz asks, speaking up. He's been so quiet and attentive that it was easy to lose myself in my conversation with Flynn.

"Well, I was thinking we could bargain with the witches. They obviously hold power in Magaelorum and the Mortal World, hiding their High Council opposition. Because they're feuding with the Nightstar Coven, we could use that to our advantage."

"I don't know, Flynn. The price for a witch's help is too steep." I anxiously shift on my feet but keep my gaze locked to his. "Many died to get me here, and I don't want to risk any more lives."

Flynn sighs and pulls me close, engulfing me in a hug. "I'm sorry I couldn't stop the summons. I thought I had everything in place, but I didn't count on the dark magic of willing sacrifices. I underestimated the alpha-mates and didn't think some would give their lives for a witch. It's why I want you to trust me now. I don't plan to pay. I won't pay. But it's risky."

"I think we need to take a vote." Caz hugs me from behind like he can't resist, sandwiching me to Flynn. "This might be too dangerous. At least here, we're safe. We know what to expect."

I bonk my head on Caz's shoulder. "Nowhere is safe. We can't spend the rest of our lives here. What would my dad say?"

"He'd want us to fight." Caz groans and nuzzles his nose

into my hair, inhaling a deep breath. "He'd expect us to do everything we can, no matter the consequences, even if it means using our very last breath."

"I'll make sure that's not the case, but like I said, you have to trust me." Flynn touches my hand. "Do you?"

I nod. "With my life."

17

Portal Shift

I PACE ALONG THE LEDGE of the small pool, staring into the glowing river water. Rubbing my hand over my neck, I imagine feeling the strange sensation of the magical collar, though Flynn hasn't unleashed me from him yet. He can't do it in the magical safety of my parents' den. Just thinking about them, about what they went through before me...why do the fates have it out for my bloodline?

"I'm all set, Lyric," Flynn says, strolling from the sleeping quarters. "Whoever enchanted this place for your parents was one hell of an amazing witch. The power source here is unlike anything I've seen. It makes me wish I could meet the witch and ask her a few questions."

Dax clears his throat. "It was a warlock. My pops told me when he brought me here to ensure I knew the safest place for Lyric. I think he only had done so because he knew something bad was coming. This was right before the Great Sacrifice."

The Great Sacrifice. Shit. Just the thought is so messed up. I can't believe the leaders even agreed to offer some of their mates as a sacrifice to the witches for more protection. And knowing how the alpha-mates have taken control over Lulupoterra alongside the Nightstar Coven...this is their fault. Dax thought the whole sacrifice thing was a setup, and the more that shit goes down, the more I realize that justice must be served with a side of fucking burning, torturous revenge. I will personally bite off the alpha-mate cocks and feed them to each other for their horrifying ways.

"I will pin them down," Sagan says, speaking from his seat on the ledge, dangling his feet into the warm pool.

"I will give you a scalpel instead, Ma Belle," Bastien says, his voice rumbly with a growl at my thought.

"Yeah, blondie. That mouth of yours will never touch any of those fuckheads' cocks." Sterling stretches his hands over his head. His muscles ripple with the gesture, and I draw my gaze down his body to check out his boner pressing against the towel slung around his waist. I know he can't help his seemingly eternal erection, but damn it. It's not helping my focus as my gaze tries to will the towel to drop to the ground.

"We will take care of them on your behalf," Dax says, crossing his arms. His words distract me from Sterling's body, and I manage to force my eyes away. "I mean it. Their fates are mine."

"And mine, Cherie. I will ensure they pay for their crimes." Antone's dark eyes shift to look at Dax and the two of them hold a quiet conversation.

I never thought I'd see the day they would stand beside each other. After Dax beat Antone into submission on the same day that Dax and I claimed one another, I was nearly certain they'd never even get within reach again. Seeing them agree on things and team up is only a tad weird, but I don't mind. Antone might be growing on me a bit.

The bastard smiles and winks at me, listening to my thought. "It's only a matter of time until I get my way. I can hear you begging me now." The words come only to me in my mind, sending hot blush across my chest.

I glower, trying to suppress any more thoughts about the asshole.

"Well, Ma Belle...this was all unexpected." Bastien turns to his brother, eyeing him like he knows Antone might've said something silently to me. He doesn't call him out though, choosing to let me decide how to handle his increasingly persistent comments, which I know to ignore. "We never anticipated that Levi was wrong in his choosing your four mates."

Okay, fuck. I can't let them start thinking Antone is about to be my mate. "*Pack* mate," I correct. "You guys share an identical bloodline, so he can just accept his omega spot." I offer Antone my best cocky-bastard smile.

The fucker winks again.

"I don't think he knew otherwise," Flynn says, speaking up, dragging my attention to him before my wolf decides she wants to tackle Antone and put him in his place—especially because I really don't want to envision him under me right now...how his muscles will flex, feeling his hairy chest against my nipples. Shit. Desperation to mate with him is the last thing I expected. If only he didn't look so damn hot and ready to—

Sagan swats my ass hard enough to make me jump. "Focus, gorgeous. Flynn asked you a question."

"Huh?" I blink a few times, blush burning my cheeks. If my guys are telling me to pay attention, I'm seriously in trouble. They usually encourage my dirty thoughts. I might be officially obsessed. Stupid vagina wanting to be a kinky bitch.

Grabbing my shoulder, Flynn shocks me with a teensy bit of his magic. "Did you ever talk to any of your dad's clients at his gym?" he asks, massaging his fingers into my skin, sending magic sparkling like glitter around me.

I automatically cover his hand with mine, pressing it harder against my body. "I guess I did."

"She did more than talk with one in particular," Sterling says from his spot. "Right, blondie?"

I crinkle my nose. "My sex life before you—"

"Was thankfully lame, but I'm only bringing it up because you mentioned the bastard was a client. It would have taken nothing short of magic to hide that from Levi." Sterling crosses his arms over his chest.

Closing my eyes, I shut all seven of their gazes from my vision. How could I have known Ambrose was a warlock? I didn't know I was a she-wolf. Plus, the guy was nothing like Flynn in bed. There was no magic. No happy endings, for me at least.

Sterling huffs. "Wow—"

I snap my eyes open to watch Dax slap his hand over Sterling's mouth before he can comment on my thoughts. Bastien and Antone look at each other in silent conversation. Caz tightens his mouth, pursing his lips. Sagan smirks at Flynn, who fidgets with his sparkling power, trying his best to ignore all of them.

"Covens are sneaky." Flynn moves and blocks my view of everyone, thankfully. "Like Sterling said, even your dad wouldn't have known. If this Ambrose was a warlock, he was probably tapping into your magic. A lot of covens are untrustworthy. Your father sounds like he was in over his head before he was even born, honestly. The old wolves set you all up for unpredictable futures."

"You think so?" I ask. I can't help it. I don't want to believe it, either. How could we be doomed like this before we were ever born? How could our species ever let it get to this point?

"Unless I can find the original five High Priestesses who arranged this and confront them, we will never know their original intentions in separating Lulupoterra from Magaelorum, or what they plan to do now. If they were ancient or if the fates had other plans, some of the High Priestesses, maybe even all of them, might not be around, entrusting their work with their covens. But witches live long lives. Hundreds of years. Those we've encountered could be who we need to face."

Damn. If only we could do the Mortal World thing and search them online to verify or some bullshit. But there is nothing like that in Lulupoterra. There isn't internet or cable. No cars. No phones. It's a miracle there is electricity. But of course, that might be because I haven't gotten away much from Lunar Crest. I've never had the chance to properly visit each of my guys' home territories apart from a day or two, in which things were fucking awful.

"We'll change that," Sagan says into my mind from his spot. "Promise."

Dax combs his fingers through his hair, turning to Flynn. "The only ones who are privy to that information are currently inaccessible. My mom would be able to tell us who accepted our fathers as sacrificial offerings." Dax frowns with his words, dragging my attention away from Sagan and our private conversation.

"We will strategize what to do about them later," Flynn says, gathering magic between his palms. "Our priority is breaking through the shield. Once it's broken, we can plan our attack."

Dax straightens his shoulders. "What else do you need? We can scout the area, track the she-wolves, find—"

"All I need you to do is hang out here where you all are safe," I say before Flynn can respond, and everyone looks at me as if I'm joking. Placing my hands on my hips, I narrow my eyes. I push away all my nerves and do my best to summon an air of authority. "I mean it. Flynn can't protect you and focus on me, and thankfully, none of you can get magically leashed, so just hang out. You will better serve me by staying safe. Come up with a list of things you want to enjoy with me when all this bullshit is over."

"You can't be serious, gorgeous," Sagan argues, speaking up before Dax can puff out his chest, charge Flynn, and demand that he come up with something else. "We can't just stay here and do nothing."

"Uh, yes you can. It's an order." I hate having to say it, but I know they will try to convince me otherwise. "Consider this some time for bonding. I'm going to need you all to be prepared for when I get back. You're going to have to fakemate my brains out. There is nothing Flynn can do to stop my damn heat except lessen the power of your swimmers."

"What if he accidentally permanently neuters us?" Sterling asks, lifting his brows. "I think butt sex is it for me until you're ready for my hose to water your garden."

I hold up my hand. "We're not discussing this now. We have—"

The ground quakes, sending me over the ledge and into the icy river. Lavender light surrounds me protectively. Flynn's magic drags me to the surface. Coughing and spitting, I heave a breath and flip my blond hair from my face. The water rushes around me, catching me in a strange whirlpool.

"Shit, someone is draining the river," Flynn says, freezing me amid the spinning water. "We have to hurry, Lyric."

I gasp. "Everyone back in the den!"

Flynn waves his hand, sending my pack flying deeper into the safety of our cave. He chants something lowly, his eyes sweeping across the water, freaking me out. I half-expect a monster to devour me. I kick my legs, but I can't move. Flynn's magic locks me in place.

"Lyric!" Dax shouts from somewhere I can't see. "Lyric!"

The river recedes another foot, getting sucked through the underwater passageway. Flynn jumps from the ledge and beside me, not even making a splash. Hooking his arms around me, he grips me to him.

"Elmurc evac!" The rocks shake and crack, splashing around us with his words. "Elmurc evac!"

Growls and yells of my name bounce off the trembling walls. The river swirls with magic, snagging ahold of me and Flynn. With a burst of power, he sends the cave ceiling caving in, the rocks crashing in front of the naturally heated pool, ensuring no one can get into the den or near my pack.

"Elmurc evac!" Flynn repeats. "Don't let go of me, Lyric. The Nightstars are shifting the magical barriers."

My eyes widen. "Why? What are they doing?"

He engulfs me in magical light, unable to fight against the power of the receding water. "We're about to find out."

The magic river sweeps us from the safety of my mom's den and out into the open of Lunar Crest. A wave of ice water crashes over us, stealing my breath. The river sweeps us away.

18

WITCH CONFRONTATION

"KISS ME." FLYNN'S THOUGHT FILLS my racing mind. "Kiss me and don't stop. I don't want to surface until we absolutely have to."

My chest tightens, my lungs ready to burst for a gasp of breath. Flynn tilts his head, pushing through the magic river current trying to rip us apart. I bend forward, the strength and power of the water unlike anything I've felt. It's disorienting and freaky-as-fuck, and I'm afraid that whatever the witches plan to do with the gateway between all the territories and the

Mortal World will ruin everything.

Sparks fly as Flynn molds his lips to mine, giving me air instead of stealing my breath away. Power zings between us, and my racing heart settles the longer he kisses me underwater, my hair swaying in the current, my body numb with cold, yet somehow, I'm no longer afraid of what to expect. Magic lights around us, filling our souls until it feels as if we merge into one entity. No witch or any amount of dark magic can ruin us. As long as Flynn kisses me, it feels as if the world will be okay.

Deepening our kiss, Flynn glides his tongue into my mouth, exploring and tasting my mouth like he can survive on this for the rest of our lives. I hug him close and squeeze him between my legs, my body determined to stay connected to him despite the rocking world.

"Brace yourself, Lyric. We're going to emerge in a minute. As soon as we do, I will unleash you. Be prepared to run. The Nightstar Coven knows we're here. We must evade them until the coven from the Mortal World can sense you. When they do, don't resist. Let them summon you. I will not leave you. I swear." Flynn slows his desperate kiss and repositions his hand to light up the glittering water with his magic. "Get ready."

I inhale another breath of magical air, feeling my lungs tighten as Flynn eases his mouth from mine. "What if Invidia gets me?" Fear steals the warmth Flynn's affection and magic summon inside me.

Flynn bows close enough for me to see the sparkling electricity in his lavender eyes even through the water blurring my vision. "She won't. Trust me."

I bob my head, squeezing my eyes shut. "I trust you."

"You're mine, Lyric. You're my familiar, my soul. I will not let anything happen to you," he murmurs, kissing me once more. "Now, get ready."

A mixture of emotions courses through me with his claim as something shifts at his need to declare something so instinctual and natural inside me. Somehow, I don't feel as if I'm a possession or a source of magic with his words. I feel stronger. More powerful. Because I know his claim resonates with everything he is, merging our souls as one.

"Three. Two. One. Run!" His call erupts not only in my mind but also in my ears as the water vanishes, leaving me gasping for breath.

Sparks of light flash and crackle around us, and Flynn flicks his wrist, throwing me from the now dry riverbed with a burst of his magic. I brace for impact, tucking my chin to my chest to somersault once before finding my balance. I catapult to my feet and charge toward the familiar tree line that'll take me into the forest growing up the hillside. If I keep running, I should reach another part of the river near the caves. I know that's where I'll find one of the gateways. If only I knew exactly how to use it. I've always entered blindly, not knowing exactly where I'd end up, trusting others to lead the way.

A long, low howl echoes through the air, and my steps falter at the familiar call of Emerson. I've never heard her wolf sound so sad. Fear clenches my chest, and a dozen thoughts swirl through my mind. Has the Omega Hunt finished? Has she been injured by one of the fucking alpha-mates in training like Fergus? Shit. I should keep running. I know I should. But she and Harlow have helped me before. I can't just abandon Emerson if I have the chance to get to her. I'm starting to believe in the supposed fates all my guys talk about. Because Emerson can help me too. She knows her way around Lulupoterra. She can help me find the right gateway to the Mortal World.

Ducking near a tree, I tug off Flynn's shirt and stretch my arms over my head. A part of me fears transforming into my she-wolf because of how the collar trapped me in the form before Flynn could work on stabilizing things, but I'm willing to risk it. I can call to Emerson and hopefully connect to her without allowing anyone else into our mind-link.

My body trembles in anticipation, my muscles tightening and rippling with a need so intense that it screams for me to get over my trepidation. It screams to be brave. I'm the fucking magical daughter of Levi and Melody, and the pack leader of Lunar Crest. I will hold tightly to the power given to me, and I will destroy anyone who tries to get in my way.

Because I'm done with all this bullshit.

I'm done with the bastard witch covens and the weak she-wolf leaders. I'm done with lycans and competitions and every damn entity in all the universe trying to get to me.

Releasing a long, loud howl through the air, I call for Emerson and Harlow, hoping they are both nearby. If I can find them, the three of us can rise together. I'll teach them what was passed to me. They will see that they are more than this life they've been forced into. Because it's time to start over. It's time to show that we are the ones who will decide who is worthy. We will decide who we want to help us lead and who can fuck off and let their damn evil bloodlines die with them.

"Emerson! Harlow!" I call through my mind with another howl. "Where are you?"

"Lyric? Lyric, help me! Please!" Emerson's cry of desperation cuts through my soul, sending me racing in the direction her howl echoes from. "Something's wrong with them. It was their turn to cross the finish line with me to protect me from the alpha-mates, but the witch—they've been spelled."

Low, guttural growls sink into my bones, sending a quiver through my body. I slink around a tree, afraid to rush into what sounds like an impending wolf fight. Emerson clings to a high branch in her human form, naked and shivering, drenched in sweat. Two wolves circle below, waiting for an opening to attack each other.

And then I see their glowing red eyes, not unlike Antone's were when he had been collared by a witch.

"Oh, shit." I recognize Alonzo, Caz's brother.

Ah, hell. I knew Invidia would do something crazy. And now I feel so fucking awful that we were forced to abandon them because Alonzo and his mates couldn't pass the protective magic of my mom's den. Hearing Emerson's pleas for them to snap out of it breaks my heart. I had no idea those against the alpha-mates have been fighting hard to protect Emerson and Harlow from those who would hurt them, but I'm so thankful, knowing they weren't chained and abused or worse. If only they didn't succumb to this fate.

It feels like my fault.

"Fuck," I say in my mind, tensing as Alonzo crashes to the ground, missing Emerson's leg.

With the whisper of my word, he and the other wolf jerk their attention in my direction. My hackles rise, and I release a warning growl. The two wolves charge in my direction, but they turn against each other, snarling and biting, ripping at each other's throats. If one of them kills the other, it'll destroy them. I know they have a bond.

Emerson waves her hands at me, grabbing my attention. I take advantage of the wolves fighting and run around a tree and in Emerson's direction.

"Hurry and transform," Emerson says to me, wrapping her legs around the branch more tightly to stretch down in an attempt to reach me.

I do as she commands, relief shuddering through my bones as I change into my human form without any problem.

Taking a few steps back, I prepare to run toward Emerson, praying she can actually lift me from the ground, so I don't have to fight the rabid-like wolves until Flynn shows. I know he should be here any second. He was right behind me.

"Hurry," Emerson repeats. "Jump."

I bolt in her direction and stretch my arms to grab onto her hands. A pop of crackling electricity startles me. I slip and crash into the ground, hitting my knees to the dirt. Emerson screams as the branch she hugs snaps from the tree. I throw myself out of the way before she crushes me and scramble to get to my feet as fast as I can.

A low whistle cuts through the air, and Alonzo and his mate freeze mid-fight. "I was wondering where they've been hiding you, pretty girl. I never expected for him to return with you to Lunar Crest of all places. How has my brother been treating you all these years, anyway? He must be desperate if he allowed me to use you to come. He always lacked in his abilities on his own, and now that Invidia seems to think she can take what doesn't belong to her... Where is my brother?"

I frown at the familiar man strolling through the trees. His rambling questions confuse the hell out of me. It's the brother of the witch who collared Antone and summoned me into a cell after I took his collar. A dozen questions flit through my mind at his comments.

"I have no fucking clue who your brother is," I say, rubbing my hand over my throat, my skin tingling. "He had nothing to do with this. It was my warlock." I don't know how else to address Flynn.

The man's eyes widen and he twists a clump of his shoulder-length, salt and pepper hair in his fingers. "Well, what a surprise. You really are just like your mother. Come closer and let me get a look at you, sweetie. I'm assuming there was a reason you were unleashed, right?"

I don't get a chance to respond or move. The man curls his fingers and mutters a spell under his breath. Pain bursts in my middle as he uses magic to pull me forward by my core. My skin warms under his ruby power, and I try to open my mouth to scream, but nothing comes out as my throat tightens.

The man is so focused on me that he misses Emerson transforming into a wolf behind him. Pushing off the ground, she collides into his back and knocks him forward. The gesture breaks his spell, sending me to the ground. I don't try to run. Instead, I rush him to fight, taking advantage of the fact that he turns toward Emerson.

"Lyric, duck!" Flynn's yell erupts through the air.

I drop to the ground on his command, expecting him to attack the warlock with magic. Instead, a burst of blue light crashes into the man, lighting him aglow. I swear I can see through his skin into his bones as Invidia materializes into view.

Two arms wrap around me, yanking me away from the witch and warlock as they each chant a spell to start a fight. Flynn's familiar scent keeps me calm, and he whispers the foreign words of an incantation too quickly for me to catch.

The world shimmers, the air looking as if heat rises toward the sky, turning the forest around us wavy. Emerson yells out my name, lunging for me, but the world around us erupts in bright, blinding light.

"Shit," I breathe, bending forward as my stomach twists and turns, the relocation worse than anything I've ever felt traveling by magic.

A wave of ice crashes over us, and Flynn releases me with a groan.

My throat suddenly tightens, the magical collar igniting to feel as if it's made of fire, burning and branding my skin with invisible chains. I can't scream or fight through the pain.

I can't breathe.

The witch with short black hair—Evelyn, the High Priestess from the lycan cabin—materializes a foot away and twitches her fingers at me in a wave.

"Oh, what a pretty girl you are up close. Has this warlock been using you? Should I punish him?" the witch asks.

Fury crashes through me, and I launch from the stone floor and at the witch. "Don't you dare touch him. Flynn is mine!"

19

Alpha-Mates

RED POWER SHOCKS ME, AND I drop to my knees. I scream out in agony as the world shimmers again, sending my stomach twisting. I slap my hands on the stone floor, coughing and dry-heaving. The stone turns to dirt, and vicious growls sound around me.

"Liet eh og chi!" Flynn's voice rips through the air.

His voice stabilizes me enough to orient myself from being forced from Lulupoterra and then pulled back again. I shove my hands into the ground and catapult to my feet. Power collides into a tree next to me, sending leaves and branches raining down. A huge wolf snarls at me, its red eyes glowing with a magical spell.

I swing my fist out to knock it away, but the beast, a man from Storm Haven, who I know is Dax's brother, sinks his teeth into my arm, yanking me down. Fire burns in his bite, my arm pulsing with agony.

Chaos swarms the area as Flynn fights the black-haired witch, and Invidia and the other warlock cast spells against each other. None of them pay attention to the wolves surrounding us, and three more wolves turn their attention to me.

"You're mine, Lyric," the wolf says, his voice penetrating my mind. "I will take you right now."

The wolf swings his head, turning into a familiar man with the same golden eyes as Dax. His dark skin shimmers with the red power stealing the golden warmth from his irises. Locking his hand around my bloody arm, he digs his fingers into the bite, making me scream.

"No!" I shout, sweeping my arms apart as hard as I can to break his grip.

His hand smashes into my throat, cutting off my airway. He's far too heavy to shove off, and the magic spelling him leaves him unfazed by my knee to his groin. Splitting his mouth into a wicked smile, he leers at me with disturbing lust in his eyes. The lack of oxygen steals my strength, my fight fizzling out. He won't kill me, but he won't stop choking me either, waiting for me to pass out.

"Lyric!" Flynn yells, his voice sounding over the pounding in my head. "I call upon the fates. Take this offering and give me more strength. Toti rem savi eticula!"

Hot blood pours across my face, and the heavy body of the spelled man sinks on top of me. Bright light flashes across my vision. Flynn flings the dead guy off of me, the heavy weight crushing me into the ground vanishing, allowing me to breathe. I gasp and spit, swiping my hands across my face to clear the blood from my lashes.

Another wolf launches at Flynn, trying to attack him from behind. I scramble away and hit my back against a tree. From my spot, I catch sight of the madness. Invidia calls upon the alpha-mates, and they lurch closer, surrounding all of us. The other warlock now shields his coven sister with magic as she shouts some sort of spell, turning the world hazy. All I can think about is how I'm out here, without my pack, and afraid that Flynn's plan to use my collar will fail.

"Blondie, can you hear me?" Sterling says, his voice echoing through my ears.

I press my back into the tree, using the sturdy trunk to stand. "Fuck, are you nearby? We need help."

"We're still trapped," Dax says. "But we are here. We can feel you, and you need to let us in. Let us give you what you need."

"I'm afraid to open my mind," I say, shaking on my feet.

"We will get you through this, Ma Belle. We are your pack." Bastien's strength zaps through me with his words.

"We stand together," Caz adds.

Sagan's presence filters into my thoughts next. "Now open that fierce mind, gorgeous."

"Do it now!" Antone's words shatter the block I hold on my mind, filling me with strength, bravery, and the knowledge that I am powerful despite everything happening.

The power witches gather comes with a price. It's summoned from outside them. But me? I'm fucking magical.

Straightening my shoulders, I savor the courage of my pack standing beside me even though they're not physically here. We're bonded by soul and no one can get between us or sever what we've grown together.

And that includes Flynn.

Rushing forward, I tackle the tan and brown alpha-mate wolf from behind, using the force of my body to knock him off his paws. We tumble across the ground as he thrashes, trying to bite and snap at me. Flynn gathers lavender light between his palms, preparing to blast the wolf.

"Nota feli coma!" Invidia cracks the ground beneath Flynn's feet, sending him crashing to the ground.

I scream and flip the alpha-mate onto his back, pinning him with all my strength.

Flynn's shout of pain grabs my attention, turning my focus to him. He summons a shield to protect himself from Invidia, but it quivers and fissures under the intensity of her power. Clenching his jaw, he holds firm, shouting spell after spell. His soul stone burns between my breasts as he taps into our bond to help himself.

"Lyric, I need a sacrifice," Flynn says, his face turning monstrous as his teeth elongate. "I need darker magic."

The alpha-mate thrashes beneath me, but the strength of my pack seeping into me from our bond keeps me pinning him. The wolf bares his fangs and snarls, trying to bite me.

"Warlock," the black-haired witch shouts. "Summon her pack. If you help us, we will help you. Command your she-wolf to do it. Make her! We will get Lulupoterra back!"

"Monnus em teps," Invidia says, her white-hair flying around her face with magic. The world quakes and two lycans appear from thin air. "Kill them, my pets!"

Oh, fuck.

"Lyric!" Flynn shouts, using a huge burst of magic to send the snarling lycan back, but it's not enough. "I need the sacrifice! I need you to do it. You're my familiar."

I suck in a breath, my body cooling at his call. Can I kill this spelled wolf? Can I sacrifice one of my species like this after everything I've lost paying the price of magic?

The lycan smashes into Flynn, swiping his dagger claws across his chest. The two other witches fight off another two, leaving me open. Invidia narrows her eyes on me, the blue light doing nothing to illuminate the darkness clinging to their very depths.

A dozen emotions cascade through me, and I try to clutch tightly to my pack's strength.

"Little she-wolves make better omegas," Invidia says. "If you help these witches, you will be theirs. At least with me, you will be with your own kind. I'll keep you safe from the big bad warlocks. Just bow."

Oh, fuck no.

I'm not cool with either of her thoughts.

"Lyric!" Flynn shouts. "Run! I can't fight much longer. Run!"

But I wasn't taught to run. I was taught to fight, and I plan on doing so until I no longer can. My guys need me. Flynn needs me. My species needs me. If I run, all it will do is give me a few extra seconds to catch my breath. Invidia will never stop. The alpha-mates and lycans won't ever stop.

I have to stop them, and I can't do it alone.

"Flynn, I give you this sacrifice!" Locking my hands to the wolf's neck, I squeeze as tightly as I can.

The alpha-mate transforms into a human, and I recognize Santiago, the man who had won Emerson's day claim my first night in Lunar Crest for the She-Wolf Games. His features twist with fear, and I loosen my hold, his familiarity smashing my ability to take his life into pieces. Maybe if it was one of the leader's asshole alpha-mates. Maybe if it was Fergus. But Santiago? I don't think he'd be this vicious without witch magic.

A shadow falls upon me. Invidia takes advantage of my hesitation, locking her hand to the back of my neck. Power sizzles across my throat, my airway tightening. My eyes bulge, and my grip loosens on Santiago.

"Eth vien lo vi." Invidia's sultry voice swirls around me, restricting my movement like an invisible rope.

"Lyric, fight!" Sterling shouts in my mind.

"Fucking fight, gorgeous! Block her! Shove her out," Sagan adds. "You can break her spell!"

A scream rips from my mouth as I summon the willpower to keep Invidia out of my head. Pain throbs in my muscles, my body trembling. Something explodes behind me, and Flynn hollers in agony. He shouts my name.

"Eth vien lo vi," Invidia repeats, sending her blue magic sparkling around me. "Be mine, beautiful she-wolf. Go on, submit and this will all stop. Give me your will and be my good little beast. Your alphas will take care of you. No one can have you again."

No. No. No. This can't be happening. She can't take my willpower and ruin the life my dad set forth for me or the life I've made into my own, using his years of guidance. I refuse to give up or give in. I won't let my pack down.

"No!" My voice breaks through my tight vocal cords, and I swivel and swing my fist, punching the bitch witch right in her crotch.

Santiago tries to take advantage of the release of my arm,

but I'm too fast for him. Grabbing him by the head, I squeeze my eyes shut and jerk his head as hard as I can until he falls limp beneath me. My heart explodes at the realization that I killed this man with my bare hands. I took his life for Flynn. For power.

I'm no better than the witches out to use us.

"I sacrifice this beast for my soul mate!" I yell, gripping Flynn's soul stone in my hand.

"My pets, stop her!" Invidia yells.

"Flow eh og monn tiaga venisima! I give this gift in sacrifice to summon my pack." Flynn's deep voice calls the words, his voice low and shaky.

Growls and snarls fill the air with a flash of lavender light. Teeth sink into my shoulder, dragging me off Santiago's dead body, and I tense at the sight of the huge red wolf. Fergus tosses me toward a pack of alpha-mates. I glower at Killian, standing naked in his human form, gripping a spelled muzzle in his gloved hands.

One of the other wolves snatches me by the ankle and drags me closer until Invidia materializes from thin air. She takes the spelled muzzle from Killian and pets his wild hair. I thrash and kick, doing everything I can to fight.

Jerking my head back, I smash it into Fergus's snout, and he drops me. It's the split second I need. I grab the scruff of his throat and flip him over my head as hard as I can. He crashes into Invidia and Killian. The muzzle clatters out of their reach.

"Li vita entianda!" Flynn shouts.

Lavender light crashes into Invidia's chest. Stretching my arms, I give control to my she-wolf. My body ripples and tenses with my transformation, and I release a howl into the air. Charging at the witch, I snap and snarl, preparing to gut her. Another alpha-mate launches at me, but a beautiful white wolf jumps from the trees and crashes into him.

Bastien sinks his teeth into the alpha-mate's throat and drags him out of the way. Growling, Sagan collides into another wolf, clearing a path for me. I kick my back legs hard into the ground and jump at Invidia, smashing into her chest. She tries to yell a spell, but I snap my jowls to her neck, cutting off her words. And I don't stop.

My she-wolf takes complete control of me, and for the first time ever, I feel the strongest as a wolf. I feel power and magic and the strength of all the men I bonded with coursing through my very soul. This witch bitch will never have me. She will never make me bow, not if I devour her.

Invidia's face morphs, her features sharpening, her teeth elongating into fangs. She takes on the monstrous form used to intimidate others, but there is nothing in the world that can scare me now. Not with the hunger of my she-wolf consuming me completely.

Tearing at her throat, I incapacitate her ability to shout a spell. My blond fur coats with her blood, and I latch on to her neck, refusing to let go. My jaws lock with my strength. The only way I'll release the witch is if she's dead. Dead and gone and unable to try to control or hurt me again.

The ground rumbles beneath me, an earthquake cracking the dirt. A tree falls nearby, cutting off Sagan, Bastien, and me from the rest of our pack. Blinding blue light erupts through the air, and a blast of energy explodes into my side. I fly off Invidia and hit the trunk of a tree. Two white-haired women and one man materialize a dozen feet away.

Sagan charges to get in front of me, growling and snarling, warning the witches to stay back. Flynn's voice rings through the air, followed by the melodious hum of the other coven. They chant a spell together, the sound like music and hope wrapped together to calm my racing heart.

And then the world shimmers.

"No!" I scream through my mind, rushing toward Bastien as he launches at the warlock.

One of the white-haired women, who are certainly part of the Nightstar Coven, shouts a spell, dropping Bastien to the ground. His wolf howls and shrieks in pain, unable to fight the magic.

"Lyric, my soul. Come to me," Flynn whispers into my mind, his voice still chanting with the other coven.

I try to push Flynn from my mind, but the world continues to haze around me. I try to snap my teeth into Sagan's tail to pull him back, but he jumps at the man, trying to fight him to get to Bastien.

He doesn't even get his teeth into the warlock.

His body sprawls across the dirt, captured in the Nightstar Coven's magic.

Opening my mouth, I howl, trying to force my humanity to break free from my she-wolf. But I can't control my beast. I can't do anything. I stand frozen in a weird foggy world, watching the warlock of the Nightstar Coven bend down and inspect Invidia. His face contorts in anger, and he gathers blue power in his hand.

Invidia is dead.

I killed her.

And now the warlock wants me.

He shouts something, but I can't hear his voice over the chanting of Flynn's spell. Over his desperate calls for his soul, for me, to return to him. I have no choice but to go. The world fogs completely, my vision turning white.

I can't do anything to get to Bastien and Sagan. I'm forced to leave them behind.

My heart stays with them, bleeding and broken. My pack falls apart.

20

Separated

I PACE AROUND THE STRANGE bedroom in my wolf form, my body refusing to release my humanity. I don't know if it's the only way I might be able to deal with the absence of Sagan and Bastien or if it's something else. Either way, I'm anxious and angry and seriously annoyed that Flynn and the other witches summoned me away from Lulupoterra, forcing me to leave part of my pack behind.

"Cherie," Antone says softly from his spot sitting on the edge of the bed. "My brother is far braver and tougher than I could ever be. It is why Levi chose him over me for you. Please trust that he can take care of himself."

I growl and whip around to face him. "He shouldn't have to! It's my job!" I shout into his mind.

My fury sets me off, and I charge toward Antone, plowing into him. He falls back on the bed, taking the force of my heavy paws on his bare chest. I snarl and snap my teeth near his face, my wild emotions needing to take out my aggression on someone, anyone, and Antone happens to be the only one here at the moment. Everyone was far too out of control with my heartache, and it doesn't help that I'm still in fucking heat. It makes it worse. I can't get the closeness I need right now. And because I haven't physically bonded with Antone, he manages to keep a semblance of his good sense.

But now I want to test him.

Antone digs his fingers into my sides and flips me off him and onto my back. "What you need is to pull yourself together, transform into that sexy, infuriatingly stubborn woman, and let me give you a proper medical exam. I can't tell how injured you really are otherwise. Your coat is filthy with blood."

"You like my filth, you bastard." I bare my fangs at him, thrashing on the bed. "And I am fucking together. I'm not injured. So, get off. I'm not transforming back. I need to be ready to bite whoever comes through that door with the only weapon I currently have."

"Damn it, Cherie," Antone says, narrowing his eyes. "I'm

giving you one more chance."

I snap at him. "Just go away, Antone. Seeing you...it reminds me that Bastien isn't here."

"But I am!" Grabbing my muzzle, Antone stops me from nipping him.

He climbs onto the bed and straddles me. I squirm and growl, trying to knock him off. How dare he restrain me like this. How dare he disobey me, ignoring my order for him to leave me alone to think things through without his suffocating presence.

"Now stop being a brat and let me examine you. I am here, and no matter what, I am not going away. So hold still so I can get this over with and give you what you truly need." Antone locks his gaze to mine and slides his big hand into my coat, combing through my thick fur to try to get a better look at my skin.

I continue to put up a fight, wiggling and moving, my body challenging Antone to give me an opportunity to break free. He clenches his teeth in determination, looking far hotter than he should. Working his way over my chest, he touches a spot on my shoulder, and I yelp in pain, unable to control my wolf's reaction.

The fucker touches the spot again. "You were bit."

A pathetic whimper escapes my mouth, and muscles spasm with my transformation. Antone stiffens on top of me as he straddles my naked body, still covered in filth from the fight in the forest. His eyes, darker than Bastien's but in the same deep-set, round shape, lock onto mine. I inhale a few breaths, his wild scent prodding at my nature as a she-wolf. It sends an ache through my body, which I know ties to my forced heat. Being in the same form worsens the strange, innate, undeniable desire coursing through me.

Antone carefully slides off me as his body arouses to my hormones calling for him to seduce the hell out of me. And right now, I won't even resist. His familiarity fills me up, and my mind begs for a better distraction than the pain still burning in my shoulder blade. The depression hurting my broken heart.

"You're not thinking clearly, Cherie," Antone murmurs, reaching for a medical bag on the floor. He shakes a serum into his palm and gently coats my skin, numbing the pain. "You don't want me. I'm your omega, remember? Last in line for—"

I grab his arm and drag him to me, pulling him to the bed. He releases a guttural moan from his lips, and I reach up and lock my hand to the back of his neck, pulling his face to mine to attack him with a fervent, desperate kiss. His thick beard brushes my chin as he molds his lips to mine, returning the affection I so forcefully push at him. I never imagined I'd kiss Antone, but damn it. He's grown on me. My claim on him allows me to feel past his asshole demeanor, where the loyal, caring mate waits to surprise me in the moments I need him to the most.

A dozen dirty thoughts swirl through my mind, shoving away all my good senses. I want to know what it'd be like to feel the coarseness of his beard scratch down my bare breast, how it would feel between my legs. If it'll tickle or if the friction will add to the ecstasy he'll summon with the flick of his deliciously soft tongue and hungry, eager mouth.

Antone growls against my lips, sweeping his tongue over mine to taste my mouth how he wants. I comb my fingers through his hair, yanking him away to guide him lower where I crave for him to go. His heavy-lidded eyes trail down my throat to my breasts, and he slides his arm under me to pull me up, taking my nipple into his mouth. I moan at the pressure of his lips sucking hard while rolling his tongue over my excited body.

"Don't think you can have your way with me," I murmur, arching my back until I plant my palms on the mattress. "The only one cumming is me until you get fucking temporarily neutered."

Antone huffs with a gruff grunt, tosses me to the bed, and flips me over. I don't have a chance to react as he spanks my ass so hard that the sting feels as if it reaches my soul. I freeze in surprise, my heart racing like crazy. I mean, holy fuck.

Fuck.

I liked that.

He was right about my kinky, needy as hell vagina wanting him to manhandle me and take control, so I could just let someone else be in charge for a while.

"Those kinds of demands get you in trouble, Cherie," he mutters, locking his hands around my ankles. Dragging me back, he pulls me to the edge of the bed until my bottom half hangs off it, and I'm bent over the mattress. "Is that clear?"

I gather the blankets in my fingers, my desperate desire turning me wet in anticipation for him to position himself behind me and thrust in while spanking me until my ass goes numb. "Antone—"

The sound of his hand slapping my ass again rings through the air. My knees weaken, and I sink deeper into the mattress, my mind whirling with a dozen thoughts.

"It's sir, Cherie. Now, tell me it's clear, and I might forgive your naughty attitude and kiss you until you feel better." His warm hand massages my ass cheek, his hulking presence behind me turning me on in a way I never thought possible. And holy shit, do I want to see where this bastard takes things.

I hum in teasing agreement. "It's clear, *sir*. I'm sorry." Hearing the word come from my mouth feels incredibly weird, yet exciting, and my body is totally here for this. I'm nearly certain not everyone in my pack could get away with this kind of kinky talk, but Antone had me when he said he'd kiss me until I felt better.

"Good girl. Now hold still. If you move, I will punish this naughty ass of yours. Because you're mine, Cherie. I will do as I please." Antone sinks his fingers into my ass cheeks, spreading my body open wider. "Understand?"

"So I can't move like this?" I say, smiling into the blankets as I shake my ass.

Antone squeezes my hips, restraining my movements. "You're asking for more punishment."

"Maybe I am," I tease. "Because I think you're full of shit. You're too scared to punish my naughty ass. Isn't that right, *sir*? You can't make me submit like you want."

Releasing a growl, Antone grabs my hair and yanks me up. He slides his hand across my stomach, holding me in place. His lips caress just below my ear, making me shiver. "Tell me, Cherie. Is this a game you really want to play?"

I dig my fingernails into the skin of his arm. "Mmmhmm. I want to see if you can really teach me a lesson."

"Then be a good girl, Cherie."

"Then make me, *sir-r-r-r*." Because I want to see exactly what Antone has in store. I want to discover if he can live up to all of his cocky-bastard talk when it comes to me.

He groans huskily, his hard-on pressing against my body as he continues to restrain me from behind. "Give me your word, Cherie. I need it to ensure I don't take things too far because you're so fucking disobedient, my spoiled she-wolf. Always getting her way."

Whoa. This is happening.

It's really happening.

"Say the word," he repeats.

"Pink," I say, popping the P and enunciating the K. "Pink because you think you can make me your good little girl."

Tightening his fingers in my hair, he stretches my neck back and sucks my sensitive skin hard enough to make a mark. I sink my nails deeper in his arm, losing myself to the ache he creates until he drops me to the mattress for a breath of relief.

And then he spanks me hard enough to make me jump. "You will be good and let me take what I want."

"You can try." I can't stop the words from coming out or the smile from lightening my words. This is way more fun than I expected.

He spanks me again.

And then again.

My ass stings and my legs go weak until I'm just hanging off the edge of the bed.

"You will hold still," he says, his hand gliding across my heated skin. "Is that clear?"

I shiver under his touch. "Yes, sir." Damn it. My body goes out of whack at the realization that Antone's about to have his way with me, and I'm going to enjoy every second of it. The fucker was right about what we'd have together as mates.

Satisfaction hums in his throat. "Good. I'm going to savor every inch of you, Cherie."

He grunts his approval and drags his hands down my hips as he lowers himself to his knees. I suck on my lip, my breathing quickening in anticipation. He slowly teases me with his finger, feeling exactly what he does to me in this moment. I moan and squirm, my desire driving me crazy.

"You're so wet. Slippery. I want you to feel it for yourself. Would you like that, Cherie?" Antone slides his finger from me and draws it higher, tracing a circle over the sensitive skin of my ass to show me what he means.

"Fuck, I don't know," I murmur, my body clenching in anticipation, my mind wandering to Sterling and our anal adventures.

He continues his exploration. "It's time for you to find out. Just remember your word."

Oh, fuck.

Antone spreads me wider and licks my clit at the same time he slips his slick finger exactly where I thought he would. The explosion of different sensations drags a loud-ass moan from my mouth. He was right about how hot and ready my body was because he's able to use my excitement to tease me in a way I had no idea I'd enjoy.

Gathering the blankets between my fingers, I lose myself to the pleasure Antone arouses in me as he licks and flicks and sucks my body while continuing to tease and please the rest of me. I moan into the mattress as I feel muscles start to tense for my oncoming orgasm. Electricity zings through me, stiffening my whole body. I cling onto the bed as if I'll fly away otherwise.

I inhale to catch my breath, my body humming and yearning for him to continue. "I need more, sir," I say, my voice nearly whining. "Please."

A crash sounds from the hallway, and Antone stops. "Fuck, pink," Antone says, growling under his breath. "Something is happening."

Scooping me up with the blankets, Antone doesn't give me a chance to react. The lust and desire between us dies with the sound of rising voices. They're not right outside the door, but they're near enough to decipher the argument between two unfamiliar people.

Antone covers my mouth with his hand, stopping me from talking out loud. "Shhh."

"If what Enrique thinks is true, I don't see why we should go for this," a feminine voice says. "We can turn him in and be done with it. It's not worth a coven war over some wolves. Pierre wouldn't have wanted this."

My eyes widen at the words. "They're talking about Flynn," I think to Antone. "But who is Pierre?"

Adjusting me in his arms, Antone meets my gaze. "I've heard that name before. Dax would know. He—"

Another crash sounds outside the door, and someone laughs. Confusion rushes through me. What the fuck is going on?

"Cherie, don't even think about it," Antone says, tightening his arms around me.

But it's too late.

Shoving my elbow into his ribs, I push off of him and nearly eat shit on the floor. He growls and lunges for me, but I dodge out of the way and bolt for the door. If anything, I just need to look. Something about the strange crashes and laughter gnaws at my instincts. Who are these witches? Where are Flynn and the rest of my pack?

I lock my fingers around the door knob to fling it open. Snaking his arm around my waist, Antone drags me back. He flips me onto my back, but I'm too quick to pin down. I sweep my leg out, knocking him off his feet. Twisting with his fall, he manages to land next to me and pulls me into his arms. He rolls over and snatches my wrists, yanking my arms over my head.

The door to the room flings open, and a woman with a long black braid thrusts out her arms. "Friyo eth flow tarday!" Blue energy blasts from her hands and strikes Antone in the side.

He hollers and flops onto me, convulsing through the shocking pain of the strange witch's power. I gasp and jerk, experiencing the same intensity Antone does because of our open mind-link to each other. A screech rips from my mouth, making me sound like a wounded animal.

"Stop! You have to stop!" Flynn shouts, his voice the only thing keeping me conscious. "They've bonded. She feels everything he does if they were—"

A burst of blue light, followed by the deep growls of my

guys, pries me from the dizzying pain. I heave a breath as it suddenly cuts off, and Sterling, Dax, and Caz rush to my side in their wolf forms. Antone groans and flips on his side, reaching out to grab my hand. Silence falls over the room, the intensity leaving all of us on edge.

"Sister!" a man shouts, stealing my attention from Antone. The warlock from Lunar Crest pushes past one of the women, who were outside in the hallway with the witch who shocked Antone and me. "You are not to touch any of the wolves."

"But he was hurting her," the woman exclaims, fisting her hands. "Just look at her. I think she was sp—"

"He wasn't doing anything I didn't ask for," I snap, finally getting my shit together.

"Blondie, damn," Sterling whispers into my mind. "You gave in to Antone's kinky shit."

"She was my perfect little brat," Antone thinks, yanking me toward him. "And the witches ruined it. I should—"

"Heather, Trinity. Out. Go find Evelyn. She needs assistance with a spell," the man says.

"But Enrique," the witch with the braid complains.

He waves his hand. "Out, sisters. Now. It's best you not be here anyway. The beasts do get a bit wild."

What the fuck?

The two witches clap their hands and vanish into thin air. I gather the discarded blanket and pull it around me, leaving Antone's naked ass to fend for himself. Dax, Sterling, and Caz remain in their wolf forms, guarding me protectively like they fear that the warlock might try something crazy.

Flynn clears his throat, drawing my attention to him as he hovers near the door. His lavender eyes flicker with power, and he looks nervous as hell. It sends panic cascading through me, doing nothing for my racing heart.

"Everyone, settle down," Flynn says, stepping forward. "I know things are intense, but you should know you're all safe. I've guaranteed it. Now, let me introduce you to Enrique Everdeen."

The man's lips split into a smile as he stares at only me. "Welcome to the Everdeen Estate. It's an honor to be in the presence of a beautiful she-wolf. Your pack is quite intriguing, sweetie. It's a shame we couldn't save them all."

My heart sinks into my stomach at his words. "I'm going back for them."

Enrique raises an eyebrow and shifts his gaze to Flynn. "She doesn't know."

I blink a few times, wishing I could read the warlock's mind. I don't like the way he says the words, and it pisses me off that he looks to Flynn like he's my master or some shit. This coven is going to be sorely disappointed if they think I'm going to put up with that kind of bullshit.

"What don't I know?" I ask, pushing to my feet. "You can talk to me directly. He's not my keeper."

Blue light sparks in Enrique's eyes. "That complicates

things, now doesn't it?" he asks Flynn. "Wild hearts should be tamed."

I stride toward Flynn, and the others stay right by my side, shadowing my every move. With my focus on my aching heart, it's easier to ignore the strange, consuming throb in my being, my nature trying to make me stupid with lust.

"Tell me what's going on Flynn," I say, straightening my shoulders.

His eyes narrow with sadness, sending panic through me. "Lyric, I'm sorry. The Nightstar Coven sealed off Lulupoterra. We can't get back in. We can't get to your mates."

"What?" I ask, licking my lips. "Then break through. You're powerful. We're powerful. We can do it."

He sighs, his shoulders slumping. "I'm sorry," he repeats. "I'm so sorry. I just don't have that sort of power."

"There has to be something we can do. I can't just leave Bastien and Sagan. I can't." My mouth dries and my whole body trembles with my panic. I refuse to believe I've lost them. My heart can't take it.

"Sweetie, you have four mates here. That is all you will require." Enrique touches my shoulder with his cool hand. "We ensured it."

Is he for real?

I shake my head and jerk away. Antone swings his fist and punches Enrique in the jaw, knocking him away from me. The others growl, and Dax launches at the warlock, ready to attack him for even touching me.

"Control them!" Enrique shouts. "Do it or I will!"

A flash of lavender light ignites in the room, stealing my vision. My knees hit the floor, my body giving out on me. I can't move or speak, and my lungs hurt, making me question if I'm even breathing.

"Collar them immediately," Enrique snaps at Flynn.

I open and close my mouth, trying to speak, but nothing works. Flynn tightens his jaw and steps toward my mates, now passed out on the floor. My mind whirls with a dozen thoughts. I can't believe what I'm seeing. What Flynn's doing. Betrayal burns hotly through my soul as Flynn quietly snaps magical collars on each of my guys. He locks them in his magical control.

"Good, now let's meet with Evelyn. She's dying to sit down for a chat," Enrique says. "We'd like for you to consider a proposition."

Flynn slowly nods. "I have one of my own."

Slapping Flynn's back, Enrique nudges him toward the door. I watch in silent horror as Flynn follows him out of the room. The door slams closed, leaving my pack and me restrained with magical collars on the floor.

I've never felt so helpless.

I'm afraid for what's to come.

What if this is it? We might never be free again.

21

Pay the Price

I BANG ON THE DOOR. "I swear to the fucking fates that if you don't let me out and take me to my mates, I will disembowel you assholes!"

My anxiety and fury have kept me going for three nights now, and the Everdeen coven is crazy if they think they can keep this up.

I don't know where Flynn is, but I haven't seen him since he collared us. Deep in my heart, I know he had his reasons, but it doesn't make this situation any better.

Taking a few steps away from the door, I roll my shoulders and sike myself up for impact. I will break down this fucking door and escape. I will. The Everdeen's magic weakens the more I fight it. I've broken out of their sedation spells every time they tried to use one to knock me out.

I rush forward and swivel my torso, hitting the door with all my strength.

Sparks shock me, sending my blond hair flying with static, and the wood cracks right down the middle. Shaking out my arm, I ignore the pain and return to my starting point, preparing to crash into the door again.

"Lyric," Flynn says, his soft voice coming through the door. "Can I come in?"

I freeze and huff a breath. "Damn it, warlock. Where have you been? Get your ass in here. You know I can't open the door."

The door creaks open, and I charge forward. I tackle Flynn, wrapping my arms and legs around him, my soul screaming to be as close as possible to him. He catches us with magic before we hit the floor and engulfs me in a hug that steals my breath.

"I'm so sorry, my she-wolf. I thought I ruined us. I was so scared." He kicks the door closed and crashes his mouth to mine like he can't help himself. "Our pack won't even let me explain myself."

I pull back and meet his lavender gaze. "What did you expect?"

"That it would've been Dax or Antone to bite me, not Sterling and Caz." He sighs and hugs me closer, carrying me to the small bed in this tiny cell of a room. "I'm sure they'll try next though."

"Take me to them." Now that he mentions them, it drives me crazy that he has already seen them before me. I miss them more than I thought possible. I hate everything about this situation. "I will talk to them. Then we'll figure out what to do and how to get out of here."

Flynn sets me on the bed and takes the spot next to me. "Lyric, do you trust me?" he asks without responding to my comment.

I suck in my bottom lip. "What kind of question is that?"

"Do you trust me?" he repeats.

Combing my fingers through my hair, I hunch forward without responding right away. "I want to, Flynn."

"But you don't." His features harden.

"I don't know anything anymore, and this situation doesn't help." I squeeze my eyes shut, trying my best to stay in control of my wild emotions. "I've been in here for days."

"I know, and I'm sorry. It's just—" Flynn tenses and whips his attention toward the door. "Someone's coming. I have to go."

I stare in shock as he vanishes, abandoning me, something he swore he'd never do.

My heart aches as it fissures, threatening to break apart. I'm so confused. I just want to know what's going on. I want to find my mates, return to Lulupoterra for Bastien and Sagan, and then find my dad. If I can just accomplish those three things, I know I can take on the damn world. I just need the people who mean the most to me by my side.

A knock thumps on the door. "Hey, sweetie. I'm coming in. Do not attack me. We need to talk."

The door swings open and Enrique peeks his head in without waiting for me to respond. He peers around the room and claps his hands, sending a strange electrical current over the walls, caging us in with his magic.

"You have a lot of nerve coming in here," I snap, getting to my feet. "Where are my mates?"

Enrique keeps his distance, hovering by the door. "They are fine. My sister is almost through with the mating spell, so you'll be able to rejoin them by tomorrow."

I don't respond. I feel deep inside that he's lying about the reason we've been kept apart. "I don't care about the spell. I want to see them now."

He clicks his tongue. "Tomorrow," he repeats. "Right now, I have something dire to discuss."

I frown. "Which is?"

"Your lost mates." Enrique rubs his hand over his black hair, pushing it back. "My High Priestess thinks the Nightstar Coven will use them to get to you. We can't allow it."

I scowl at him. "Oh, fuck off. You can't speak of me like you don't want to use me for anything apart from power."

"What if I told you we have thought of a way to get them back? Would you hear me out then?" Enrique crosses his arms over his chest. "I'm sure you'd prefer for your pack to be together."

My heart stalls for a moment before restarting to thud in overdrive. "I'm listening."

"As you know, the Nightstar Coven sealed off Lulupoterra, but we figured out a way to re-open it for us. At least, temporarily," he says.

Nerves tighten in my muscles. I don't have to hear what he has to say to know I won't like it.

"But we need you," he adds. "We need you to create a lycan curse. They are the only creatures who can cross realms without paying a huge price. If they open a gateway, we can use it to get through. We can get your mates."

His words put me at war with myself. Could I agree to this? It would mean cursing a human and binding them to witch servitude.

On the other hand...I really fucking want my mates back. I hate thinking about the torture they're going through being with the Nightstar Coven.

"What do I need to do?" I ask, licking my lips. My heart already makes up my mind for me.

"We just need your she-wolf to help us activate the spell,

but I have to warn you. There is a price," he says.

Of-fucking-course. "Name it."

"You will bring us a she-wolf of our own, and one of her alpha-mates." His eyes narrow, darkening in a way that makes my skin crawl. "Since you've been claimed by the Tenebris Coven, we can't have you, so my High Priestess would like a replacement."

Fuck.

Can I do this?

Can I be the woman who dooms my species after everything my dad did to ensure I was strong enough to save us? If I want to get my mates back, I don't think I have a choice.

He clears his throat. "You have thirty seconds to decide."

I nod my head before my mind can catch up. What am I doing? "You'll help me get my mates if I help you with the lycan curse and bring you your wolves?"

"Yes," he says.

Why does it feel like I'm signing away my soul to the devil?

Maybe I am.

"Okay. I'll help you." I straighten my back. "But you have to take me to my mates first. I don't do anything without my pack."

"Very well." Enrique claps his hands, engulfing me in light.

I lose my balance and drop to my knees, only to have cool

hands lock under my arms to pull me to my feet. Growls echo through the stone room as Dax, Antone, Caz, and Sterling slink from their spots near the wall.

My heart ricochets around my ribs. "Thank fucking fuck. Stop it with the growling and transform so I can hug you."

"Lyric," Dax says into my mind. "Your eyes."

Flynn spins me around and cups my face, getting a better look at me. "What have you done?"

"I did what I had to do," I snap, tugging away from him. "I'm doing what we need to unite our pack again."

Flynn links his fingers to the back of his head. "What you agreed to…this will bring their war directly to us."

"This is our war." Turning to my pack, I look at each of my mates. "This is our future at stake. I am your leader, and I will do whatever it takes to keep us together. Do you understand?"

The four of them howl, and Flynn turns his back on me.

I grab him by the shoulder and spin him around. "Will you stand with me? I can't do this without you. You're part of our pack too."

Slowly nodding, Flynn says, "I told you you're my soul mate. I'll never abandon you or our pack."

I wiggle my fingers, getting my guys to come closer. "Are you ready to fight with me?"

Dax, Sterling, Antone, and Caz finally transform into their human selves. "We'll fight with you, always. You're our mate and leader," they say in unison.

Flynn rubs his hands together, sending sparks through the air. "We will not only fight together. We will win."

He's right. We will win. Together.

Lunar Crest and Lulupoterra is ours.

To be continued...

Other Reverse Harem Novels by Ginna Moran

THE WOLFPACKS OF SHADOW MOON ISLAND:
Wild Wolves
Savage Wolves

THE VAMPIRE HEIRS WORLD

La Vega Vampire Showstoppers
Vampire Nights
Bloody Nights
Renegade Nights

The Divine Vampire Heirs
Blood Match
Blood Rebel
Blood Debt
Blood Feud
Blood Loss
Blood Vows
Blood Holiday

The Royale Vampire Heirs Series:
Rebel Vampires
Rebel Dhampir
Rebel Match
Rebel Heir
Rebel Fight

Academy of Vampire Heirs Series:
Dhampirs 101
Blood Sources 102
Coven Bonds 103
Personal Donors 104
Blood Wars 105

THE MATES OF MAGAELORUM WORLD

SERIES IN THE MATES OF MAGAELORUM WORLD

The Pack Mates of Lunar Crest:
The She-Wolf Games
The Wolf-Mate Trials
The Omega Hunt
The Witch Chase

Fated Mate of the Dragon Clans
Caged by Her Dragons
Freed by Her Dragons
Saved by Her Dragons

SEVEN SINNERS WORLD

The Seven Sinners of Hell's Kingdom:
Her Personal Demons
Her Deadly Angels
Her Darkest Devils
Her Sinful Saints
Her **Twisted** Sinners

SAINT VISTA PACK REGIMES

The Knotty Girl Club

STANDALONES
Fame
Rise from the Flames

Acknowledgments

THIS BOOK WOULDN'T HAVE BEEN possible without the support and excitement of my team. I want to give a huge thanks to Felicia, Heather, Noel, Bailey, and Katie for your hard work. I appreciate you with my whole heart!

About Ginna Moran

GINNA MORAN IS the USA Today Bestselling author of over seventy novels including the popular The Pack Mates of Lunar Crest and The Seven Sinners of Hell's Kingdom reverse harem novels.

She always carried a fascination for all things paranormal and wrote her first unpublished manuscript at age eighteen. Her love of the supernatural grew stronger through her adult life, and she now spends her days with different creatures of the night. Whether it's vampires, werewolves, dragons, fae, angels, demons, or mermaids, Ginna loves creating and living in worlds from her dreams.

Aside from Ginna's professional life, she enjoys binge-watching TV, crafting and design, playing pretend with her daughter, and cuddling with her dog. Some of her favorite things include chocolate, mermaids, anything that glitters, learning new things, cheesy jokes, and organizing her bookshelf. Ginna is currently hard at work on her next novel and the one after, and the one after that.

www.ingramcontent.com/pod-product-compliance
Lightning Source LLC
Chambersburg PA
CBHW031615180726
48284CB00005B/1561